That Constant Coyote

Books by Gerald Haslam

FICTION

Okies: Selected Stories
Masks: A Novel
The Wages of Sin: Collected Stories
Hawk Flights: Visions of the West
Snapshots: Glimpses of the Other California
The Man Who Cultivated Fire and Other Stories
That Constant Coyote: California Stories

NONFICTION

Forgotten Pages of American Literature
The Language of the Oil Fields
Western Writing
California Heartland: Writing from the Great Central Valley
Literary History of the American West
Voices of a Place: Social and Literary Essays
   from the Other California
Coming of Age in California: Personal Essays

That Constant Coyote

California Stories

Gerald Haslam

Foreword by Ann Ronald

The University of Nevada Press   Reno & Las Vegas

The author wishes to thank the California Arts
Council for its support of his literary efforts.

University of Nevada Press,
Reno, Nevada 89557 USA
Copyright © 1990 by Gerald Haslam
New foreword copyright © 1990 by
University of Nevada Press
Manufactured in the United States of America
Design by Richard Hendel

Library of Congress Cataloging-in-Publication
Data appears at end of book

The paper used in this book is a recycled stock
made from 30 percent post-consumer waste
materials, certified by FSC, and meets the
requirements of American National Standard
for Information Sciences—Permanence of Paper
for Printed Library Materials, ANSI/NISO Z39.48-
1992 (R2002). Binding materials were selected for
strength and durability.

19 18 17 16 15 14 13 12 11 10

9 8 7 6 5

"Earthquake Summer" copyright © 1983 by
Bilingual Review. All other previously published
stories in this volume were copyrighted by Gerald
Haslam in the year of original publication:
"Upstream" from Cache Review, November–
December 1982; "The Great Waldorf Astoria
Caper" from The Comic Spirit, California State
University, Long Beach, 1983; "That Constant
Coyote," "Sin Flick," "Vengeance," "Trophies,"
and "My Dear Mr. Thorp" from Snapshots:
Glimpses of the Other California, Devil Mountain
Books, 1985; "Sweet Reason" and "Someone Else's
Life" from The Wages of Sin, Duck Down Press,
1980; "Rider" from Main Trend, fall 1981; "The
Horned Toad" from New Arts Review, January
1983; "Hawk's Flight: An American Fable" from
Open Reading, fall 1972; "California Christmas"
from Okies: Selected Stories, Peregrine Smith,
Inc., 1975; "King of Skateland" from Sree, 8
summer 1977; "Joaquin" from Hawk Flights:
Visions of the West, Seven Buffaloes Press, 1983;
"Another California" from The Californians,
January–February 1988; "An Old Intimacy"
from Voc Feminae, California State University,
1988; "Tarzan's House" from Redneck Review of
Literature, spring 1989.

For Suzanne Tumblin,

Clark Sturges, and

Gerald Locklin,

three of the good ones . . .

Contents

Foreword

For many readers, John Steinbeck's California is the most familiar literary one. No one who has read *The Grapes of Wrath* can forget the heavenly panorama of "distant cities, the little towns in the orchard land, and the morning sun, golden on the valley." And no one can forget the disillusion that ensued, the "putrefying ooze" of fruits and vegetables rotting while children went hungry, the dilapidated migrant camps in which they lived, the torrential rains that came, then the sickness, the unbearable poverty, and finally the floods.

Steinbeck did not leave a legacy of literary negativism about California's Central Valley, however. Quite the contrary. He bequeathed a vision of the land's fecundity coupled with a heritage of both realism and optimism that subsequent generations of California writers have been quick to embrace. One of the most successful, one of the most perceptive, one of the most articulate of those Californians writing today is Gerald Haslam.

Haslam loves fiercely his native land and identifies with its many contradictions. Born in 1937 in Oildale, then a tiny town just outside Bakersfield at the southern end of the San Joaquin Valley, he is a fifth-generation Californian. As a boy, he worked the ranches and farms; as a young man, he worked the oilfields like his father. He was a roughneck whose mother insisted upon a Catholic education, a competitive high school and college athlete who surreptitiously began writing at the same time. He was a rebel who even then was moving slowly toward his cause.

The rebel won out for a while. He flunked out of Bakersfield Junior College, suffered through a stint in the Army, and then returned home. Back in the Central Valley once more, Haslam began to settle down. He returned to school and improved his grades, married, started a family, and saved his money. Soon he was able to transfer to San Francisco State, where he received his B.A. degree in 1963 and his M.A. in 1965. The title of his Master's thesis—"The Language of the Oilfields"—gives a clue to the tenor of his mind and to the direction in which his future was unfolding.

Part of Haslam was ready to be an academic. To prepare for a life as a scholar, he entered the Ph.D. program at Washington State University. But part of Haslam was compelled to be a writer, and the creative spirit did not function well within the strictures of academe. When the two parts mixed unhappily, he left graduate school and found a job as an instructor at San Francisco State. The next year, he found an even better position at Sonoma State where he still teaches today. Meanwhile, he wrote. And he wrote. And he wrote. He did receive that academic stamp of approval in 1980 when the Union of Experimenting Colleges and Universities granted him a Ph.D., but after 1966 the heart of his career was always his writing.

That was the first year—1966—when pieces by Gerald Haslam began to appear in print. Two were revisions of his academic work, one was a short story called "The Trinket." Before long, Haslam was publishing more and more frequently. He wrote a monograph on William Eastlake for the Steck-Vaughn Southwest Writers' Series, and another on Jack Schaefer for Boise State. He wrote a number of articles about black American literature, about Mexican-American literary figures, about our linguistic differences, and even about Henry James. In just a few years, he compiled a personal bibliography that many academics would envy. In the meantime, however, he was working just as seriously on the craft of fiction.

Short stories by Haslam could soon be found in *Flight*, in *Arizona Quarterly*, in *Journal*, in *Ecolit*, in *Opening Reading*, and in *Dakota Farmer*. Best of all, his tales could be found in a collection all his own called *Okies: Selected Stories*. Published by New West Publications in 1973, *Okies* was a success. A second edition was published the next year, and after that a third—this time by Peregrine-Smith. Haslam's reputation was growing, as was his creative output. The son of Steinbeck had found his place, back in the Central Valley of his native California. In an essay called "Writing About Home," Haslam explains the importance to him of his boyhood surroundings. *"Home* [italics his] is the place you cannot leave no matter where you go. You carry its imprint in your soul." Then he adds, "When critics ask me why I continue to write about Oildale, about Bakersfield, about the Central Valley, I tell them that the place is sufficient, even though my talent or craft may not be." So home—*home*—became the wellspring of his fiction, a place of complex dimensions that provides the setting and source of all his best writing.

His is not the raw fiction of the untrained eye, however. As Gerald Locklin rightly notes in his Boise State University pamphlet about Haslam's career, this Californian sits "astride two worlds." His Oildale experience has been tempered and honed by the classroom, so that Haslam is "a writer shaped almost equally by formal education and the School of Hard Knocks." Thus, the Central Valley native brings to his work a perspective at once intellectual, physical, personal, and philosophical. Locklin suggests that this complexity "may create tensions in his life, but those tensions become resonating chords in his work." In turn, Haslam's stories resonate with the felt images of a man who has been there, a man who has left and yet will never leave, a man who has created his own native voice.

After 1973, that voice found its way into print with increasing frequency. A list of the separate stories and where they were published would take pages. During those formative years Haslam even tried a novel, *Masks,* brought out by Old Adobe Press in 1976. But his real medium has always been short fiction rather than long and, despite good reviews of *Masks,* he has not produced a second extended narrative work. He has, however, put together several more collections of stories. Duck Down Press/Windriver Books published *The Wages of Sin* in 1980, Seven Buffaloes Press published *Hawk Flights* in 1983, Devil Mountain Books published *Snapshots: Glimpses of the Other California* in 1985, and Capra published *The Man Who Cultivated Fire and Other Stories* in 1987. Now the University of Nevada Press is bringing the best of those stories together, along with some new ones, in *That Constant Coyote,* the book you hold in your hands.

Meanwhile, Haslam's work has been moving in some rather interesting new directions as well. Nonfiction has been flowing from his pen—not the sort of academic nonfiction with which his career began, but more personalized narrative incantations of his native land and of those who populate it. Like his fiction, his nonfiction first was published in scattered places—the *Nation, The Californians, Bakersfield Lifestyle, Pacific Discovery*. Lately, he has begun gathering those essays into more coherent arrangements. One collection appeared in 1987, *Voices of a Place: Social and Literary Essays from the Other California*. Two more—*California's Heartland: The Great Central Valley* and *Coming of Age in California*— are on their way. A look at their tables of contents and, more specifically, an examination of their subjects and subjectivity, leads us straight to the core of what Haslam means to say to his readers. As a matter of fact, *Voices of a Place* quite possibly is the very best guidebook to *That Constant Coyote*.

Haslam's own preface explains the rationale behind his *Voices*. In its pages he hopes to "give a genuine sense of the golden state's complexity by exploring some of the people, some places, some activities that do not conform to this state's stereotype. Since I am rooted in what has been called 'the other California,' no other locale of the land or the heart more intrigues me. It is, to borrow Judith Wright's eloquence, 'my blood's country.'" That blood's country is no longer Steinbeck's alone, but is Haslam's also.

The first chapter of *Voices* examines the land itself. Interspersing his own words with those of authors from preceding generations—yes, Steinbeck is there, on page 1 in fact—Haslam reconstructs the contemporary California landscape that is the background for his fiction as well as his nonfiction. He describes "a varied place where once elk and antelope roamed, where grizzlies prowled and marshes hid legions of red-wing blackbirds." Now, he reports, "at least some of the land is toxic, . . . beginning to evidence the ravages of overpopulation," and he warns that, "with all its apparent open space, the valley is vulnerable: it cannot feed the nation if it is paved; it cannot provide water from contaminated wells; it cannot grow crops in poisoned soil."

Haslam does not mean to preach, however. Instead, he means simply to image the land as it is today. So he concludes his opening essay in a stunningly visual sentence, where he compacts the central California earth and its residents. "On summer afternoons when the sun begins to slip

beyond the Coast Ranges and the frequently polluted sky hovers dangerously on the cusp of red, irrigators lean against their shovels and gaze
westward across textured croplands, wrinkled rows in soil shadowed by
clods, certain that this their reality is sufficient." The reality of those
irrigators, the reality of all the men and women who, in one way or
another, live close to the California land, is the reality as well as of Gerald
Haslam's prose.

The third essay in *Voices* talks about some of them, those so-called
Okies, a catch-phrase for all the migrant workers who "drifted west from
across the Great Plains and rural South; the Dakotas, Nebraska, Kansas,
Missouri, Oklahoma, Mississippi, Texas, New Mexico, and Arkansas."
Products of rural poverty and victims of mechanized farming, they struggled through the Central Valley in the 1930s, picking cotton for 50 cents
a hundred pounds, potatoes for 15 cents an hour. Now fully integrated
in the California scene, their heritage remains an important ingredient
nonetheless. Haslam explains that fact. "Within California's rapidly
changing, trendy society, Okies have exerted a tempering, though spicy
influence like the country cooking they favor, still retaining strong family
ties, clannishness, traditional sex roles, sometimes absurd rites of passage,
church affiliations, and a belief in America's promise (for they are proof
that, however raggedly, it can be fulfilled)."

That Okie heritage and that Okie spirit belong to the majority of men
and women who populate Haslam's fictional worlds. He catches the lilts
of their voices, their attitudes, their body stances, their poses, the eccen-
tricities of their souls. So those whom *Voices of a Place* describes and
defines on paper, *That Constant Coyote* brings to life. This is not to say
flatly that all of Haslam's characters bear the stamp of Oklahoma, but
rather to generalize about the earthiness of his people. They belong to
that California landscape of red sky, textured croplands, wrinkled sod; they
are genuine; they are spicy; they are real.

Actually, they appear in many shapes and colors in *That Constant
Coyote*. The protagonist of the title story seems conventional enough, but
then we meet a rapid succession of distinctive faces—an Indian brave, the
wrestling champion of Taylor County, migrant workers, an erstwhile black
cowboy, a retarded rollerskater, an aging movie queen, a boy with a speech
impediment, a Japanese-American, the last of the Tubatulabals, the Di-

vine Len Schwartz, and a host of others whose lives are touched by Haslam. A look at one or two of these characters reveals their special natures.

Some of them may remind the reader of the creations of Flannery O'Connor, or William Faulkner, or even Charles Dickens. They could be called "grotesques." This is a literary term denoting someone whose eccentricity controls the characterization, so that a reader finally sees the oddity as a metaphor and the person as a device. The characters in Haslam's "Vengeance," for example, are just such people. The ostensible hero wears a protruding hearing aid, and speaks a broken line. "I sneen nya Namar! I wont my nike!" His enemy, Lamar Studly, is an overweight, beer-drinking bicycle thief. Studly's father presages an older version of the youth. "Like the heavy boy, the man wore a dirty t-shirt without sleeves; and his thick arms were rippled with fat that stretched his fading tattoos into textured frescoes. Perched jauntily on the side of a head that might have been a pale pumpkin was a greasy baseball cap, and a toothpick extended from the man's mouth like a serpent's single fang." Almost unreal because their intrinsic traits are drawn so broadly, the three together nonetheless portray a realistic truth. Young Bertil may not speak so clearly, but his mind is devious and more than a match for the lumbering Studlys. What could be grotesque turns out to be hilarious when poetic justice prevails and the Studlys go down to defeat.

For every such caricature, however, Haslam designs a story of everyday life. "An Old Intimacy," for example, explores a family encounter with an old friend. The men are older now, and the passions of youth juxtapose ironically with the pressures of the present. Where once they fought violently over a girl, now they stand helpless and silent at the edge of a field poisoned by groundwater herbicides and pesticides. Where boys used force, men draw from the strength of wisdom. Haslam needs few words to visually describe these characters, for they are our neighbors and we know them.

One way we know them is by the sounds of their voices. For many years—since long before his M.A. thesis on the language of the oilfields, in fact—Haslam has been listening. Sometimes he hears rural speech, and replicates it closely in his text. "'Is you the rasslin champeen a Westbrook County?' the man asked softly. 'Yep.' 'Well, suh,' the man continued to look down and to speak in a voice barely audible, 'My name Rufus

Tuhnuh. I's champeen down Tayluh County, and I walk up heah hopin' maybe we might could seen who best in bof counties.'" And sometimes his cadences sound more citified. " 'He *lost* the car,' she pointed out as though speaking to a dullwitted kid. 'What am I supposed to *do*? You don't seem to understand. I just can't *stand* having him drive anymore.' Her voice deepened and her chin began to tremble. 'You've *got* to help me.' "

One story in *That Constant Coyote*, where Haslam invents a series of letters to the editor of a poetry journal, directly makes fun of the ways people think and talk and write. "The world will soon end unless human beings begin to love one another in God's fullness. Thusly, I am submitting to you the enclosed three brief poems celebrating our Oneness with the Eternal." Or, "THE BARD HATH LONG SINCE/ GRIPPED MY HEART,/ SO WITH THESE PRECIOUS LINES/ I PART." Or, "How dare you refuse to publish a work by 'one of the signal poets of our time.' Just who do you think you are? No wonder you're stuck in California!" Or, "I've never wrote anything before, but here's a poem that makes the boys at the bar where I hang out laugh."

Such playfulness highlights a good many of Haslam's creations. Some would say, in fact, that his pranks from the Tejon Club are direct descendants of "The Notorious Jumping Frog of Calaveras County." Certainly "The Great Waldorf Astoria Caper" ranks alongside the tall tales of Twain and Harte and Ambrose Bierce. Part of the flavor comes from the language. "When me and Earl and Bob Don seen the woman he brung in with him, well we was semi-stunned. Nedra, ol Shoat's wife, was a looker. Oh, she was all painted-up with purple eyelids and lips like slabs a liver, and her hair it was lacquered. She even had false eyelashes about three inches long. But her basic equipment looked damn prime to me. While we's all noddin and shakin hands and sayin how pleased we was to meet her, me I's thinkin baffled'd be a better word."

Part of the flavor comes from storyline itself. In this case, the boys of the Tejon Club set out to embarrass their buddy's new wife by making fun of her plans to erect the Oildale Waldorf Astoria and by erecting, instead, an outhouse so labeled. "I hustled three broken-down ol chairs and a spittoon from the card room, then set em up on front of the shitter along with this other sign I made with a markin pen and a tore-off cigarette carton, 'Lobby.'" Then Dunc added another sign, "Shoats best erecshun," and Nedra's embarrassment was almost complete. Such fun is overstatement, of course, but stories like "The Great Waldorf Astoria Caper," "My Dear Mr. Thorpe," and the Divine Len Schwartz's "Tower Power" are just plain good sport.

If Haslam is a man with a fine sense of humor, though, he also is an author who knows when to be serious. Many of his best stories engage the reader in profound ways. The theme that recurs most often is one that stretches from youth to old age. Initiation and death, the two bookends of maturity, inform the cycle of life as envisioned by Gerald Haslam. Some, like "Hawk's Flight," "Rider," "The Welder's Cap," and "Tarzan's House," focus on the dilemmas of the young. Others, like "That Constant Coyote," "Joaquin," "Dancing," and "The Hearse Across the Street," on the dilemmas of the old. In every case, the author pinpoints a moment in time when a man or woman, boy or girl, comes face to face with him or herself. Sometimes his characters blink; more often they do not.

In "Hawk's Flight," for example, an Indian boy demonstrates more bravery than the cavalry that captured him. Facing his own death squarely, Hawk first manages to kill "the savages' leader." The other cavalrymen fire point blank at the boy, "yet Hawk stood straight and tall, making no attempt to flee or dodge." Less compelling, perhaps, but no less poignant, the behavior of the children who hide from their brutal father in "Tarzan's House" is another kind of initiation into a painful maturity. Here the children are not aware, as the reader is, of the consequences of their acts. But their innocence only underscores Haslam's theme—the sometimes harsh continuity between father and son.

"Dancing" and "The Hearse Across the Street" look at that continuity from the perspective of age. The former story shares a genuine relationship between father and son, while the latter shuts out a daughter who cannot understand. In both cases, Haslam presumes a movement from one generation into the next, a movement that he has observed personally in such essays as "An Affair of Love," "Pop: A Love Song for my Father," and "Homage to Uncle Willie." Indeed, the recurrent analysis of change and transition is so important to Haslam that it dictated his choice for the title of this book.

"That Constant Coyote" follows a man dying of cancer out to the far edge of his property for one last overnight stay in a grove of redwoods where five generations had camped. "Sipping brandy, I'd looked carefully at those trees and stumps, their shadows and shapes, thinking that my grandfather, my father, my son and grandson, all of them had known or did know this place." The brandy, the narrator's own "personal chemo-therapy," turns out to be "strong stuff." A dream sequence follows, bring-ing three of those generations together in a oneness as much spiritual as alcoholic. "'We met in your blood,' the larger man said." Then, "in the breathless night, their faces finally coalesced," and the narrator begins to understand the truth of that unity. "Agreed, we hover in time like spar-rowhawks in wind. . . . Agreed, our lives have passed through redwood exclamations. . . . Agreed, we never were what we used to be. . . ." And yet, so often, Gerald Haslam characters are just that—exactly what they used to be, with only ironic variations, extending the designs of both heredity and environment from one generation to the next.

Two of my favorite stories in *That Constant Coyote* reiterate this theme from a double point of view. That is, one generation addresses its maturity while an older generation confronts its mortality. "The Horned Toad" places boy and great-grandmother side by side. In this winsome tale, first published in *New Arts Review* in 1983, a young narrator learns a genuine compassion that earlier had eluded him. Confronted with the death of an animal he wrested from its natural environment, the boy acknowledges, "if I had left it on its lot, it would still be alive." Confronted with the death of his great-grandmother, the boy recalls the lesson he learned, remembers the burial they shared, and insists that her body lie next to her husband's in Arroyo Cantua. Ironically, it is the boy who must remind his parents of the efficacy of place, and it is the father who must then draw upon his son's newborn wisdom. "When you're family, you take care of your own," the tale seamlessly concludes.

Not all of Haslam's stories rely on family to make tangible the rites of passage or the passing of time, however. "Someone Else's Life," published first in *Ecolit* in 1975, then reprinted in *The Wages of Sin* before being reprinted here, brings together a man and his boyhood mentor instead. "He was a foreman in my father's packing shed, a tough, stringy man with a face at once emaciated and powerful. . . . Wade took me fishing." But, as the narrator explains, "Wade taught me far more than how to catch fish—catching fish often seemed little more than an afterthought on our trips; he had shown me how wildness could strip—as from an ancient, exfoliating stone—layer after layer of civilized complexity." Wade also taught the narrator about evanescence. "Just always be sure ya remember what's real," he bids, "and keep a tight hold on it." Although Wade himself cannot clutch reality tightly enough, and neither can the narrator exactly, their story, somehow, does just that. For their story is what is real, and their friendship the cement, the "tight hold" that binds these men with their fates. Their story is also the vehicle whereby Haslam can signal once again that critical moment when maturity and mortality meet face to face.

In many ways, "Someone Else's Life" brings this introduction full circle. Its first paragraph returns us to a California of three or four decades ago, the terrain of Haslam's youth. "Our fishing trips never really began until we drove past the last houses in the orange grove marking the eastern boundary of town and burst free into treeless, rolling hills, driving east until mountains loomed from smog before us, brown and bleached at their roots, yet ascending into distant blue shafts far above the thick warmth of flatland air—into cool, thin purity." Without the smog, the view could have been Steinbeck's in the 1930s as well. Then the last paragraph thrusts us toward the California present. "The Corps of Engineers dammed the canyon the year I returned from the Army," the narrator reports. "It's a water-skiers' lake now, oily, with supermarkets and trailer parks and honky tonks growing around it, and neon lights to guide lost travelers in from the threatening dark."

In the context of the story, such a juxtaposition between a canyon where boys could grow and an oily lake where men might not is a metaphorical restatement about the lives of the narrator and his mentor. In the context of Haslam's career, it reminds us of the two Californias—past and present—which are the heartland of his prose. "*Home* is the place you cannot leave no matter where you go," we recall Haslam saying. He sees that home as Steinbeck saw it—the land's pristine potential succumbing to the fatal demands of mankind. "Today, when natives return," Haslam writes in *Voices*, "they find cultivated fields where a year ago they hunted rabbits, stucco houses where ten years before almonds were harvested, McDonalds' homogeneity replacing the Chat'n'Chew's intimacy. Amidst the area's considerable wealth, they discover the stumps of antique groves cut and torn from the earth, favorite streams dammed and tamed, old stores boarded and blank, and they die a little."

Refusing to despair, however, Haslam instead turns that Central Valley landscape into his Athens. As Steinbeck and William Saroyan understood as well, "In this locale are all the great subjects, all the grand dramas and they, in fact, are not only the themes of my stories and essays, but in a sense they are the setting too, for they are finally a terrain of the heart." Populating that terrain are the folk of Oildale, "the mix of people here-abouts that most compels." Populating that terrain are the folk of *That Constant Coyote*.

Ann Ronald

University of Nevada, Reno

Preface

At twenty-one I was drifting: working on a ranch in Utah for six months, then back home to California's Great Central Valley, soon to become a soldier. I toiled during the interim at a packing shed near Delano, loading boxcars with crates of table grapes. The fruit was picked by Mexican and Filipino adults who labored in searing sun, while cooler and more desirable jobs in the shed—jobs such as mine—in those years went exclusively to whites, often just kids.

Two of the loaders with whom I worked that summer were cousins, lanky men from Oklahoma who could outwork the rest of us. They were afflicted with an eerie condition I'd never seen before and haven't seen since. The slightest poke anywhere on their bodies would cause them to explode into a spasmodic jerking and jolting while they repeated whatever word they had last heard: A wickedly uttered "Baloney!", accompanied by a swift finger to the short ribs, would lead to "Ohhhhhh, baloney!" and a raggedly choreographed dance. Most of the guys said, though not in the presence of the cousins, that they were goosey.

Few people ever poked them twice, I can assure you, for they were tough, stringy men honed by hard work, unwilling to accept abuse and quite able to dispatch smart-assed kids like me. One day, following a lunch in an iced boxcar—it was well over 100 degrees outside—one of the goosey cousins challenged me to a playful wrestling match. I was a weight-trained ex-college football player but the wiry man gave me all I could handle until, just as he encircled my neck with a muscular arm and proclaimed to our assembled buddies, "Now ol' Gerald's a-gonna git the *Ja-pan* sleep hold," my elbow dug into his belly.

"Ohhhhh sleep hold!" he cried as his right leg described a violent arc and he jolted across the boxcar, spectators scrambling over one another to avoid his swinging boot.

I sat on the floor watching the quick chaos, then burst into uncontrolled laughter just as my erstwhile opponent swirled and menaced, his fists coming up, "You done that on purpose, Gerald!"

Before I could reply, the angry man's cousin said, "Cool off. You give him the Ja-pan sleep hold, but he give you the wild goose hold," breaking the tension. Everyone erupted in laughter.

Who *wouldn't* write about that?

I was born and my life has been shaped in the rural and small-town West—places like Oildale, Arvin, and Penngrove, California; like Fillmore and Kanosh, Utah. In my house, Spanish and English mingled. The farms, the ranches, the drilling rigs where I worked were populated by a strange—perhaps amazing—collection of characters. I boxed and played ball, boozed and brawled, with extraordinary specimens. And all of it in places themselves possessed of a haunted, haunting beauty—vast plains shimmering with mirages, desert tracts over which dust devils danced, the high meadows of the Sierra Nevada.

So what did I do when I determined to become a writer? Naturally I set my stories in Paris and New York and San Francisco—places I knew nothing about but which seemed to me uniquely suitable for literature. Who writes about *Oildale*?

Well, as it turns out, I do.

Fortunately, a friend named Dorothy Overly who knew my ambition took me aside and firmly advised that if I was determined to grind out short stories, I had better write them about what I knew and stop imitating others. I was offended, of course, and paid no attention to Dorothy's advice for a long time, but slowly the wisdom of her words sunk in and I began trying to capture the people and places I actually knew. Not until fifteen years later—a solid education that did not include a creative writing major, countless literary experiments and abundant rejection slips, marriage and a stable lifestyle—did a collection of my short fiction manage honorable mention in the 1971 Joseph Henry Jackson Award competition. All those stories were set in the Great Central Valley and all its characters were Valley folks. That small success confirmed my suspicion that only my own limitations would preclude outstanding literature from my rural realm—the place, the people, the situations were potentially the stuff of great literature. I dug in and, two years later, a polished version of that manuscript was published as *Okies: Selected Stories* and received excellent reviews.

A strange thing began happening during those years while I struggled to produce fiction that was true to locales and locals long ignored by others: The more I read and wrote, the more I perceived, the more sensitive I became to the wonders around me. I began asking questions such as why love between a titled couple in England was intrinsically more important than love between cotton pickers in Arvin or between a cowpuncher and a honky-tonk queen in Springville. It isn't, of course, and that realization was prime: there were stories that needed to be told because the human condition does not limit itself to specific, elite areas or specific, elite perceptions. Take smells, for instance.

When I was a kid we would pile into the car and drive south from Oildale's vague sulfuric belch, toward the Kern River where clear mountain fragrance cleansed our nostrils. We'd cross the bridge, leave the snow melt and riparian forest, then our noses would fill suddenly with the heavy fecundity of cow and hay and manure as we passed Peacock Dairy. Another mile—that deep barnyard aroma fading, fading—and we'd reach a traffic circle where Padre Garces stood in stone and Highway 99 sliced Bakersfield's edge, auto exhausts briefly stealing our breaths. After negotiating that barrier we'd at last enter Bakersfield and the scorched stench of heated pavement, the scorched surge of sweaty bodies, the scorched allure of theater popcorn, all blending with quick sights and sounds that filled us: the big city.

Years later, writing about my home region, I viscerally remembered those intimate aromas, intimately partook of them once again, as urgently as front-seat sex: they had been part of me and still were despite the passage of years. In fact, very little was completely gone. Like lives touching, experiences bump and blend and leave their singular impressions. Being human and alive is no simple matter, I realize, but it certainly is interesting, and my little part of the West hid wonders to be reckoned with.

I dedicated myself to expanding my craft so that I could be a faithful reckoner, reading especially writers such as Mildred Hahn, Jorge Luis

Borges, John Steinbeck, Franz Kafka, Flannery O'Conner, and William Saroyan. I was influenced not by their styles, but by their freedom, their ability to evolve unique forms to convey their fictions—"Barshi's Horse He Made It Flew," "The South," "The Chrysanthemum," "The Bucket Rider," "Everything That Rises Must Converge," "The Daring Young Man on the Flying Trapeze"—great stories all. Open yourself, never say no to an idea, don't assume that you know the absolute boundaries of anything, and be willing to work for years to develop your craft so that you can reveal your vision—these and other generalizations dawned and the writing, some of the writing at least, slowly began to work, to *feel* right.

The bottom line is that as my own craft slowly expanded, so did my concept of the rural West—like Huckleberry Finn, I came to see more of what had always been there. I've never regretted having built my fictive firmament here for it is the world writ small and life is lived no less intensely here than anywhere. I understand now that there was passion to spare in that packing shed and on those fields near Delano, passion and pain, wealth and grinding poverty. And there were people, my people.

Gerald Haslam

That Constant Coyote

Agreed, water ouzels dance through the mad music of mountain streams. . . .

Agreed, quaking aspens disintegrate in wind. . . .

Agreed, I never was what I used to be. . . .

Agreed. Agreed. Agreed.

But don't tell me what's done's done. I've lived too long and held the sticky hands of too many grandchildren, stood watching day slide into earth like a sharpened shovel while our generations clasped. I've gazed ahead into a past as jagged as the crazed castrato calls of evening coyotes. My own coyote, the very one whose song had haunted my sleep as well as my stock—only days after a state hunter had poisoned him and buzzards had disrobed his bones—appeared this morning in triplicate, gloriously alive, from a den above our high pasture on Brekenridge Mountain: the same flesh multiplied, pups probably wiser because of their father's recent fatal mistake. Despairing for my feathers and my wool, I welcomed the old scamp back, even tripled. State hunter be damned. Age teaches you to appreciate characters as much as character. I'd missed the quality of our continuing contest. In fact, I'd been missing a lot of things recently.

I watched my multiplied nemesis pounce on bugs and, one-third of him anyway, trap then lose a mouse. You're young again, old-timer, I thought, you'll learn. You'll nail the next one. I observed him wrestle himself down an embankment, snapping and yipping while young momma coyote—the old scamp always did favor youthful consorts—trotted heedlessly ahead past a stand of aspen, scanning for breakfast.

Finally the quartet—momma in the lead—bounded out of sight into an arroyo near Bear Creek, and I hiked back to my pickup, swigged a shot of pain killer, and headed home, satisfied that in this remote region, at least, the eternal struggle would be renewed. Bouncing back toward breakfast, I couldn't help but chuckle at the irony of it all, my genuine joy at seeing the old lamb stealer after all the cartridges I'd wasted trying to plug him.

Damn his old carcass, but every spring it seemed he'd lose his taste for mesquite berries and mice and garter snakes, and commence cropping my sheep. Every spring, about two lambs in, I'd lose my patience and whistle a few 30-30 protests toward him. In fact, I don't know if I ever really wanted to ventilate the pirate, and it was my son who had called the state hunter. After a few seasons I'd finally figured out that the old boy had to be feeding his own youngsters that lamb, the same way I was feeding mine. He needed a better food-source for those fuzzy bundles than the spring rodent crop provided. I became more tolerant then, a tad more.

Most of all, I've come to admit that I liked the mangy old coyote, with his desire for young sheep and young lovers. Once, long before this damned disease got me, my son and I were visiting the redwood grove where we've kept our family camp for nearly a century; I was reading, my boots propped up on an ancient stump, while the horses blew and my kid cooked coffee. All of a sudden I sensed eyes on me. I figured it had to be the mystery story I was enjoying, and chuckled at myself. A minute later Len, my son, whispered, "Would you look at that."

I looked. Not fifty yards away on the edge of a clearing sat the old boy staring in my direction. "He probably checked at the ranch to make sure we left our rifles home," I told Len.

"Then trailed us," he added.

"He probably just figured this was a stag party and followed us all the way up here. After all, he *is* a senior partner in this outfit."

Len laughed and finished the coffee. I kept reading, but every time I looked up, there he sat, although once or twice I caught him snapping up grasshoppers like a bum snitching hors d'oeuvres: what a character.

The grove, with its ferns and creek and giant trees, sat in a canyon on the far edge of our property, fully ten miles from the ranch house. My grandfather had bought that corridor of land specifically so we could own it before some renegade loggers cleared those beautiful trees the way they wanted to harvest every other accessible redwood in the Sierra. At one point, he'd even posted a man there to protect our timber. Over the years, several chairs had been carved out of small stumps, and one large table had been made by smoothing a large one, the remains of a titan felled by lightning. Two hollowed trees—both still living—took the place of tents; we'd been sleeping in them as far back as I can remember. We had also over the years hammered a few cabinets and boxes on snags, constructed a corral, and built a large fire ring.

There was something enduring about that place. On the stumps I could read carvings made by my grandfather and his pals eighty-some years ago, and I could imagine a lively Texan who had come to California with guts and ambition and built a small empire. He and his pals had slugged down whiskey and told lies and roughhoused in this very place when Cleveland was president, and now my grandkids and their friends were adding their carving to the stumps, their lies to the echoes.

Last month, when I returned from San Francisco after hearing that my cancer was inoperable and enduring three weeks of chemotherapy and counseling, I lit out for the grove. I had enough platinum floating through my system by then to start a jewelry store, a strange fate for a guy who even refused to wear a class ring. Moreover, although my oncologist had assured me that I withstood the effects of the toxin remarkably well, I was feeling punk. My gray locks were evacuating in clumps, and eating was no longer a pleasure. Hell of a note.

At least I was over the initial shock and depression. When the local doc had given me the bad news and urged that I travel north so that specialists at the University Medical Center could treat me, I had slipped into a sump of self-pity. Brandy hadn't helped, nor had my wife's deep concern. We hadn't told the family, of course, and didn't intend to until death was just around the corner. But I had remained low until I got things into perspective.

On the day after I returned home from the Med Center, Doris and I had saddled up our horses, loaded Molly, our favorite pack mule, then we'd ridden to the grove for a weekend. It had been a good journey, with trout working the creek along which we traveled, aspen groves shimmering in the breeze, and—a real rarity—a pine marten humping along a deadfall across the water. By the time we'd arrived, we were in good spirits. That's when Doris told me, casually yet tentatively, that the state hunter had killed the old coyote.

"He *what?*" My fuse was short after all that chemotherapy.

"He poisoned that old nemesis of yours."

"Well, *that's* just great," I replied sarcastically.

She stopped and stared at me. "Clint," she said, "you've been after him for years."

"*I've* been after him. It was between us, not some damned state hunter."

"Men!" Doris shook her head and began brewing coffee.

That night I'd sat at the fire after Doris turned in. Sipping brandy, I'd looked carefully at those trees and stumps, their shadows and shapes, thinking that my grandfather, my father, my son and grandson, all of them had known or did know this place. I had never met my dad, and hadn't ever seen my granddad either—both were killed young—but we had all three shared knowledge of this grove, of that bedding place within the hollowed goliath where my dad was built who built me on a feather bed who built Len in the backseat of an aging car, who built Timmy and Karen God knows where, all of us products of the same lightning that emptied the tree. Strong stuff, brandy, my personal chemotherapy. I turned in, snuggling next to Doris in the redwood's hollow.

She was snoring. I didn't blame her. This whole damned thing had been harder for her than me, I'm sure. I only had to die. She had to live with it and with the uncertain future. My future was certain. They told me at the Med Center that I had only a matter of months, and they put me in contact with the folks at the local hospice—most of them old friends—so I was downing, along with my brandy, a concoction they gave me to dull the pain that was already invading my middle.

I snuggled there next to my best pal, but my eyes, booze and drugs dimming them or not, would not close. I gazed through the frayed branches of redwoods at more stars than generations of my kin had a right to expect. Then I heard voices. . . .

I started, jerking my head to the side and saw two figures plop on the stump next to the fire ring. Well, if trespassers wanted trouble they had it. I wasn't in any mood to reason with anyone, nor was I too keen on avoiding trouble anymore. Deciding not to awaken Doris, I crawled out of my bag, pulled on jeans and boots, then slipped on my down vest.

"What do you two think you're doing here?" I demanded in a tense hiss soon as I approached the stump. Both men smiled at me in the dark. "I asked you a question," I said.

The larger of the two turned toward the other and said, "You tell him. He's got your personality."

I heard the other one reply, "The wages of sin." They both laughed.

"I'm waiting," I pointed out, in no mood to play.

"Clint," said the smaller man, "you always did have more guts than good sense."

I looked hard then, but couldn't recognize either of them, not exactly anyway. They were kids, maybe friends of Len's, but his pals would know better than to sneak up here without permission. Still, they were vaguely familiar, even in the dark and they didn't seem intent on mayhem, so I said, "You boys should've told us you were coming up. A midnight visit might buy you a 30-30 greeting."

I could see them smiling, then the smaller man said pleasantly, "Why don't you sit a spell and talk. We can't stay long."

"I didn't hear your horses," I said. "Did you hike in?" I remained a little irritated but their manner relaxed me. Besides, I figured I had enough juice left in me to take them if they got frisky.

'We didn't ride in," the larger man said.

"Hell of a hike," I said, still trying to see them clearly in the darkness.

"It's all of that," the larger man replied.

Away, far to the north, I heard a coyote cry.

"This place doesn't change much, does it, Dad?" the smaller man said to the larger.

Dad? Hell, they both looked less than thirty in that light, or lack of it.

"Did Len put you up to this?" I asked.

"Oh, in a way," responded the smaller man.

"That kid," I said.

"He's a good one," the smaller man said. "Like you."

"Like me?" This was getting silly. "Look, boys, I'm tired. Why don't you roll out your sacks and we'll talk in the morning."

"We'd like to," replied the larger man, "but we've only got a little while. We just came to tell you that we're with you in this, and that everything'll be alright. Play out your hand."

"Play out my hand?"

The coyote yipped once more.

"The years don't mean one hell of a lot, but how you live does," the larger man continued. "Lenny here didn't get much of a stake, but he did his damndest."

Before I could speak, the smaller man added, "Dad did the same. You've done a job and you're leaving good stock in that boy of yours, and his kids. We're proud of you, aren't we, Dad?"

I squatted next to the fire ring. "Let's start this all over again," I suggested, wondering whether mixing brandy with painkiller was such a good idea. I felt okay, but this conversation had me befuddled.

"You don't recognize us, do you?" asked the smaller man.

"No."

"And you invited us to stay anyway?"

"Why not?" I asked. "I learned a long time ago to trust my instincts. You two're alright, but I don't remember where we met or your names. I figured we'd shake all that out over coffee in the morning."

"We met in your blood," the larger man said.

"In my blood?"

"Did you expect us to wear sheets and rattle chains?" the larger man asked.

I said nothing, but searched—really searched—them with my eyes in the gentle darkness. The smaller man wore a uniform and not a recent one. As near as I could tell, it was a doughboy's outfit from World War I. The larger man wore jeans, a rough flannel shirt and a Mexican sombrero; he had a pistol strapped high on his waist, I realized. In the breathless night, their faces finally coalesced, finally became those in the fading photos on the mantel at home.

My granddad had been killed at twenty-nine, victim of a badger hole up on Tejon Ranch that broke his mount's leg and collapsed the big bay onto Grandpa's chest. Three other vaqueros buried him in an oak grove near the cabin. Grandma outlived two more husbands.

My father was vaporized by a German artillery round in France when he was twenty-one. He had lived with my mother, his high school sweetheart, for only a week before shipping overseas to make the world safe for democracy. Momma never remarried.

Which leaves me. Somehow I survived both horses and wars, further building the cattle business Grandpa had started, Grandma had built, and Momma had managed. I'm almost three times as old as my dad and granddad, and have lived to see two further generations of us raise old Ned. And now I've got this cancer, or rather it's got me.

"We figured you'd come back here just like we did. It's the center," Dad added.

Feeling suddenly relaxed with my hallucination, I nodded. "You two want a drink?" I asked. They did—my kind of ghosts.

Sunshine warmed my face when Doris poked me. "Hey night owl," she said, "I thought we were going fishing."

"Huh? Yeah, oh yeah. My kingdom for a cup of coffee." I smacked my brandy-befouled lips—ugh!—then leaned on one elbow.

She brought me a metal cup full of strong brew. "You must've really been dreaming last night. You were talking to yourself, carrying on."

"I was?"

"You sure were." Her face suddenly turned grave. "Clint, were you in pain?" Her eyes glistened.

"No, not at all." I sat up fully. "Hey, don't let it get you down, hon'. I sure as hell don't like it either, but it's out of our hands, so we can't let it ruin what we've got left."

Her hand was on my face and, with the morning sun behind her, she appeared as young as that first morning when we'd awakened in the midst of these same massive trees. "I know," she said. "I know we'll both die and so will everyone else. But it's just that we'll be separated." She did not blink, that good, brave woman who has made my life so, so . . . so desirable. Thank God for Doris. Leaving her was what I really hated.

"You know what I feel like doing?" I asked.

For a second a startled look crossed her face, then she smiled. "I thought you were sick."

"Sick, not dead."

Her smile broadened. "You know what *I* feel like doing?" she asked, unsnapping her denim shirt.

Far off, beyond our grove, above on a ridge somewhere, that coyote sang. I caught it through our pounding breath and, for an instant, a flash, I realized that I'd never before heard one call this late in the morning, then I sensed our breath, our breath, felt it.

Agreed, we hover in time like sparrowhawks in wind. . . .

Agreed, our lives have passed through redwood exclamations. . . .

Agreed, we never were what we used to be. . . .

Agreed. Agreed. Agreed.

Hawk's Flight: An American Fable

Awake early, he had crept sleepily up the gully to relieve himself. He was not yet old enough to stand guard, and on mornings like this he was grateful to be sleeping inside beneath warm robes. There had been no one visible when he started up the gully, so he hadn't walked as far from home as usual. Still he walked too far. Savages leapt upon him before he could shout a warning and, in the instant before he was beaten unconscious, he realized fully it was the attack they had for so long dreaded.

He vaguely perceived that morning, yet through haze he heard shouts and screams from his village, frenzied yips of savages, pops and cracks of rifles. A child flashed up the gully past him with a mounted savage behind her. In a moment there was a scream, then the horseman rode back down the gully breathing hard. Painfully turning his head, he saw where the girl lay, her crushed head in a pool of blood, her tiny features stunned and askew.

Struggling to rise, he glimpsed, before collapsing, men trying to defend their families—his own father perhaps—and he caught the hot leer of one savage's eye. He knew he was done, that everyone was done, as he slipped back into the void.

How many hours or days or weeks they dragged him, leather thong round his neck, he could not say. He had stumbled and staggered barefoot over rocky ground for endless miles. When he fell, they jerked him until he was unconscious from choking, but always stopped to revive him just in time to deny him merciful death. Yet he was dead, he had died with his family back at the village.

They dragged him finally into their compound where villagers beat and spat upon him. Children threw rocks at him, shouting in their incomprehensible tongue. He did not have to know their words to understand what they said. He was taken before their chief, a small, decorated man. There was a good deal of loud talk, again incomprehensible, then he was forced into a small wooden hut.

He needed water; he needed food; he needed rest. Lying painfully on a grass-covered corner of the hut, sleep came to him finally in the heat of the day. And he lived again in his dreams: Hawk flew wind away from the savages toward the hills where his people lay; his mother and father and sisters and brothers waved to him as he flew beyond them toward Sacred Spring.

Before the Spring, he knelt and asked what his people had done that their homeland should be invaded by savages. But Sacred Spring did not answer. Are we to submit? he asked, incredulous. Are we to not fight back? The Spring gurgled, then belched forth red: blood flowed from wounded Earth. But I am only one, he said, and not even a warrior. Become a warrior, ordered Sacred Spring. I have no weapons, he said. Then it came to him: he was Hawk and he had the wind.

He awoke to find a cup of water and a metal plate with a few pieces of dried meat and hard bread on it. He wanted to bolt the food, but Hawk's battered face made chewing difficult, so he broke both meat and bread into tiny pieces which he softened in his mouth, then swallowed. Just as he finished his meal, he heard voices outside the hut, and gruff laughter. There was one small, low window in the dark hovel and suddenly a stream of urine sprayed through it. The laughter grew louder, some words were shouted, then the voices grew faint. Hawk peered out the window and saw three of the savage warriors striding away, their blue uniforms dark as death over the bright earth of the compound.

It was nearly night when several blue warriors threw open the door of his hut and pulled him out. Prodded to their chief again, Hawk felt strengthened from the food and able to breathe and draw life from the air. This time there were other human beings present, though they were of a rival clan. As the pale chief spoke, one of the human beings said to Hawk: "Now listen to this. I will tell you what their chief says." The man spoke poorly, but at least he could be understood. "The white chief says you and your clan have hurt many of his warriors. He says you are dangerous vermin. He says you must be an example. He says they will pull your neck with a rope until you are dead. He says their god will protect you." The human being who was not of his clan could not resist a comment of his own: "You and yours are lice," he added.

Hawk turned to face the other human being. "At least we have not become savages," he spat, and the other human being was ashamed and angry. He knew that Hawk, a boy not yet a warrior, had bested him. He said something to a savage in the strange tongue, and the blue warrior struck Hawk hard across the face. The other human being was even more ashamed when Hawk did not flinch.

Back in the wooden hovel, the boy again curled on the grass to sleep. His face hurt badly where the savage had struck him. He could neither open nor close his mouth. His head pulsed with pain each time his heart beat. He could not sleep and was sitting up when a very pale young savage visited him, accompanied by blue warriors. The savage held two pieces of wood tied together to represent the four sacred directions. The direction stick told Hawk that the savage was a shaman. So Hawk listened respectfully to words he could not understand while the pale shaman gestured and babbled. When the savage finally quieted, Hawk mumbled no, only that. The pale savage seemed to understand, and departed. He had been a weak shaman with no real power.

Hawk found himself feeling a strange kind of pity for these hopeless creatures who possessed no magic at all, no union with Earth or Sky, only the ability to hurt and kill. He could not even hate such creatures for they were beneath hate. They were sad and dangerous like a broken rattlesnake thrashing around wildly to kill whatever neared it because it could not save itself. They had great skill at destruction, but he could sense no life force in them.

Hawk flew wind again that night, flew high to the zenith where Old Man of the Ancients resided; Old Man was growing impatient with the savages. Hawk flew to the nadir and Earth Mother wept angrily over her torn land and dead children. It was a bad dream because the savages killed everything and everyone. And, in the instant before he awoke, the shattered, bleeding face of the little girl he had seen in the gully flooded him. It was a very bad dream, for he knew he must kill a savage.

They came for him early next morning, a mass of blue-shirted savages who bound his arms with leather straps, then led him around a building into a square where it seemed all the pale villagers were gathered around a wooden platform. As he was thrust up the steps, he saw a rope—the rope for pulling his neck—draped over a crossbeam. Hawk was placed beneath the rope and the savages' chief stood at the front of the platform and spoke loudly to his people. At the same time, the wan shaman stood directly before Hawk, muttering tensely and senselessly into his face, holding his sticks in one hand. Another savage knelt behind Hawk and began to bind his legs. Hawk knew it was time, and he repeated to himself a warrior's song he had been learning as part of his training:

> Let us see, is this real,
> Let us see, is this real,
> This life I am living—
> You Powers who dwell everywhere,
> Let us see, is this real,
> This life I am living—

He leaned forward and bit the shaman's pallid white nose, at the same time kicking the man who sought to bind his legs. Then Hawk darted across the platform and kicked the startled chief behind a knee and the enemy leader collapsed directly in front of him. One more kick with all his leg behind it and Hawk felt the pale chief's head crumple. He had killed the savages' leader.

From all around him, blue savages fired their weapons, yet Hawk stood straight and tall, making no attempt to flee or dodge. Bullets smashed into his body, but they were too slow, for Hawk flew wind once more, high over the frantic scene and away, over plains and deserts, over brooding hills, over bleeding Sacred Spring. And Sacred Spring called to him as he soared: "Ho Warrior!"

Sweet Reason

Clutching the white-gloved hand of an aging Negro gentleman, tilting her pert head to one side, the moppet began to dance, pale little legs thrusting from a skirt stiff with petticoats. Faster and faster moved her white shoes, while her lithe body—with its hint of awkward provocation—matched the old man move for move.

Then the screen went black, or for a moment I thought it had, snapping me out of my reverie. Uncle Fate Newby had risen and passed his huge frame in front of me on his way to the aisle then out of the picture show. He made no apology or complaint. He simply departed.

Later, when we were all seated in the cab of his truck jostling back toward the farm, I asked Uncle Fate—who had not volunteered any information concerning his departure—why he'd left. I wondered if it had been the sight of a black man dancing with a white girl, since the local klavern of the klan had tried to make an issue of it soon after the movie began showing in Westbrook County, parading around in sheets one hot afternoon.

Squinting straight ahead up the dirt track, his lower lip snug over a quid of snoose the size of a pinecone, Uncle Fate grunted, "Y'all believe in that?"

"In *that?*" I responded, a tad arrogant for it was the summer after my first year at the university, and I had returned home more than a little aware of my family's lack of sophistication. "*That* what?"

Uncle Fate spat out the window. "That there girl?"

"Shirley Temple?" chimed in Emily Anne, my younger sister, who sat between us on the truck's seat.

My uncle nodded. "Y'all believe in that?"

"Uncle Fate," I answered with great patience, "what's there to believe in?"

"That ain't no real girl," he said.

"Huh?" I stammered, and Emily Anne immediately burst into raucous laughter, sounding like a John Deere trying to start on a cold morning.

"That ain't no real girl," Uncle Fate repeated.

Emily Anne, despite receiving little encouragement from nature, spent a good many of her waking hours before our parents' full-length mirror rehearsing Shirley Temple's routines against the day Hollywood talent scouts would flock to Westbrook County, so Uncle Fate's pronouncement left her snorting and gasping, poking me in the ribs all the while.

"Sure it is," I asserted. "It's gotta be a real girl."

"That ain't no real girl. Ain't no real girl can do that stuff. That there's a shrunk growed-up woman."

My sister shrieked at Uncle Fate's explanation, nearly shoving my floating rib into my throat with her sharp elbow. I poked her back, then asked, "But how can they do that?"

"They got ways," he snorted.

"Look, Uncle Fate," I replied calmly, having determined to employ the clear logic I had so lately acquired, "Shirley Temple is a little girl with special talent and good training. There's no trick about her."

Still guiding the truck over that rude country road, my uncle swiveled his huge head to face me. His tone, always gruff, softened slightly. "Boy," he said, steadily ignoring Emily Anne's antics, "that ain't no real girl," and I knew the discussion was closed. Even Emily Anne swallowed her laughter and emitted thereafter only a few choked snorts.

You see, Uncle Fate Newby didn't cotton to uncertainty. He lived in a known cosmos largely of his own creation, and few of his fellow philosophers have been better equipped to define the limits of reality. He was not only the most prosperous farmer in our region, but he was also Westbrook County's catch-as-catch-can wrestling champion, an honor he had won as a youth and defended year after year at the county fair. Even though he was well into middle age, his six-feet, nine inches and three hundred pounds remained invulnerable. They also tended to make him a persuasive advocate for any position he favored. He was a master of sweet reason, never raising his voice to win a point.

Like the time he joined Momma and Daddy and me for a holiday weekend at the university, and I decided to treat us to one of my new-found delights, brunch at the Palace Hotel. No sooner had the genteel waiter delivered eggs baked in square stoneware dishes and garnished with cheese and parsley than Uncle Fate pushed the plate away, reached into his vest pocket and withdrew his snuff tin, then tamped half a bushel into his lower lip.

"What's the matter, Uncle Fate?" I asked with a smile to hide my embarrassment.

He glanced from mother to father to me. "What *is* that?" he asked.

"Eggs," I chuckled. "The cook breaks them into these special dishes, mixes them with a sauce and sprinkles cheese and greens on them, then bakes the whole works. Try them. They're delicious."

"Them ain't eggs," said Uncle Fate.

I called the waiter, an old-world genius of his craft, and asked him to please detail the ingredients of the dish for my uncle. "Why it is baked egg, sir," he smiled, then followed with approximately the same recipe I had cited.

Uncle Fate replied with quiet assurance, "Them ain't eggs."

The waiter and I exchanged knowing glances, then he said to the vast man seated before him, "My dear sir, I assure you . . ." He did not complete his statement for his eyes met my Uncle's and suddenly the waiter nodded and said, "Yes, sir," apparently swayed by sweet reason, then withdrew.

Through all this, my mother and father had continued eating, ignoring the exchange. Uncle Fate said nothing of his triumph: indeed, he hardly seemed to have noticed it. I, on the other hand, seethed. Thank God, at least Emily Anne hadn't been there to gloat and giggle.

She was present, however, that hot noon when Uncle Fate retired from wrestling. In fact, Emily Anne fetched me from the house so I could see the action. It was dinner time, and Momma had sent my sister out to fetch Uncle Fate from the cotton patch near the county road where he was inspecting the results of last week's chopping. Just as she reached him, she noticed a black man approaching from the road. Since it was not uncommon during those times for men seeking work to wander from farm to farm, and since my uncle was in the habit of feeding any hungry man, whether he had work for him or not, Emily Anne and Uncle Fate waited while the stranger approached.

The black man walked directly toward my uncle, removed his hat and held it in front of his chest with both hands. When he was close enough to speak, he looked at the earth in front of his feet and asked, "Is you Mistuh Fate, suh?"

"Yep."

"Is you the rasslin champeen a Westbrook County?" the man asked softly.

"Yep."

"Well, suh," the man continued to look down and to speak in a voice barely audible, "my name Rufus Tuhnuh. I's champeen down Tayluh County, and I walk up heah hopin' maybe we might could see who best in bof counties."

Uncle Fate eyed the man, who was large by normal standards, and young, then shook his head. "Sorry, Rufus, but I got dinner waitin'."

The black man, his voice still soft and without a hint of demand, said, "I's walked a pow'ful long ways."

"Is that so? Where ye walk from, Rufus?"

"Bridgeville, Mistuh Fate."

"Ye walk all that a-way just to rassle me?"

"Yassuh."

Uncle Fate turned to Emily Anne and said, "Go tell your momma I'll be late for dinner." Then he turned, slipped off his galluses and his shirt, and carefully removed his hat, placing it atop his shirt on the ground. "Go own," he urged Emily Anne as the black man piled his own shirt and hat on the ground near Uncle Fate's.

By the time I got out to the field, having sprinted all the way, a cloud of dust was rising. Both men were covered with dirt and Rufus Turner's hair had caught thistles and twigs. They were both on their feet, circling each other, and Uncle Fate's huge white body heaved for breath, while the black body, glistening where sweat trailed through the dirt, breathed easily. Fate was stalking the man, who darted this way and that when my uncle closed, smoothly avoiding his slow swoops.

Neither man was speaking; both meant business. Yet I could see that Uncle Fate was growing frustrated, his face bright red, his mouth agape, while his opponent continued moving quickly in and out of range, forcing my uncle to pursue him. No sooner had I arrived than Uncle Fate misread a feint and lunged toward the swift younger man, missed, and nearly fell to the ground. He was tiring and Rufus, coiled and lively, seemed full of fight. I suddenly didn't like the look of things.

A moment later I liked them even less. Just as Uncle Fate turned toward him, the Taylor County champion shot both his hands at the red face, causing my uncle to lean back and raise his heavy arms to ward off the blow, then the black man swooped low and tackled him above the knees, felling him with a dead thud that I was certain had ended the match, especially when the black man swarmed up my uncle's body, wrapping his own powerful arms around the prone man's, encircling his neck and chest in the process. He was only inches away from pinning Uncle Fate, and all three of us knew it.

Protruding beyond the hunched, clasping black body was my uncle's head, swollen with fatigue. I saw his eyes close and veins begin to bulge on his forehead, saw his features gradually erase as he strained, his face purple. Everything—Uncle Fate, Rufus Turner, even the earth—seemed to quiver for a long moment until, like two powerful springs releasing, the thick black arms popped apart and the black man recoiled onto his haunches, stunned.

He recovered quickly, though, leaping up and crouching, poised and ready, while Uncle Fate struggled to rise. Once on his feet, my uncle had trouble even raising his arms and he stood stiff-legged, swaying in front of his antagonist, his eyes still fiery but his body empty. The Taylor County champion, along with me, sensed that the match was over, that the big man was spent if not broken. It was the first time I'd seen Uncle Fate lose, and I think I admired him more for how he was losing than for any of the times I'd seen him win.

Carefully, Rufus Turner circled the exhausted man, who stumbled trying to face him. Then, just as it became clear that Uncle Fate could no longer even turn fast enough to keep his opponent in sight, the black man feinted a dive at Uncle Fate's legs, then zigged rapidly to his right, only to slip in the loose dirt and fall on his side.

So fatigued was Uncle Fate that, with Rufus Turner on the ground in front of him, he barely managed to lunge before the black man scrambled to his feet. When he finally did, though, his three hundred pounds leveled his opponent. Staggered by the impact, the Taylor County champ's normally swift reactions deserted him and, for an instant, he lay passively under Uncle Fate, whose thick white arms moved—his right through an armpit and over the dark chest, his left through the other armpit and behind Turner's thick back—big, pale hands edging closer together atop one black shoulder just as Rufus began to stir with some purpose, then struggle with considerable power to release himself, but Fate's hands had joined, and he arched on his toes until his full weight and strength bore down on his opponent.

Unwilling to concede, Rufus Turner bridged up on his neck, lifting Uncle Fate off the ground, and I heard both men grunt like battling boars, but my uncle's weight and strength, coupled with the crippling hold he had locked on the black man, were too much, and the Taylor County man's strength finally failed. He collapsed flat against the ground under Uncle Fate.

The winner rolled onto the ground next to his vanquished opponent and lay gasping like some huge sea mammal suddenly dropped on the field. Rufus Turner rose, shaking his head, and walked to a nearby irrigation ditch where he drank and washed himself, then stood drying in the sun while my uncle still gasped on the earth. When he was finally dry enough, Rufus Turner put on his frayed workshirt, buttoned the bib of his overalls, and placed his straw hat back on his head. He returned then to Uncle Fate, who had just managed to sit up, his face now ashen.

Holding his hat in front of himself just as he had before, and looking at his feet, the black man said, "Much 'blidged, Mistah Fate." He turned to leave, but my uncle's voice stopped him. "Have ye eat dinner, Rufus?"

"Nawsuh."

"Then ye better come along to the house fer vittles." Uncle Fate extended a hand toward me and I steadied him as he rose. He bathed in the ditch then slowly dressed himself and finally we trudged home, Rufus Turner and I both having to slow our walk in order not to pull away from him.

Once home, Uncle Fate told Momma to feed Rufus and she did, though her real concern was for my uncle, and her face could not hide it. Soon as he had disappeared into the house and Rufus was eating, she asked me what had happened. I told her and she only shook her head. "The old fool," she muttered.

A few minutes later, Uncle Fate reappeared, shuffling slowly to the serving porch where Rufus Turner ate. In his hand he carried one of the silver cups he won annually for his wrestling at the Westbrook County Fair. He placed it in front of the black man and said, "Rufus, you champeen a both counties now."

The black man blinked, then stood and looked at his feet. "Nawsuh, Mistuh Fate, you done whup me, suh."

"You champeen now, Rufus," Fate repeated softly.

"Mistuh Fate, suh, I cain't take . . ." Rufus paused. He had looked up and his eyes had met my uncle's. "Thank you suh," he said, and he picked up the silver cup in one large hand.

Rufus Turner walked back to Taylor County and Uncle Fate went to bed for two days. When he finally arose, having ignored my mother's requests that she be allowed to call the doctor, he devoured a huge breakfast, then strided out of the house toward the field he had been inspecting when Rufus Turner interrupted. Emily Anne and I scurried after him.

Halfway to the field my sister, who not-too-secretly coveted her uncle's silver cups, whined, "How come you went and give that nigra your cup?"

"He warn't no nigra," replied Uncle Fate without breaking stride, and I have to admit that caught my attention since I'd seen the black man.

"Was so!" sassed Emily Anne.

"He warn't no nigra."

Not wanting to sound like my sister, but curious all the same, I had to ask, "What was he then?"

Uncle Fate stopped and looked down at the two of us, then answered: "He was champeen a Taylor County."

California Christmas

Things was powerful hard that first winter after we come to California. Daddy, and other farmers too, I reckon, just figured the sun shone all the year round out West and jobs went a-begging, but that ain't how it was. We was camped with some other folks right alongside the Kern River near Bakersfield. Daddy he'd found him a little work in the crops around there, and he had signed for a job with some oil companies; he was waiting to be hired and just hanging on with what he could pick up at day labor. Them oil fields looked mighty good to men with families to support; they looked like hope. Daddy figured he could make as much wages just working around Bakersfield as he could trying to follow crops all over the state; anyways Momma was sick and our truck was about give out. So we stayed in Riverview. Besides, there was always that chance he could get on with an oil company; he just pined for that.

It rained some that winter and the river climbed up the levee and really scared us; we didn't have much left, but we sure didn't want to lose it. But praise Jesus the levee held. Mostly it was just cold and terrible foggy, a grainy grey fog that even made breathing hard. None of us never seen nothing like it back home on the farm, and it got lots of folks to talking about how much they missed Oklahoma. Us kids didn't have good clothes or even shoes, so we couldn't go to school. Momma said she surely prayed Daddy'd get steady work so we could go, but she wasn't going to send us looking like scarecrows because she knew what would happen. It just seemed like folks wasn't too friendly toward us in California.

Daddy had fixed up a cabin out of whatever wood he found and cardboard. We lived in it, bundled up in all the clothes we owned, and still cold. It must have been comical to see us looking like pale-faced Eskimos, but we didn't laugh none then, I'll tell you. Old sunny California just froze us half to death.

I don't believe none of us kids would have remembered Christmas that year, except one day the sun broke through so a bunch of us we walked all the way to Oildale and seen a giant Christmas tree in front of the grade school there. That done it. We hustled ourselves home and commenced worrying poor Momma, us not realizing she was poorly. Momma she looked mighty sad, like she was gonna bawl, and she told us not to think too much about it. Well, before long we taken every kid from the camp to see that big old tree with its electric lights and fake snow. It looked ready to sprout presents any time.

Come the day before Christmas, Daddy couldn't find no work. He just fussed around the cabin, patching here and there and working on the stove. After while he went outside and squatted with other men talking about hard times. Well, all of a sudden up drives these two big shiny cars and out steps a preacher and some ladies. The preacher he opened the back of his car and commenced unloading big baskets filled with food and one filled with presents.

What's this? Daddy asked them. This is our annual Christmas basket program for the needy, said the preacher. What church? Daddy asked him. The preacher he looked kind of confused and I figured he'd ask what difference it made. Community, the preacher finally answered. Daddy looked around at the other men; Just what I figured, he said. I knew I seen this preacher before. Member when we tried to worship at your church last summer and you run us off? Now that preacher he surely didn't want to remember.

One big old fat lady stepped up in front of the preacher real uppity like. Here we are trying to help you people, she kind of hollered, and this is the thanks we receive. Daddy he said real quiet: Why don't you folks help us by letting us worship Jesus with you then? Now wait a minute, the preacher sputtered, but a man from camp he said: We'd rather a decent church for our kids than all that food. You've got this all wrong, the preacher said, and that fat lady fumed at us. Daddy cut them both off: You folks think you're too good to pray with us. Well then we ain't good enough to take your handouts either. Get the hell out of here! All of a sudden Daddy sounded dangerous. I guess being hungry, and seeing folks sneer at his kids, and knowing his wife was sick, and not finding work, I guess it all just welled up.

The fat lady had been pouting and glaring, but when she looked at Daddy's face, she waddled back to her car without saying nothing. I thought Daddy might sock her. One little guy from our camp he said to the preacher: You better get out of here, mister. Them townfolks climbed all over each other getting back into their cars and the preacher reloaded his baskets in a big hurry and got back into his car. As they pulled away, the fat lady put her big old face out a window and said she was going the sic the sheriff on us. Daddy he spit a great big goober on her car and didn't miss her face by much.

Them rich people was so busy scrambling away that they plum forgot their basket of presents, and all us kids gathered round and, without touching nothing, stayed mighty close to it. Daddy looked like he'd kick that basket clean into the river, but another man came over and he said maybe Jesus hadn't forgot us after all. He said we shouldn't be sitting around feeling sorry for ourselves, that we ought to hold a worship service right there on the riverbank next morning. Daddy he agreed with the man and said it was true, the baby Jesus was born in a pretty humble place his-ownself.

Everything changed that quick. An old man said his boys and him had caught them a mess of carp and the women folk could cook them up for Christmas dinner. Another man said his family had some extra beans and Daddy said we had coffee to share. Other folks said they could fry some pan bread and boil some syrup. Everyone was grinning and looking excited, then Daddy said: If that shurf don't show up, I reckon we just might can find something to do with these presents too. He winked at us kids, and the men all laughed.

That evening we built a huge bonfire and everyone gathered round it in thick fog to sing hymns and Christmas carols with the Kern River a-sucking and a-gurgling in the background. About the time Momma was fixing to put us kids to bed, up pulled a car. We couldn't make it out clear through the fog, but one man said: I believe it's the shurf. Daddy he tensed up and I seen him reach into the pocket where he kept his knife, then I heard Momma whisper his name—Roy—and she touched his arm. The car's door slammed and a deputy came out of the fog and kind of stood on his heels a-looking at us. It seemed like nobody was breathing.

Evening, the deputy finally said, everything all right? Daddy said things was fine. The deputy, he said that a big fire was sure welcome on a cold night and folks agreed; Sholy, one skinny lady said real loud, it sholy is. I heard you folks singing, the deputy told us, so I just thought I'd stop in for a minute. You're welcome, the same lady said. The deputy reached for a pocket and I could feel Daddy kind of stiffen, then the deputy said he had him a couple of kids at home and would it be okay if he give each of us a piece of hard candy. We couldn't hardly believe it; we hadn't had much candy since we left the farm. Daddy hesitated, but Momma said much obliged, so he kept quiet and the deputy give each of us a piece all wrapped in paper. Merry Christmas folks, the deputy said and off he went.

After the car pulled away, Daddy he shook his head. Damn, he said, it's like folks out here just change the rules come Christmas. And I'm thankful they do, Momma said. A man said it's Jesus makes em change. Jesus he's a workin man hisownself. He don't forget workin folks. Amen, a lady added. Besides, another man said, these ain't bad folks out here. They're just skeered, skeered as they can be. They figure we might get their jobs, see. A lady said maybe we ought to pray for them, so we did.

Christmas morning every kid in camp had a gift. My sister Vondalee she got gloves and my big brothers, Earl and Larance, both got little metal cars; me, I got a small square box and inside was a whistle. It was the best present I ever got, and I still got it hanging on my key chain.

That morning we had us a real back home worship service for baby Jesus and we all said a special thanks for being so blessed. We ate carp and beans, and drank coffee. Then we had us some pan bread with syrup for dessert. Lord, was I stuffed. Everyone gathered round the fire after we ate and told stories about home and other Christmases. All the folks was smiling at each other, and pretty soon Momma and Daddy stood right there with their arms around each other, us kids giggling and pointing. California didn't seem half bad.

Rider

⚡ ⚡ ⚡ ⚡ ⚡ ⚡ ⚡ ⚡ ⚡ ⚡ ⚡ ⚡

"Ol' Jesse Stahl ride any bangtail ever foaled," the old man wheezed.

"Jesse black?" asked Charles, his grandson.

"As coal," chuckled Grandpappy, "and hard. *Hard.* Yessir, Jesse 'bout the hardest ever they was, 'ceptin' maybe Jackson Sundown. Jackson ride too. And Bill Pickett. Yakima Canutt. They ride, boy. Ain' no riders like 'em today."

"All them dudes brothers?"

"Colored," answered Grandpappy. "Colored mens."

"Damn," exclaimed Charles, "I never see *them* in no movies."

"One time me and Jesse, we at Pendleton and he clownin'. Come time for saddle broncs, and he cain't find his boots, so he wear these floppy ol' shoes he clown in. They so big he cain't fit 'em in the stirrups, so he tell the boys to jam them devils in for him. This white buckaroo, he say, 'But what if you gets bucked off? You be killed.' Ol' Jesse he look dead at the boy and he say, 'I ain' gon' *get* bucked off.' He right. He work that horse till it ready to drop. I ridin' pickup, but he cain't take his feets outta them stirrups, so we have to cut the saddle loose to get him off. Jesse he look at that white boy and he grin: 'What I say?' he ask him. Me and Jesse, we cut some rusty capers together," the old man continued, his red-rimmed eyes drifting, floating on his face for a long moment. "Ol' Jesse," he sighed.

"Stop it, Pappy!" snapped his daughter. "Them old days don't put no grits on the table. Leave the boy be. Don't give him no crazy ideas."

The old man said nothing more. He tightened within himself for he

was hot, damned hot, but he resolved not to fight in front of his grandson.
The boy had seen enough of that. Later, when Charles had gone out,
Grandpappy cornered Joletha: "Looky here, girl," he growled, "don' you
never talk to me like that again in front of the boy or I go up longside yo'
head. I means it! Don' you want that boy to grow up straight?"

His daughter rolled her eyes. "Oh, Pappy . . ."

"I means it! I really means it! You a good momma, baby, but you don'
know what it like for a boy to grow. That boy goin' find him some way
to be a man, and I reckon what I gives him a damn sight better 'n what
the street give him."

Joletha ran a hand through her hair. "I don' know," she shook her
head. "Those stories of yours like fairy tales. We scufflin' to eat, and you
carry on 'bout cowboys 'n' Indians."

"Nawsuh!" Grandpappy wouldn't give. "Nawsuh. Ain' no play actin'
'bout it. I tell Charles 'bout workin' cattle and 'bout rodeoin'. Tha's all."

Joletha hushed him. "Pappy, don' you see it all the same for Charles?
He no closer to bein' a cowboy than bein' a Indian. You gotta *see*. Them
ol' days over. They *be* over."

She was right, of course, and he knew it. Oh, there were still ranches,
but they were few and growing fewer. In fact, Grandpappy himself had
been too late for the open range and long cattle drives, and that had finally
led him to spend nearly thirty years on the rodeo circuit. When he grew
too stove up to compete any longer, he had repaired to Wes Cooley's
spread at Glenville, and he'd still be riding there if Wes hadn't died,
leaving the ranch to his citified nephew who turned it into a summer-
home development. The nephew had asked Grandpappy to stay on as "a
touch of the old West," but he didn't intend to be anyone's buffoon.

So he'd moved in with Joletha. He knew he could have found a cabin
near Glenville and remained his own man, but there was the boy—his
grandson—growing up without a father.

And Charles did listen to him, especially since the night Lonnie, the
boy's main man, had been blown away on the street. Lonnie's death had
deepened Charles. He spent much more time within himself. But he also
spent even more time with his grandfather, and the old man gave what
he sensed the boy needed, answering his questions, telling him tales,
teaching him practical skills. He even managed to scratch a few dollars
together so that he and the boy could travel by bus to Golden Gate Park

and rent mounts. He noted with pride that Charles was a natural, sitting the horse as though born in a saddle.

But the high point came the day when Charles brought home from the library a book about Negro cowboys. Since the boy was no reader—he had left school in ninth grade, and only sporadically even glanced at a newspaper—his grandfather, a great believer in learning despite his own limited formal education, had felt matters were moving in the best possible direction, especially when Charles opened the book and showed him on a list of the outstanding rodeo riders the brief notation that proved he—a stove-up old man—he too had lived: ". . . from Langston, Oklahoma, came a bull-rider *par excellence*, Charlie 'Bo' Howard."

It flooded him with memories, glistened his eyes: the good old boys, the *hombres del Campo*, the horses and snaky bulls and the gals. Mostly it brought back Marlene, Charles's grandmother. Half-Kiowa, she could ride the wind. When she had died—Joletha just a baby—it had killed a part of him that had never come back to life, and it had probably made him a tougher rider. He just didn't give a damn after that. In Mexico he had even ridden fighting bulls.

"Who write that book?" he asked. "I never know I be in no book."

When Charles had shown Joletha, even she softened. "Your Granpappy a cowboy," she had acknowledged to the boy, and she had patted her father's back.

Two days later detectives picked Charles up for rustling a horse from the mounted police stable in Golden Gate Park. While neighborhood young bloods had cackled over Charles's feat—ripping off a pig's horse—Momma had not been amused. They had no money for a lawyer, and she was concerned that her son, juvenile or not, would be prosecuted for felony grand theft, as one city man had warned. Fortunately, the public defender made a deal, pointing out that Charles had really just engaged in a prank, and that he had made no effort to really steal the animal, but had merely taken a joy ride. Ninety days' probation was all the juvenile judge had given the boy. Momma had been relieved at the outcome.

But Grandpappy was livid. "You don' never steal nobody's horse, nigger! Never!" The boy grinned, only to feel his grandfather pop him hard across the mouth. "Don't gi' me no sass," the old man warned. "They's things a man don' do, and horse stealin' one of 'em."

Charles could have flattened Grandpappy easily and he knew it, but he was so stunned by the old man's anger that it didn't occur to him to strike back. "Yes sir," he said.

"Ain' nobody ride with no horse thief," his grandfather explained. "Ain' nobody share they grub with no horse thief. Horse thief no better'n a re-rider. If you be a man, act like one."

The boy had rocked on his heels, undecided whether to leave this bent old man who hovered before him and return to the street brothers while he was still a celebrity. "What's a *re*-rider?" he'd finally grumbled.

"A re-rider? That what we calls all them boys what holler for extra tries at the rodeo," the old man explained. "You know, carryin' on 'bout how they wasn' ready or some such. Always got excuses. Low, boy, low-life folks."

"Uhm," nodded Charles. He began to say something when his grandfather interrupted him to tell him about the rodeo.

"If you ready to be man, they's a rodeo up at Guerneville this weekend. I save a little money so's you can go and watch some riders work, and I buy you somethin' too." Grandpappy shuffled to his drawer and returned with a large shoebox. When he opened it, Charles saw a bright new pair of cowboy boots. "These workin' boots," Grandpappy explained, "the kind real riders wear. They go with that sombrero I buy you. Maybe you ready for 'em."

They spent that afternoon talking about bull riding, the techniques and tricks Grandpappy had learned during his years in the arena. He told the boy of his failures and his triumphs. "One time this bull name Screwtail he throw me, then he worry me till he knock this out," Grandpappy said, pointing at his drooping left eye. "Then ol' Manny Rojas, he put it back in and carry me to the hospital. That way back in '28 at Clovis, New Mexico. A mean damn bull. Flat snaky."

"Knock your *eye* out?"

"Clean out."

"Damn!" exclaimed Charles.

"Double damn. But I ride that rank Screwtail a month later at Flagstaff," Grandpappy chuckled. "He a bad bull though."

"Damn," the boy repeated.

Saturday Charles caught a ride as far as Cotati with one of Momma's friends, then hitchhiked to Guerneville. A Volkswagen with three long-haired young white men picked him up and they shared a joint with him as they drove. They dropped him next to a parking lot and small arena nestled in a wooded canyon. There was no town visible, though cars were streaming into the lot, and large numbers of people wandered up the road from the direction he had not traveled. The people were an oddly mixed lot, not at all the John Wayne-Gary Cooper-Clint Eastwood types he had expected. Oh, there were plenty of what could be called cowboys, lean mostly, and white, sipping on beers or pulling on bottles hidden in paper bags, but there were also large numbers of hippies smiling and carrying on. Although he saw a few other black people, he felt suddenly alone, very alone. He knew no one here, and this wooded canyon was no Golden Gate Park snuggled in the comfort of his city; this was the sticks.

"Lookin' for somethin'?"

Charles turned to face a white sheriff, and his belly swooped. The pig didn't smile. "What?" asked Charles.

"You look like you're lookin' for somethin'," explained the sheriff. "Late entries sign up at the van over yonder." The uniformed man pointed toward a mobile home parked near one wooden grandstand, and Charles saw a short line of cowboys waiting in front.

"Thanks," he said warily.

"Good luck," winked the sheriff as Charles walked toward the van, and the boy realized the pig had seen a rider, not a nigger. Alright, he thought. *Alright.*

He joined the line, his eyes averted, and he was again surprised as several of the others waiting greeted him as though they knew him. Next to him a pimply-faced boy sporting an enormous black hat nervously fingered several crumpled bills. "What're you entering?" the kid asked Charles.

"Ah . . . novice bull ridin'." Saying it aloud made it real. Charles would indeed do what he had hardly been considering. There had been no talk at home of him riding, but within himself he needed to try, to find out who his grandfather really was.

"I'm gonna go in calf roping and bulldogging novice," the kid told him. "I'd try bull riding, too, but I ain't got enough money."

"Money?"

"For the entry fee."

Charles gulped. "How much it cost, man?"

"For novice events, five bucks per."

Charles had six dollars and change in his pocket. That left him eating money anyway. He smiled.

"Where you from?" asked the other novice.

Hesitating, Charles answered, "Glenville."

"Glenville? Where's that at?"

Because he didn't know for certain, Charles merely replied, "South." It seemed to satisfy the black-hatted kid.

After paying his entry fee, the other boy turned towards Charles and shook his hand. "Take 'er easy," he said.

Handing the beefy, red-faced man who registered entries five dollars, Charles said, "Novice bull ridin'."

The man took his money and began filling out a form. "You put in some practice ain't you, son?" he asked. "We don't want any of you boys gettin' hurt."

"Yessir."

"Name?"

"Charles . . . Charlie Howard," he quickly improvised, and the red-faced man looked up at him, searched him it seemed.

Then he handed Charles a piece of white cloth with the number N-27 printed in black on it. "Wear that on your back," the red-faced man instructed. "There's safety pins in that box. And Charlie," he said, and the boy looked at him, "good luck."

After checking the schedule of events posted on the mobile home's side, Charles wandered to the refreshment stand, bought a hot dog and coke, then leaned on one end of the grandstand to eat. Sensing eyes on him from the passing crowd, he was immediately pulled toward that storm of discomfort that often swept him when he left the certainty of his neighborhood and found himself in what he considered the white world. Glancing furtively for somewhere else to eat, he noticed a small blonde girl wearing a fringed cowboy hat approaching him followed by two adults. She stood directly in front of him so he could not avoid her, and he stopped chewing.

"Can I have your autograph?" the little girl asked, handing him a program. He was stunned, having forgotten that he'd had his number pinned on by another novice. He nearly dropped what was left of his hot dog while signing her program. The parents both smiled at him as they left.

He understood then why people gave him a second look: he *was* a rider. Why not? He pushed his straw Stetson back farther on his head and smiled at passersby, feeling easier. Then he heard a somehow familiar voice: "Say brothah!" He turned to face a small, rugged-looking black man dressed in expensive western clothes.

"What's happenin'?" Charles ventured, uncertain.

"Alright, brothah," replied the man, "Alrighty. I'm Boise Jones." They shook hands. "You new, ain't ya? Wanna taste?" The man extended a paper bag from which he had been sipping.

"No thanks."

Charles decided immediately that this was not a man to bullshit, seeing the ridged eyebrows, the askew nose, the gold teeth, the gnarled hands. "This my first rodeo," he acknowledged sheepishly.

"Alright. We all gotta start, bro'. Who you been ridin' with?"

"Well," tempting lies crossed his mind, but Charles decided to stick with the truth, "I just ride a little in the city. My people be ranch folks, but I come from San Francisco." As they talked, passing cowboys and gals hailed Boise Jones: "Hey, Boise!" "Catch ya for a snort after while, Boise!" "How they hangin', Boise?" Jones smiled and nodded and called out friendly greetings.

"Shit, bro', they's all kinda good cowboys come from big cities. What you enter?"

"Bull ridin'."

Boise Jones removed his hat, wiped his forehead, then replaced his hat. "Whew! You sure pick a pisser to start with. Whyn't you switch to somethin' else, just for a start I mean?"

"I can't."

"It's your booty, blood, but if you want some help, count on ol' Boise. First time the worst." The older man shrugged and smiled. "I gotta make it. Lemme know if you want help. Sure you don't want a taste?"

"No, man," smiled Charles. "maybe after."

"Maybe we rub this on your *outside* after," laughed Boise Jones as he swaggered off toward two blonde women in tight jeans who had just smiled as they walked by. Charles's eyes followed the cocky figure until Jones disappeared, arm in arm with the women, into the crowd.

When he saw the bull he'd drawn—young and small by rodeo standards, but awesome to him—he wished he could disappear into the crowd as Boise had. A thick-shouldered tan beast, the bull was fully rigged when Charles climbed to the top of the chute as he'd seen the other three novices do, and looked down on the back he had to straddle. He froze there until he heard a voice—"Come on, son, you'll be alright"—and looked into the eyes of the red-faced man who had registered him.

The man smiled, and Charles managed to force a smile, then lowered himself onto the thick back, sensing power like that which had so astounded him the first time he had mounted a horse. This time, though, no saddle sat between him and the animal, so every twitch of the bull's thick muscles twitched Charles, filling him with the impression that he sat on moving, liquid metal. He perched wide and low on the bull, afraid to place much pressure on it, but the animal seemed to accept him passively. "Tighten up them knees," advised the red-faced man.

"Not that way or you get your hand caught," barked Boise Jones, suddenly near him, as Charles wrapped his grip—wearing a glove loaned by one of the white novices. "Pull that line through there. Yeah, that's it, now over. You got it, bro'." Charles could not clearly see the dark mask that instructed him through the chute rails, but he listened.

Another face popped in front of his, this one painted a ghostly white with a red nose and blue slash mouth. It wore a small derby hat perched on top of the orange-wigged head. "Don't worry, boy, I'll keep this rank bastard off'n you. You just ride 'im," advised the clown.

"From Glenville, California, on Thunderbolt Two, Charlie Howard!" the announcer brayed, and there was light applause.

Beneath him the bull surged, lifting Charles as an ocean wave lifts a swimmer, and the boy jerked his legs free. "You're okay," the gateman assured. "Just gimme the nod when you're ready."

Slipping back onto the bull, he was swept with terror once more and had to grip himself hard to avoid flinching. That was all the sign the gateman needed.

In the first bolting instant Charles felt himself burst from the chute, his arm and grip hand in the lead, his butt and legs in only momentary contact with the bull. Below and in front he caught flashings of animal, of fence rails, of dirt. He sought desperately to reconnect his butt and legs, to tighten his knees, but the force beneath him dodged and swirled so that he couldn't even breathe, only hold on and try to press himself downward.

Then, after a nauseous swirl, the bull reversed directions, and Charles sensed an electric jolt on his arm and hand, a release, a weightlessness, ended by broken slashes of motion, by bumps and shouts, by spreading numbness.

He leaned against the fence when he came to, the clown patting his back. "You done real good, boy. Real good. You sure that's your first bull? Rode 'im like a champ. Give 'im all he wanted, by God."

A gate opened, and he was urged out of the arena, only vaguely aware of the crowd's applause and the announcer's loud appeal: "Let's give one more hand to young Charlie Howard from Glenville!"

Boise Jones and the red-faced man helped him to the bed of a pickup, where he sat, still dizzy, tasting blood and feeling the cold spot where his lip was split. "Hey, Velma," called Boise, "bring me a couple ice cubes for Charlie's lip, willya?"

"Shore thang," replied a stringy woman, and off she scurried.

"You with us?" asked the red-faced man speaking directly into Charles's face.

Charles nodded. "Think so . . ." he managed to reply.

"Hell yeah, he with us, ain't ya bro'?" laughed Boise.

Charles tried to smile.

"You may not know it, son," the red-faced man said, "but you're a bull rider. You damn sure ain't no re-rider. You carried yourself out there like you been at it for a while, and I know you ain't. Didn't he do good, Boise?"

"Damn rights! I though he maybe bullshittin' at first, Red, but the boy a rider. A *nachal*. A pure *nachal*. Where you learn all that in the city, bro'?"

Charles's head was clearing now, making sense of what they said. "My granpappy tell me."

"Your granpappy?" asked Red.

"Yeah. Bo Howard my granpappy."

"Bo Howard! Bo Howard your granpappy? Shee-it, man, no wonder, you got it in your *blood!*" Boise Jones poked Red in the ribs. "Was he a rider? Was ol' Bo a rider? Hah!"

"I seen ol' Bo oncet years ago when I's just startin' out myself, and he was already a ol' fart then. But ride! That's gotta be the greatest bull rider ever there was. I haven't heard of him for years. When did he die?" asked Red.

"Die? Granpappy?" Charles was confused. "He ain't dead. He stay with me and Momma right now. He wait for me at home."

"Bo Howard's alive!" exclaimed Red. "Be damned. Where'd you say you're from? Glenville? I'd sure be proud to meet your granddad."

Charles averted his eyes. "I stay in San Francisco. Granpappy he stay there too."

"The city?" laughed Red. "Hell, I'm from the city myself. Butchertown. Lived there all my life. We're practically neighbors. Listen, son, you got wheels?"

"Naw."

"What the hell," grinned the ruddy-faced old cowboy, "lemme run you home whenever we finish here. Maybe I could meet your granddad: I'd be damned proud to do that."

"I wouldn't mind pickin' up a few pointers from that ol' man," acknowledged Boise Jones. "*Hell* no. I might just drive to the city with you boys my-*damn*-self."

Still vaguely disoriented, holding ice cubes against his split lip, Charles grinned sheepishly through the sudden attention he was attracting, for several other riders had joined Boise and Red and were patting his back or shaking his hand. He didn't even notice his name being sounded over the public address system: he had won novice bull riding and was being paged to collect his award, a belt buckle. Boise had to send him toward the judges' stand.

"He's gonna be a goodun, Boise," Red grunted, his eyes following the slim youth who walked away from them toward the award ceremony. "Yessir, a real goodun, maybe."

Jones nodded. "Yeah, he got it, the . . . what do you call it . . . the *style*. He ride that rank little bull like he's part of it. I never seen a purtier first ride. *Stylin'!* Ain't this a bitch; Bo Howard's kin and we tellin' *him* what to do."

Red nodded. "We're a couple pistols, we are."

"That there kid's the pistol," interjected the clown, who had just joined them. "He's somethin'."

Charles returned carrying the large boxed buckle, his gaze still not entirely clear. Boise Jones handed him the rumpled paper bag and said, "Here go, blood, you earned that taste."

Charles blinked and his eyes seemed finally to focus. He hesitated, then grinned. "Maybe I rub it on my *outside*," he said, and everyone laughed.

The King of Skateland

They had been bright colors once—orange and pink and yellow and green—all long since faded on the curved metal walls of a Quonset hut so squat that it appeared to have grown from its unpaved parking lot like a mutant toadstool, except a toadstool would have been cleaner, without *Trini de Loma* or *E. B. sucks*, written on its sides. And a toadstool might have been safer, for at Skateland the underworld met the over, stringy shitkickers cuddling song leaders who wouldn't dance with them at high school, while honor-roll boys puffed clandestine joints and coveted the knowing bodies of Saturday-night girls.

The King already roared the boards that evening, circled like a predatory bird, leaving ripe girls breathless with his moves, with his glances, so almost no one noticed the new guy. They should have, for the vast Chicano had never before entered Skateland, and his browless face—a battlefield of pimples—appeared to have been roughed out in sculptor's clay, then left unfinished.

He lurched to the rental counter, taking no notice of the woman's expression as she handed him skates, then he hulked his shapeless body to the benches. Seated, he began a tortuously slow lacing of the shoe skates after clumsily removing his battered sneakers. Tiny eyes intent, thick fingers stiff and awkward, he hunched over the skates with spittle glistening his heavy lips, not hearing the metallic music or noticing the whir of the King's skates. The Chicano tried several times to tie the laces before succeeding, then he sat back as though exhausted, his little eyes bright but empty.

Meanwhile Rex Ray Maytubby, the King of Skateland, performed and no one else dared join him on the floor. They waited, as usual, until he picked a partner from the panting pack, thus signaling others that his solo was over and that they were free to skate. But the new guy didn't know the rules.

Soon as he'd caught his breath, he lunged onto the King's floor and began skating, slowly and awkwardly at first, like an engine warming up, then faster and more smoothly. The King, meanwhile, heard the crowd gasp and the echoing sound of the hulk's skates. Turning, he first noticed that everyone's eyes seemed to have left him, to be following a large dark clown around the rink. Swallowing anger, the King immediately sensed there was no reason to duke the Mexican. No, let him skate. He was a perfect foil for the King's own spectacular moves.

Increasing his speed, the King quickly caught the clown and circled him several times, mugging for the audience, while kids on the sidelines whooped and whistled. The hulk seemed not to have noticed, making the whole thing even funnier, so the King slowed and began imitating the Mexican's orangutanal style, scratching himself under one dragging arm, while more laughter rippled from his crowd.

Rex Ray laughed so hard himself that he hardly noticed the first time he was circled by the shapeless Chicano, hardly believed the sudden burst of speed that carried the clown around him once more, that carried the hulk around a third time before he—the King, the King after all—could recover. It was unreal, and the sidelines fell suddenly quiet.

Skating backwards now, in front of the Mexican, Rex Ray Maytubby scowled into his antagonist's expressionless face. The King opened his mouth to tell the bastard off, but suddenly faced nothing; the Mexican had whirled and was skating backwards next to him, his own brown face still blank. When the King turned to warn him, the hulk was moving away, faster and faster, until Rex had to really pump to catch him. When he finally managed to overhaul the speeding Mexican, he was so breathless he could hardly speak. The big clown still looked fresh.

Then the music stopped, and so did the Chicano, immediately. He again hulked awkwardly as he shuffled from the floor to the benches, ignoring the King, who did not ignore him, scorching a scowl in his direction. Rex Ray Maytubby stalked from the floor into a clutch of young guys, the ones who tried to imitate him, his boys. "Who the hell *is* that guy?" he panted, his face tight.

For a moment no one answered, then a thin, pimply-faced kid responded: "They call him Cheetah. I know his brother."

"It's gonna be his ass, man," growled the King. "His ass."

"Don't let his brother hear you say that, man," warned the pimply boy, only to have his collar suddenly twisted tight in the King's fist. "What?" spat the King, "What did you say to me?"

"Not me, man," gasped the wide-eyed boy, his voice trembling. "Him. His brother."

"Shit!" The King released him. "I don't care who his brother is."

The pimply kid still trembled. "Don't get hot at me, man. I'm only tryin to tell ya."

"Who? Who the hell is the big dummy's brother?"

"Tony Cavillo."

"Hah!" laughed the King. "He's nothin', man. Nothin'." All the while a slug crawled into his belly. He wanted no part of Cavillo, who was what Rex had always wanted to be, a genuinely hard dude. Cavillo didn't have to bully teenage punks.

A couple other kids looked at him strangely; not aggressively, just strangely, as though they knew what he was thinking. "What's so damn funny?" he growled at them.

"Nothin'." answered one. The other just backed off.

"Nothin'," mimicked the King, as he spat on the floor at the dude's feet. "Nothin'," he mimicked again. Then he slapped the chump who hadn't backed off, popped him hand-print hard across the mouth. The kid made no effort to defend himself, but he stood his ground and for an instant the King nearly let it all go, nearly swarmed the punk, but he didn't, and he noticed in the eyes of the other young dudes a look he hadn't seen before. He scowled them down.

More music rasped from the amplifiers, and Rex Ray Maytubby hesitated, looking toward Cheetah. "What's wrong with that bastard?" he asked no one in particular.

"He's a re-tard," answered the same kid who had told him Cheetah's name. "I seen him in the re-tard class at school."

"A re-tard," mumbled Maytubby. Well no damn dummy was going to humiliate the King. He skated back onto the floor, feeling eyes on him and hurried to catch Cheetah, who had slipped out soon as the music started and who already floated over the boards. What was worse, after the Mexican had preceded him onto the floor, everybody seemed to forget themselves, joining Cheetah without waiting for the King.

This time Rex speeded immediately next to the Chicano and bumped him. "Get off the floor," he hissed. The blank face registered nothing, but the King was suddenly airbound, afloat from a bump that caught him just as he lifted to increase his own speed and sent him out of control against the far wall.

That tore it! Everything on the floor stopped but the music and the Mexican. Rex Ray began his stalk, fists clenched white against his sides. Cheetah ignored him, weaving in and around stopped skaters, denying Rex Ray the comforting ritual of bluff-and-attack he used to start fights, denying him in fact the fight itself, for in his combat posture he could not catch the unaware Chicano. And the King heard, hardly believing, people laughing at him. In Skateland. Hell, he was trying to fight, and they were laughing at him.

He began jostling anyone in his way, cursing them, swinging his elbows as he clammered to reach Cheetah. "What's wrong, Rexie?" he heard a girl snivel. Spinning around he spat: "Nothin'. Not a damn thing," and again he heard small clusters of laughter.

Then some dude whispered "What about Cavillo?" Hinting, the King knew, that he wasn't really trying to catch the dummy. "Who said that?" Rex Ray demanded, and people edged away from him without answering.

"Maytubby!" It was Mr. Karabian, the owner. He usually let kids settle their own problems—outside—and he had seen Rex Ray around for so many years that he kept a special eye on him. "What's going on here?"

Even the King didn't cross Mr. Karabian. "That guy pushed me," Rex Ray answered.

"No trouble in here. You know that. Go outside and settle things."

"Right," barked the King. "Outside, and I'll settle things fast."

Mr. Karabian waved at Cheetah, who continued skating alone now that other skaters had left the floor, but the large Chicano seemed not to notice. Finally, Karabian walked onto the boards and grabbed Cheetah by an arm, not roughly, but firmly, and told him he'd have to leave. Cheetah didn't understand. He knitted his thick brows and chewed the words he'd heard as he was led to the benches. Only when Mr. Karabian began unlacing the shoe skates did the Mexican grasp that he must leave, and his heavy face softened, tears welled in his small, dark eyes, then he mumbled something about having spent all his money and not wanting to leave.

"Tough shit," called the King, who had already removed his shoe skates and pulled on his gear-jammer boots. "Listen to the big chicken cry. Wait'll I get through with him," he called to his clutch of admirers. "He won't come back here no more."

Together with his entourage, the King paraded out the door into the parking lot, followed by Mr. Karabian escorting the large, weeping Chicano who still whined that he wanted to skate, and that he'd spent all his money to get in. Soon as Karabian deposited Cheetah on the lot, the owner turned and reentered Skateland, leaving him to his fate.

Rubbing his eyes like a little boy, Cheetah continued sobbing, turning his head to look in the door, impervious to the King and the small crowd that surrounded him. "What's a matter, man?" sneered the King, buoyed by the certainty of another triumph. Cheetah ignored him, so Rex slapped the Chicano sharply on his turned-away face. "I said what's a matter, man?" Cheetah faced him then, the large brown mask empty, without understanding what was happening and, for an instant, the King almost felt sorry for him, only for an instant. It was clear he could taunt this retard for awhile, could milk drama like a bullfighter controlling a bull; the King knew how to please his fans. Even the tinny music that muffled from Skateland seemed to fit this melodrama on the parking lot.

Few noticed the long, low sedan that swooped slowly onto the far end of the lot, then killed its lights, the driverless sedan, or so it appeared for no heads showed until one erstwhile skater looked closely and saw four sets of hooded eyes just above dashboard level like cobras in a basket. He shuddered as the big car crept slowly closer, crunching and cracking across the lot, closer and closer, the dark eyes within haloed by shining black hair.

Most spectators didn't realize what was happening until they felt the car bump them, almost gently, then they scrambled to avoid being crushed by its slow, inexorable progress, the crowd splitting into two groups with the dark sedan between them in front of the taunting King and his bewildered foil. Then the car's lights flashed on and the King quickly shielded his eyes. "Shut those damned lights off!" he shouted. Nothing happened, so he advanced several menacing steps. "Shut em off, I said."

From the car shot a staccato voice. "Ven aqui, Cheetah."

Something close to a smile crossed the big Mexican's face as he clumsily turned and waddled to the car, then lurched into its backseat. Spectators had spread—more than a few heading for the safety of Skateland—and the car sat nearly alone in front of the King, who remained shading his eyes.

"Hey, guy," burst the machine-gun voice from the car, "come 'ere."

The King hesitated. He wanted to return to Skateland's comforting certainty, but the voice from the light was insistent, and he—the King, himself—had created the situation, so he had to see it through. He swaggered toward the car and, when he reached the front door, demanded: "Whataya want, man?"

For a long time—an eternity it seemed—no answer came from the car, and the King felt drums beating within his ears. Then Tony Cavillo's voice fired from a window: "You don't like my brahther, guy?" Before Rex Ray could answer, the car's door clicked open with the crispness of a gun cocking; the King suppressed a shudder as Cavillo unwound from the door, more and more of him, his thick shoulders at the King's eye level, his hair a black burst of danger. Cavillo hovered in front of the King, swaying slightly, his darkly slitted eyes impassive as a serpent's. Fear burrowed into the King's belly. "You don' like my brahther?" Cavillo hissed. "You tol' the man on him?"

The King tried to laugh it off. "Naw," he explained, "we was just messin' around and old man Karabian he . . ."

Smack! Cavillo slapped him so fast he didn't see the dark hand move; he only jolted back a step. "Don' lie, you bahstair. Why you tol' on Cheetah?"

"I didn't." Rex tried to lift his arms, but they felt heavy, asleep. His whole body felt drugged.

"How much money you got?"

"Wait a minute," the King tried to give his voice a hard edge. "Wait just a damn minute."

Smack! His head bounced back again, and he distinctly felt his hair fly up as he was struck and staggered back another step. Cavillo menaced, walking forward. "How much money you got, guy?" he repeated.

The King backed away. "Wait a minute," his voice began to whine. "Wait."

Without turning, Tony Cavillo called to the car: "Cheetah, cuanto cuesta?" There was a pause, then a voice grunted "Cincuenta," from within the dark automobile, and Cavillo once again addressed the King. "Four bits. You go buy my brahther a ticket, bahstair." He feinted another slap, and the King flinched.

Rex Ray Maytubby was broken and, worse, he knew it. He turned his empty body and dragged slowly away from Cavillo—feeling almost like crying—until he reached the ticket office. Once there, he noticed the eyes of the kids—wide eyes and laughing eyes and sad eyes—watching his humiliation, but he was so blank that he could neither snarl at them nor even laugh. He didn't care. He just wanted out.

Handing the small green ticket to Cavillo, Rex Ray Maytubby waited. "Tiene huevos, gabacho?" Cavillo taunted. Harsh laughter ripped from the car. "No," Cavillo answered himself, his tongue flicking over his lips, "no tiene." The tall Chicano loomed in front of the King, over him, still swaying slightly, a grin slitting the dark face. "Go away, bahstair, and don' come back here no more. You don' like my brahther. I don' like you." The hooded eyes riveted Rex Ray Maytubby, who slowly slumped away toward his wheels.

"Cheetah, de prisa!" called Cavillo, and his brother lurched from the car, and took the small ticket, clutching it in a thick paw. Cheetah hulked happily to Skateland, past kids clustered staring out the door, until he disappeared into music and light, into the sound of singing skates.

Upstream

That morning when my uncle Arlo Epps stalked out from the cabin buck naked, he declared, "I'm a unsheathed soul!" Then he dove right into the Kern River and swam, angling kinda upstream to fight the current so that, whenever he finally turned directly into it, he just hung in that swift water, about halfway across, straight out from where I stood watching him.

"An unsheathed soul?" I asked myself. That sounded more like some preacher than my uncle.

He sure picked a terrible place to swim, the river right there, just below where Kern Canyon opened into the Southern Sierra, because that water it was snow melt straight from the high country, and it come down fast and freezing. Directly above where Arlo took to swimming, there was these rapids couldn't no boat get through and, at the canyon's mouth, this cataract was boiling.

At first I just stood there and watched him, stunned I guess. Once Uncle Arlo got turned into the current, though, and chugged into a rhythm that held him even with me—slipping back, then pulling forward again—I hollered at him, "Uncle Arlo! Uncle Arlo!"

"Leave the ol' fool be," snapped Aunt Mazie Bee leaning on the dark cabin's doorway. "He's just a-tryin' to attract attention." She disappeared back into darkness talking to herself.

Me, I spent most of that morning watching my uncle surge, slip back, then surge again, as he tried to hold even with the cabin. You know, I'd never even seen him naked before, let alone acting so crazy, so I didn't know what to do. A couple times I asked Mazie Bee if we shouldn't try to help him some way.

"Help him?" she finally huffed. "Arlo Epps is a growed man. He can just take care a hisself."

"But he might get drownded," I insisted.

"Hah!" was all she said.

I wasn't surprised at her acting so hateful toward him. They'd had an argument that morning, as usual. I'd heard them rumbling at one another through the walls. It went on longer than most and I'd begun to wonder if there'd be any breakfast at all, then he'd jumped into the river. As a matter of fact, there wasn't no breakfast, but I never really noticed because I was so worried about Uncle Arlo.

Come midafternoon, me avoiding chores to watch him fight that current, still figuring him to collapse any second, I determined to rescue my uncle. Without asking permission, I pulled our boat, the Packard Prow Special, out from the shed and dragged her to the river's bank.

The Special was this old wooden dinghy that Uncle Arlo he'd took for a dowsing job years before. She'd never looked too great but, in spite of her one-lunged motor, he'd been able to use her on that river without no trouble. What give the Special class, though, was that Packard hood ornament Arlo'd wired to her prow. He'd traded for it at this yard sale and he kept it shined, something that really ate at Aunt Mazie Bee. She said it just showed how foolish he was. She said that all the time.

Anyways, I launched the boat and managed to maneuver it into position next to my uncle, that bright ornament pointed upstream toward the canyon. I leaned over to talk to him, but was shocked by what I seen. He was so *white*. I'd always seen his arms from the elbow down, and his face, all real tan, but the rest of him—the part his clothes hid—was the color of a trout's belly, and it seemed like he shimmered in that clear, rushing water like some kinda ghost. It was scary. "Uncle Arlo," I finally called, "Please come in. You'll get drownded for sure."

My uncle he just kept on cruising, his face out of the water every other stroke. His eyes they looked real big and white, but I couldn't tell if he recognized me. "Shall I bring you some dinner?" I yelled. "You gotta eat." He never answered, but those two-tone arms kept stretching, those white eyes turning.

Then he done something that surprised me. This fat stonefly it come bouncing down the water toward him. Just before it reached his face, he twisted his body and snapped the big insect into his mouth. "Crime-in-ently!" I gasped. I surely wasn't gonna mention *that* to Aunt Mazie Bee.

Whenever I chugged the Packard Prow back to shore, I hurried to the cabin and confronted my aunt. "You *gotta* do something," I insisted. "Uncle Arlo'll get drownded for sure."

"He'll no such a thang," she snapped. "Arlo Epps won't act his age is what he won't. He just wants attention, but what he needs is to brang some money in this house and stop his durn dreamin'."

"But Aunt Mazie Bee . . ."

"No buts! Now do your chores!"

Well, I stayed up all that night, or tried to—I reckon I mighta dozed some, leaning against the Special there on the bank. Not much, though, 'cause in the moonlight I could see him, out there holding against the current, that white body almost flashing like a fishing lure, never still. Just about dawn, I snuck in the cabin and brewed coffee, then filled the old thermos bottle. I knew my uncle he had to be froze by then and I was determined to force some hot coffee down him. I carried it to the Special, then bucked the river's swirl out to Arlo and positioned the boat right next to him. He didn't pay me no mind. "You gotta drink some coffee," I urged. "Uncle Arlo, pleeease." He kept pulling against that rushing water, snapping at the morning's hatch of mayflies. I finally give up.

That afternoon, a reporter and a photographer from the Bakersfield newspaper they showed up. My aunt'd called them. "I thought you wasn't gonna give Uncle Arlo no attention," I hissed to her out the corner of my mouth.

"Hesh up," she snapped, "or I'll peench a chunk outta you. Besides, I'm not a-givin' him the kind he wants, I'll tell you that much. We gotta live some way, don't we?"

That reporter he was a stout gent that chewed on a unlit cigar. His partner was a little weasel lugging this big, giant camera, and with a fat bag hanging from one shoulder. He listed whenever he walked.

After my aunt got done telling her story, that reporter he just closed his notebook and put his stub pencil away. "Lady," he said real tough, "you must think we were born yesterday. Nobody could do what you claim your old man's done. We weren't born yesterday, right Earl?"

"Right," agreed the photographer.

"Ask the boy," snapped Mazie Bee, unwilling to back down.

The reporter he wiggled his wet cigar at her, then he turned to face me. "Well, boy?" he demanded.

I looked at the ground. "It's true. Honest."

We was standing on the river's bank, maybe a hundred feet from where Uncle Arlo worked against the current. The reporter he stared at that pale form that the rushing water made look like a torpedo, then he asked, "What's that guy wearing?"

I looked at my aunt and she looked at me. "Well, he left in a big hurry," she finally said.

"Yeah, but what's he wearing?"

"Nothin'," she choked.

"Nothing? You mean he's bare-assed?"

"Yeah," I gulped, and my aunt she looked away.

"For Chrissake, Earl, get a picture of that nut!"

"Right," said the photographer.

"What'd you say his name was," asked the reporter, and Aunt Mazie Bee she smiled.

The story with a picture was in that next morning's paper and the crowds begun arriving before lunch. My aunt she was ready for them.

Mazie Bee stationed herself at the gate in a warped wooden lawn chair we'd salvaged years before from the river. She also had me set up our old card table—that we got cheap at a yard sale—and she put on it a cigar box to hold all the money she planned to collect, plus a can to spit snuff juice into. Across her lap she laid our old single-shot .410 that Uncle Arlo'd swapped for way back when. Finally, she tied on her good sun-bonnet and waited. "Ever'body pays, buster," she told the first arrival. "That'll be two-bits." Then she spit into the can, "Ptui!" and give me a I-told-you-so grin.

Whata buncha jokers turned out. While my uncle was struggling out in that water, pick-ups and jalopies and hot rods sped to the fence, and out spilled the darndest specimens I ever seen: mostly young studs with more tattoos per square mile than the state pen. All colors and shapes, sleeves rolled up and sucking on toothpicks, gals parading in bathing suits and shorts, giggling and pointing while boyfriends they scowled at each other.

"Hell, I could swim 'er easy," claimed one old boy that had a pack of cigarettes rolled into a sleeve of his t-shirt, and the crowd cheered. A minute later he was into a fight with another guy that had his sleeves rolled up too, and the crowd surged and tugged for a minute, then cheered some more.

Aunt Mazie Bee hardly seemed to notice the goings on. She sat counting quarters and filling that spit can. Once she called, "No rock throwin', buster," and she gestured with her scattergun. The old boy quit flinging stones at Uncle Arlo right now.

A little later, after she'd sold a couple old tires for a dollar and this beat-up bike seat for thirty cents, a great big pot-bellied devil without no shirt on he swaggered up to the doorway of our cabin, but my aunt never blinked: "Nothin' for sale in there, buster, but you about to buy this .410 shell." She clicked back the hammer, and he lost interest in the cabin. A hour later she sold the lawn chair to a Mexican man for seventy-five cents and took to accepting bids on the card table. I never liked the way she was eyeing the Packard Prow Special.

It was about dark, the crowd finally drifting off, whenever that Cadillac it swooped up to the gate. Out of the driver's seat come this big, tough-looking guy in a suit and tie that went and opened a back door. A short, fat guy—in a suit and tie but with a hat too—he squeezed out. The two of them they paid my aunt—by now she was sitting on a nail keg—then they trooped through what was left of the picnickers and beer drinkers, the crowd kinda opening and staring real quiet as them two passed. Those two looked like they'd showed up at the wrong place.

On the point closest to Uncle Arlo, they stood for a long time, those two, not talking to one another that I could see, their eyes on them two-tone arms, on that two-tone head, and on that ghost of a body in the current. Finally, the fat man he called to my aunt in this high-pitched voice: "Lady, you got a boat we can use?"

Mazie Bee's eyes narrowed. "Fer what?"

"For five dollars."

He was speaking my aunt's language, so even before she answered I was trudging to the Special. I knew I'd be ferrying the fat guy. There wasn't room for three in the special, so the fat guy's driver he stayed on shore while the two of us chugged out, the current jerking and pushing us around till I got that hood ornament pointed upstream and we moved toward Uncle Arlo. That big shot he clung to the boat's sides tight as he could, and I was half tempted to dump us both just to keep him away from Arlo because there was *something* about him. He didn't fit.

Whenever we finally maneuvered alongside my uncle, the fat guy he raised one hand, signaling me to stop, then grabbed the boat's side again right away. He watched the swimmer for a long time, then rasped to me, "How long you say he's been at it, boy?"

"Two days nearly."

"Two days without stopping?"

"Uh-huh."

"Take me back," he ordered. "I seen enough."

Soon as we hit shore, the fat man and his pal they joined Aunt Mazie Bee in the cabin after she give me the .410 along with orders to make sure nobody got in without paying, and not to take less than twenty cents for the nail keg. She carried the cigar box with her.

Half an hour later, my aunt walked the fat man and his pal to that Cad', shook hands, then come back to the gate as they drove away. "Well, I sold him," she announced, her hands on her hips, her chin out, grinning.

"Huh?"

"Your uncle, I sold him to that there Mr. Rattocazano of Wide World Shows. Your uncle's a-gonna be famous and we're agonna be rich," she told me real proud.

"But you can't *sell* Uncle Arlo," I protest. "You can't do that!"

"I can so!" she asserted. "Besides, I never exactly sold *him*, I jest sold that Mr. Rattocazano the right to exhibit him. Course, we gotta git him declared crazy first, but Mr. Rattocazano says his lawyer'll take care a that in no time. They'll brang him and the sher'ff out tomorra."

"The sheriff?"

"To declare Arlo Epps nuts and take him. He's been crazier'n a bedbug for years. Now he can finally support us."

"But Aunt Mazie Bee . . ." I complained.

"You jest hesh!" she snapped. "This here's growed-up's business."

Tired as I was, I couldn't sleep that night for worrying about my uncle, that never hurt a soul, being declared nuts and took to the nuthouse or stuck in some kinda freak show. No sir, was all I could think, not to my uncle you don't. It seemed like to me that Aunt Mazie Bee was the one gone crazy.

Before dawn, I crept out to the Packard Prow Special and hit the river. Soon as the engine coughed me out alongside Uncle Arlo—him not looking any different to me than he had that first morning, arms reaching for the water in front of him, head turning regular to breath—I hollered at him, hoping the river's growl would cover my voice. "You gotta come back, Uncle Arlo," I pleaded. "The sheriff's gonna come and take you away. They say you've went crazy." His movements never changed, so I added, "I brung a towel."

His face kept turning, his arms pulling, but I noticed his eyes roll in my direction: He seen me. We seen each other. A real look. So I told him again: "You gotta come in. The sheriff's coming today, and a lawyer too. They'll take you to the nuthouse or the sideshow, one." I extended that towel.

His body it just shimmered in that hurried water, and his arms kept up their rhythm, but the look on his face it changed. Then, sure as anything, he winked at me. That was when I noticed that the Special it was gradually falling behind him. I thought for a second that the sick old motor was giving up but, no, it sounded the same as always. Then I realized that he was moving upstream, real slow but moving, toward the rapids and that cataract.

I opened the throttle of the Special and caught Arlo, but not for long. We was getting close to those rapids, and he was moving faster all the time. Them two-tone arms they was churning faster and his two-tone face hardly seemed to be sucking air at all as he dug in. The Special was wide open but it was lagging farther and farther behind, so I throttled back the engine to hold even in the current, not wantin' to get into the rapids.

Up ahead, I seen my uncle slide into them, kinda bounce but keep swimming, around curling whirlpools, up swooshing runs, over hidden boulders, not believing what I was seeing with my own eyes, until pretty soon he reached the boiling edge of that cataract. I couldn't hardly breath.

For what seemed like a long, long time he disappeared in the white water and I was scared he'd finally drownded. Then I seen this pale shape shoot up out a the water, looking less like a man at that distance than some fair fish. The current it drove him back, but a second later he come out of that froth again, farther this time, almost over the worst of it, but not quite and he fell back into that terrible foam. I figured him a goner for sure, and I squeezed my eyes closed not wanting to see what happened. A second later, I couldn't resist squinting them open. 'Come *on*, Uncle Arlo," I heard myself rooting, "*make* it!"

Then he exploded, a ghost that popped from the cataract like . . . well, almost like an unsheathed soul, smack into the smooth water above. I couldn't believe it, but I cheered, "Yaaaay!"—my heart pumping like sixty. Whenever I rubbed my eyes and shook my head, he was stroking up there out of sight into the canyon.

I plopped in the wiggling Special, breathing real heavy, and I wiped my own face with the towel I'd brung for Uncle Arlo. He was away and I was exhausted, so I pointed the Packard Prow toward the bank. Whenever I got to shore, Aunt Mazie Bee come out from the cabin. "Where's your uncle at?" she demanded, her eyes searching the river.

"He drownded," I replied.

She glanced from me to the stream and back, made a clucking sound with her mouth, then said, "He *would*."

Earthquake Summer

A brief eternity after I coaxed my eyes open and glimpsed the picket fence differentiating our small patch of lawn from thousands of cultivated acres surrounding it, something shifted. I snapped awake, seeing a canteloupe sky pushing darkness above the nearby foothills. Across the yard, Uncle Pedro and Aunt Beda, my two-year-old cousin Linda lying next to them, did not stir under their blankets.

Then I truly felt it, a slow shrugging beneath me as though the earth itself was rousing. At that moment our ranch dogs began to howl. Still not moving, I watched my uncle's head jerk up. The earth shuddered once more.

"What's wrong?" I heard my aunt whisper.

"It's nothing." Tio Pedro answered. "Just a little one." He rolled onto his feet and stood lean in his jockey shorts surveying the hills, then walked to the yard's edge and urinated. When he returned and reached for his levis, Tia Beda urged, "Come back to bed."

Smiling, he asked, "The baby?"

"She's asleep." I heard them chuckle privately when he crawled under the covers and I rolled my back toward them.

When Pedro awakened me later—"Hey Junior! You gonna sleep all day?"—the sun was over Bear Mountain and I was amazed to find I'd fallen back asleep, dripping with perspiration now beneath my blankets. "No more pocket pool this morning," he winked, extending a cup of sugared coffee. "We got work to do." He moseyed back toward the house. Sitting up, I saw that Aunt Beda and Linda were gone, their blankets empty on the mattress. Beneath me I felt a tiny jolt, then a shrug, as I sipped the sweet brew.

There had been rumblings from within the earth almost all summer, ever since the first violent jolt nearly destroyed Tehachapi, a small town in the mountains just east of us. I'd been alone in the house that morning, my aunt, uncle, and cousin having driven up to a dance at Balance Rock the night before, one of their rare weekend escapes. It had still been dark when my bed lurched, then began to shake, the house groaning around me as I lay there too terrified to move, not knowing what was happening. When all motion stopped temporarily, I had run outside into the cries of frightened animals and seen lights snapping on at ranch houses far off across the flat fields, just as another sharp lurch knocked a knick-knack shelf crashing loose back in the living room, terrifying me. I had thought—I could not help thinking—that the world was ending.

Since that initial quake, heavings within the earth had occurred often, though irregularly, and most ranch folk had, like us, begun sleeping outside. And we were quick to find a doorway if a shake caught us within a building. In fact, a lot of front-yard conversations were held that summer all over Kern County, because the slightest tremor sent folks scrambling outside. Life at our ranch, like others, went on. We irrigated our crops and repaired our equipment and fed our stock, and we probably all slept better outside anyway, where day's heat didn't linger through the night the way it did indoors.

I finished my coffee that morning and ate a bacon-and-egg burrito on the way out to a 40-acre grid we had been clearing since high school let out and I had begun my summer vacation. It was land newly acquired from an absentee owner, a plot that joined Pedro's and one on which we had hunted but that had, as far as we knew, never been cultivated. My uncle had coveted it for years. Whenever he didn't need me for other jobs, he would assign me to the new spread. I had pretty well cleared it and was beginning—with occasional help from Pedro—the boring job of turning the soil over, plowing, disking, and plowing once more.

We jostled out the dirt ranch road, dust pluming behind like a hawk's burnished tail, to where we'd left our big Caterpillar diesel, me pointing out an old car that had been parked at the field's far end on the county road the evening before. "That old rattletrap's still there," I said.

Pedro nodded. "I noticed. I hope somebody comes out and tows 'er away."

I climbed onto the tractor and coaxed it to life, while Pedro puffed a cigarette in his pickup's cab. It was an old Cat, and he wanted to be sure the darn thing started before leaving me. Once it snorted and pooped its way into a rhythm, he built his tail of dust back along the ranch road toward the barn where he was repairing a truck.

Only fifty or sixty yards into the field, I heard a harsh clank from the gang plow I was pulling and felt the rig halt for a moment, then jolt free. I threw the transmission into neutral and jumped down to check for damage. Sure enough, I'd hit another of those Indian mortars, a big one; this field was full of them. It was a large round granite boulder that had been hollowed to crush acorns or something. I was afraid I'd broken a plow blade on it. Pedro had done just that last week and we'd spent a long afternoon at the blacksmith's shop in Edison, the smith teasing my uncle—"God damn, Pete, you ain't got but a hunert-sixty acres out there, how's come you went and hit a little ol' rock no bigger'n a horse turd?"— while we sipped from cans of beer. I hated to think what kind of static I'd have taken if I'd chipped that blade.

Anyway, I hefted that big stone bowl up onto the Cat's floor so I could dump it with the rest of them along the road near where the old car was parked. I noticed some funny kind of material edged up out of the dirt in the hollow where the mortar had been so, before I climbed back onto the rig, I walked back and tugged it; all I got was a handful of rotten fiber that looked like old reeds or something. To hell with it. I turned to get back to work, but glimpsed something small, black, and shiny where I'd torn the material loose. I reached down and unearthed a nearly perfect obsidian arrowhead, the nicest I'd ever seen.

Checking to be certain Uncle Pedro wasn't nearby—he'd be quick to give me hell if he thought I was loafing—I grabbed my shovel from behind the Caterpillar's seat and took a couple of bites from the earth with it, finding that the material I'd torn was part of a larger piece, a mat maybe. I dug more, clearing away in the soil a couple of heavy pestles, and several more arrowheads, which I pocketed, before reaching a lump where the mat bundled. I'd already dug a good-sized hole, and the bundle promised a real treasure of arrowheads so, first searching for a telltale dust plume from Pedro's pickup, I decided to dig the whole works up then cover the excavation and get back to business.

After carefully scooping around the bundle, initially with the shovel, then manually so I wouldn't burst the material and spill its contents, I finally worked both gloved hands under it and lifted as gently as I could. It started to move, held for a moment, then gave, fragile material tearing free in my hands, exposing parts of a skeleton folded within it.

I tumbled back onto my butt, then stood, peeping over the edge of the hole to make certain I'd seen what I thought I had, wiping my gloves on my Levi's all the while. Just then the earth, like me, shuddered. I had been right the first time; it was a small skeleton, with the outline of a skull imprinted on a part of the mat that had not torn. Then I noticed that lady.

She was stalking toward me from the country road through heat shivers like some kind of apparition. An old woman it looked like, with a dark shawl and long gray hair tumbling down her back in the windless sun. For an instant, I thought of *La Llorona*. Assuming she was Mexican, I spoke to her in Spanish, but she seemed not to understand until I switched to English. "What are you doing here?" she finally challenged.

"Me? I work here." Her tone and questions surprised me, and I was more than a little shaken to begin with. "What are *you* doing here, on my uncle's field?"

"This is our land."

"Your land?"

"Yauelamni land. Ours."

The woman stood directly in front of me, her face creased like a rotting pumpkin, her eyes dark and curved obsidian, hiding a certainty that made me back up a couple steps and wish that Uncle Pedro was with me. "Yauelamni land?" I sputtered. "Whadya mean? What's that? This is Garcia land, ours!" It really wasn't. We only leased it from a man named Antongiovanni.

The old woman eyed me and I eyed the road, searching for Uncle Pedro's dust, hoping for it this time: no luck. "Boy," she said, her voice softer, "this is our land. The land where my people lived and died. My great-grandfather and grandmother rest here somewhere. The bowls you dig up were ours. I mean you no harm, but this is our land, and I intend to let my ancestors rest here."

That stumped me.

"You feel the rumbles from within?" she asked.

We had just experienced a faint quiver, so I nodded, my own demeanor changed. "Yes ma'am," I replied.

"When did they start?"

"I don't remember. Whenever that Tehachapi quake happened."

She nodded. "When did you start working this field?"

I had to hesitate, then it dawned on me that I had begun clearing the field the day before Tehachapi was leveled. I said nothing, shrugging my shoulders instead.

"This is sacred land, boy. Do not desecrate it."

Just as I was about to howl for him, Uncle Pedro whizzed up the road, dust billowing, halted his pickup, then pounded across the field. "Okay, payoso, que pasó?" he demanded.

"I hit another one of those chingasos," I explained, pointing toward the stone mortar on the Cat's floor. "Then I saw this material and dug to check on it"—I nodded toward the hole—"and found that skeleton down there."

Uncle Pedro's eyes bugged as he followed the line of my finger. "Hijole!" he exclaimed.

Before he could say more, I continued: "Then this lady she came over from the road." Pedro didn't hear me. He was leaning into the hole I had dug, looking none too steady.

The old woman moved between us and knelt at the hole. She reached in and touched the yellowed bones, pulling the torn mat to cover what I had exposed. "You see this fiber; it is tule. My mother may have woven it. This was her home."

Uncle Pedro recovered. "Who the hell are you? Is that your old jalopy parked out there?"

"This is our land," the old woman asserted again.

"Listen, lady," my uncle roared, obviously upset by the skeleton he'd seen, "get the hell outta here. This is my land. I paid for it! I'm gonna farm it!" Then he turned toward me. "We gotta call the sheriff, I guess and report this body. Damn! That means no more plowing today. You can come in and clean the corral."

I nodded, not the least unhappy to escape the field.

"And you," Pedro hissed to the lady, "better not only be off this land but away from it or I'll have the sheriff run you in."

The old woman stood. "This is sacred land. You will never work it. Earth Mother will not allow it. She will shrug you away."

"Get away from here," Pedro warned, his voice cold and ominous. I could tell he was scared too. There was something strange about that lady. "Get away or I'll use the shotgun I keep in that pickup."

"No you won't," she replied. "I only ask that you allow the dead to sleep."

Uncle Pedro looked at me, then back toward the old woman. "The dead? You mean there's more?"

"This was my village. Everyone rests here."

"And that means we'll be breaking plow blades and uncovering skeletons as long as we work it?"

"It means you will be disturbing Earth Mother."

Much to my astonishment, Pedro said simply, "Okay," then paused, "we'll quit. Junior, cover that skeleton. I'll call the Eye-talian and tell him to keep his graveyard. Are you happy?" he asked the old woman.

"Thank you," she said.

As we drove back toward the house, I had to ask, "Why, after all that work, are you giving up on the 40 acres?"

Pedro grinned. "Are you kidding? I'm not giving up. We'll just let La Bruja there go on her way, then finish with the field. We're in no hurry with it anyway. Besides, if she was to make a stink about those bones we'd have the county historical society and the sheriff and the newspaper and every other damned bleeding heart in Kern County out here in our way. We've got plenty of work to do without worrying about that acreage right now. Let it rest a week or two."

Four mornings later the lady's rattletrap disappeared. She had spent most of those days just walking over the land. I'd see her out there through heat shivers like a ghost, slowly floating over the forty acres. She never built a fire to cook that I noticed, but I did see her climb from that old car one morning, so I suppose she slept in it.

One odd thing, though, I didn't notice any earthquakes during that period. Of course, if they're little or you're driving, or just concentrating on something else, you don't always notice them. I remember how Aunt Beda at breakfast mentioned to us how nice it was that they'd finally stopped. "Don't count on it," my uncle had laughed. I told him, then, what that lady had said about why the earth was shaking and he'd laughed again. "Hey, Junior, don't you know where quakes come from? There's cracks down in the earth called faults." I noticed Aunt Beda seemed to be listening carefully. "When one of them moves, the crust up here where we live moves too. I read about it in the paper. And guess what?"

I shrugged.

"We've got one of those faults, the White Wolf, running right under our ranch. Don't let that witch spook you," he winked. "When our place shakes it's because of that fault, not because of any Indians." I still didn't like it, but decided to say no more.

After we'd eaten, while Uncle Pedro stood in the yard jawing with a fertilizer salesman, I asked Aunt Beda what she thought caused the quakes.

Tia didn't reply immediately. She wiped her hands on her apron, then picked up her ever-present glass of iced tea and sipped from it. "The scientists," she finally acknowledged, "say there is a great crack in the earth beneath us. The scientists say it is moving, moving us."

I nodded. She had told me nothing new.

Then she added. "The scientists do not say why it is moving."

"Why?" I asked, for she had paused to once more sip tea.

She smiled and in her large, dark eyes I seemed to sense the same hidden certainty I had seen in the old Indian woman's. "Because, Junior, God wills it. If there is a crack, God put it there. If it moves, God moves it."

I said only "Oh," before walking out of the house to set water in a field I was irrigating. It was then I noticed that the old car was gone. When I finished moving pipes, I walked over to where it had been parked and saw that all the mortars and pestles, and everything else I'd dug up and piled near that road, were also gone; how could that old woman have hefted all that stuff? Good riddance, in any case. I felt better without her hovering across the field.

At lunch that day Pedro said I could get back to plowing the new ground tomorrow. It had rested long enough. He winked at me, "Unless you're afraid of the Indians."

"I'm not afraid of anyone," I snapped. He had hit a raw, adolescent nerve. All he did was laugh.

The next morning I managed to crank up the old Caterpillar and begin my rounds. It was the first day of plowing when I hadn't hit several of those mortars. In fact, I didn't hit anything. I just plowed along. It was as though someone had cleared all the stone bowls out of the land during the days we'd rested it.

I can't tell you exactly what time the quake hit because you get lulled driving a tractor and everything becomes automatic. I was probably asleep on my endless rounds, but when that big cat jumped it nearly tossed me like a rodeo bull. "Jesus!" I burst. I thought I'd hit something, or maybe driven into a ditch. I'd never felt a tractor leap like that before. I killed the engine, but the Cat kept moving, jerking back and forth like we were plowing. I swear I could see the ground surging and it wasn't the only thing: my belly was surging too. The land was shuddering me off itself like a fly-plagued mare. Uncle or no uncle, I wasn't plowing that field anymore. I climbed off the tractor and walked uneasily across the undulating earth. I no sooner got clear of it when the quake stopped.

An hour later, Linda, Aunt Beda, and Uncle Pedro drove up our dirt track from the country road. They had gone to Arvin shopping for groceries that morning. Before I could say anything, my uncle—his face pale and tense—said, "That last big one just knocked down the center of Bakersfield we heard on the radio. It killed some people. And it cracked a bunch of places in Arvin too. We were in the Safeway and it knocked cans and stuff all over hell. There's wires down. We were damned lucky to get home as quick as we did." He was gasping for words. "Where were you when it hit?"

"In the field," I mumbled.

"Oh Christ," he groaned, "I forgot."

"The field of the Indians."

"I know which field."

Trying to keep my voice calm, I asked, "What're we gonna do?"

"Help me carry in these damn groceries," he snapped, turning away.

I hefted two large brown sacks, saying to him all the while, "I'm not gonna plow that damn thing anymore. I'll do anything else you want me to, but I'm not gonna plow that field. It doesn't want us out there. By the five wounds, Tio, I'm not gonna do it." I hadn't called him Tio since I was a little boy, and I think it was only then he realized how frightened I was, and only then I acknowledged to myself the degree of my fear. I was fighting not to cry.

Pedro stopped before we reached the house. His voice softened and he put a bag down and encircled my shoulders with one of his wiry arms. "What happened out there today, Junior? What exactly?"

He stood there with his arm around me—I was as big as him then—while I explained and choked back tears. When I finished, he whistled through his teeth. "Okay, maybe I was wrong. Maybe she was a bruja. You're right, something is strange."

We talked no more about it that day. I spent the afternoon first helping my aunt and uncle restack bags of gypsum that had been tumbled by the earthquake, then checking the spread for any other damage. We were mostly worried that a water line might have ruptured, but none had. We listened to the radio too, hearing reports of devastation all around us. Aunt Beda was on the phone a lot, assuring relatives in Texas and Los Angeles that we were okay.

After supper, Pedro gave me the pickup's keys and told me to go to town and have some fun. I did, too, taking my girlfriend to a drive-in movie, and a drive-in restaurant; I wasn't exactly anxious to go inside any buildings. I couldn't forget that field.

The next morning, Pedro jabbed me awake, holding my coffee as usual. "Come on, night owl, we got work to do." I sat up, yawning and stretching, not asking my uncle aloud, but searching him with my eyes. "You take care of the field of the Indians," he directed. "Clear our equipment off and bring it back of the barn."

"We're not gonna work it anymore?"

"No," he shook his head sadly. "I called the Eye-talian last night. We could've really used it, too," he added, then he turned away and headed for the kitchen.

There weren't any more major shakes that summer.

Joaquin

She hadn't really known what to expect, of course, but in some snug corner of her mind redwoods loomed, with shaded ferns and a lazing brook beneath them. The limousine, however, was not a snug corner, so she sweltered as the caravan motored from flat valley land into low, brown foothills, the road ahead diaphanous with heat. "Jeez," she groaned to herself.

Through the car's windows she saw only a few charred-appearing oaks with dull cattle clustered in their meager shade, plus an occasional coyote carcass stiffening on barbed wire, those things and an invasive glare that made her happy she affected dark glasses. So this was the famous Mother Lode. Like everything else in California it was fake. Mother must have really been loaded. "Jeez," she again complained privately.

To the three reporters who sat—two in jump seats, one up front with the chauffeur—interviewing her, however, she remained professional. "Breathtakin' place you boys got here," she smiled.

"And why, exactly, are you folks filming in Hornitos?" asked the surly older newspaperman from Fresno.

Because that jerk Roger wants authenticity even if I have to sweat my ass off, she thought. She said, "Well, Roger Carson, our producer, feels we can only achieve depth, honey, if we work where it all really happened. And you boys know I like *depth*," she growled. The older guy only blinked, but the two younger journalists began hyperventilating.

"Don't mind if I stay cool, do ya boys?" she crooned, unbuttoning the top of her blouse so that a slice of her creamy cleavage was suddenly visible. "I'm a little hot, with you good-lookin' fellas in the car," she winked.

Unimpressed, the older gent asked, "What exactly is this picture about, Mae?"

Mae? How does this old fart get off calling me by my first name? He's just showing off for the youngsters. "Well, boys," she replied pleasantly, "It's about that Mexican bandit, Joaquin . . . ah . . . Joaquin what's-his-name."

"Murrieta," interjected the older reporter.

"Murrieta," Mae smiled, thinking *kiss off*, "and about his love for a fandango dancer. That's me."

The cub from Merced finally worked up enough courage to speak. "Who . . . who plays Joaquin, Miss Lamont?"

She flashed her eyes at him. "One of my favorite leadin' men, Pedro Suarez," she confided, "a real man's man." I would land that fairy again, she groused to herself: Hollywood's prime butterfly.

"He'd better be if he's playing Joaquin," observed the old-timer. "Locals claim the real Joaquin was, to put it delicately, generously endowed. And, or so rumor has it, his . . . ah . . . business had a prominent scar inflicted by a jealous husband's knife."

"He had a what?" Mae demanded, her tone so harsh that it left no doubt that the journalist had gone too far. Who did he think he was, anyway? If anybody's gonna talk dirty around here it's me. She glared at the gray-haired man, and he averted his eyes. She'd have him off this story so fast his shorts would be singed.

Just as she was about to tell the old boy off good, the other young reporter, this one from Madera, said, "You know, Miss Lamont, authorities claimed Murrieta was killed by Harry Love's Rangers over near Coalinga on the other side of the valley, due west of here, but no one around this area believes it. They say it was Joaquin's *mozo* they killed, and whose head they chopped off, and that Joaquin was smart enough to lay low and use the confusion to go legitimate. Rumor is he'd accumulated a lot of loot by then."

"Is that right?" she cooed, not forgetting the old bozo, who'd be looking for work tomorrow. "What finally happened to him then?"

"No one knows for certain, ma'am. He just sorta disappeared."

"He went back to Mexico, or so they say," offered the old guy tentatively, but Mae ignored him. He was a cooked goose, she'd see to that.

"We're almost to Hornitos, Miss Lamont," pointed out the youngster from Merced.

"That's good, honey, 'cause I'm a little *hornitos* myself," she said, crossing her legs and hiking her skirt, "if ya get my meanin'."

The hayseed gulped and blinked his eyes.

Early morning and Mae sat under a vast oak tree grouching to her maid. She had long since disposed of the old reporter from Fresno, and now fretted over the inactivity; every day she spent sitting around this burg meant one more day stuck in the sticks. "Jeez, Hazel, I'm sweatin' like a nickle whore. We'll never get this damn picture shot."

The large brown woman just chuckled. "Well, Miss Mae, I thinks we get it shot. Mr. Roger just slow."

"Slow ain't the word for it, honey," sighed Mae. "Where the hell's he off to now?"

"Negotiatin' somewhere one of the boys told me."

"Pour me another drink from that thermos, willya?"

Hazel hesitated. "You sure you needs another one, Miss Mae?"

"*I needs, I needs.* Besides, that's just gin and tonic. Somethin' to keep me cool."

Hazel handed her another drink—her fourth that morning—then continued sorting and straightening costumes. Mae Lamont sipped while fanning herself, buzzed slightly by the gin, but not relieved by it. Even in the oak's shade heat assaulted her. Jeez, what a place. It could be worse, though, she admitted, watching the prop and equipment men lugging gear in open sunlight on the village's unpaved square.

As befitted a star, Mae Lamont's trailer was parked on the square's edge next to the gnarled tree, apart from the rest of the company, so she sat in regal isolation: painted, coiffed, bedecked and sweating. "Who's that creepy bastard?" she asked after a moment.

Glancing across the town square, Hazel caught sight of a tall man wearing a wide-brimmed sombrero leaning against the post office's adobe wall; he gazed steadily toward Mae Lamont's trailer. "You mean him? He just some old man from hereabouts. Mr. Roger he say that man a rancher."

"Mr. Roger?"

"Yeah. They talkin' the other day."

"Well, you tell Mr. Roger to run him off," ordered the blonde. "He gives me the creeps."

"Can't."

"Can't?" Mae snapped. "Don't forget who's star here!"

A patient smile slit the large brown face. "Now, now Miss Mae, don't go gettin' your dander up. I means we can't run that old man off because he own some buildin's we usin'.' "

"Dumps, you mean," grouched Mae.

"Dumps, then," chuckled Hazel, who busied herself straightening Mae Lamont's wardrobe. "He still own 'em."

Hell's bells thought the star as she sipped her gin and tonic. Sitting around this narrow spot in the road while some creepy dime-store cowboy gave her the eye. Jeez, they should have shot a couple of scenes by now. At least they were going back to the studio to shoot interiors. Now she sat in the middle of nowhere getting tight while nothing happened. Typical Roger Carson production, she acknowledged. That guy could screw up a two-car funeral. Good thing for him his father-in-law owns the studio.

She peered across the square into the verandaed shade where the tall rancher coiled against the wall. It was hard to make him out clearly, but he appeared to be one of those fair-skinned Mexicans Mae occasionally encountered in Southern California, the kind with burnished pink skin and blond hair, and he was still staring toward her. She thrust her chin forward and boldly returned his gaze. The more she looked, the more she saw: the man was older than he first appeared, but there was something about him that was young indeed, something that had fooled her when she had first caught sight of him. She decided it was his carriage, the way he leaned against the wall as though he could spring from it. An odd old bird. She drained her glass.

To hell with it, she mused, glancing around for Hazel, then deciding to forgo a refill. She needed a nap. Just as she contemplated lifting herself from her folding chair and repairing to her trailer, she noticed her co-star, the diminutive Pedro Suarez, flitting across the square toward her. "Jeez," Mae commented to no one in particular, "if his fans ever saw that butterfly strut he'd be out sellin' shoes in no time." Still, he was a good guy. "Whadya say, Pete?" she smiled.

"Ah, Mae, *mi corazon* . . ."

"Knock off the Spanish, Pete, I happen to know you're of the Hebrew persuasion."

Pedro Suarez smiled. "Just trying to set the mood, my dahling."

"What I'm in the mood for, you can't give me," Mae winked, "or won't."

"I could try," he grinned.

"Yeah," Mae returned his grin, "but what'll yer stunt man pal say? What's on yer mind, sweetie?"

Pedro swept into a folding chair next to hers and crossed his legs, bouncing one on the other, "Well, I just heard the wildest rumor, dahling, that there's an old man around here who actually claims to have known the real Joaquin Murrieta." He crooked one hand at the wrist and pointed across the square: "That's him over there, I think."

Mae Lamont followed the line of Pedro's finger and met the eyes of the old Mexican, who nodded and touched the brim of his sombrero. Looking away, vaguely disturbed, she remarked, "I d'know, Pete. Remember when we shot *The Flame of Chihuahua* down in El Paso how all those old women claimed to have been old lovers of Pancho Villa? Jeez, let a camera appear and so do the yokels."

"Well, my dahling . . ."

"What's all this 'dahling' jazz? Can't you say 'darling' anymore?"

"Now, now, pussycat, allow me my small peccadillos."

"Yer small *what*?" Mae Lamont guffawed. "You can come up with the damndest stuff. I'll bet you've got a small peckerdillo all right! Ha-ha-ha!"

Pedro Suarez raised his eyebrows and pursed his lips. "Puss, puss, puss," he said. "As I was trying to tell you, Roger told me . . ."

"Roger!" Mae snorted. "Hah! He doesn't know his ass from his elbow! If he hadn't married into the studio that klutz'd be sellin' Fuller Brushes, and screwin' that up too. Jeez."

"You are outrageous today, my dahling, don't be a puss. Besides, Roger is a very nice boy."

"In other words *you* know his ass from his elbow."

A broad grin cracked Pedro's chiseled features. "You have a filthy mind," he observed, "and I love it." Mae slapped his knee. "Oops," her leading man said, "here comes the man of the hour now, and he's bringing that old bandito with him."

The old man swaggered on slightly bowed legs, large shoulders swaying over lean hips, as he walked next to Roger, who seemed to be cantering. Their costumes, too, were in sharp contrast: the producer in English riding clothes, an outfit he affected on the set, while the Mexican wore jeans and a faded denim shirt along with his wide-brimmed hat.

As the two men neared, Mae noticed with increasing interest how the old man's heavy shoulders undulated beneath his shirt, and that his belly was flat. There was a muscular leanness about him she'd never seen in an old man, and she'd seen plenty, having launched her career by reviving the fading lust of several prominent figures in the film industry, big bombs with small fuses as she recalled. This guy didn't move like any old-timer she'd ever seen; he moved like a young buck costumed in an old body.

"Mae, Pedro, allow me to introduce Mr. Joaquin Tee-john," blustered Roger, who as usual managed to sound sincerely impressed.

"Tejon," corrected the old man quietly.

"Oh, yes," nodded Roger. "Mr. Tejon, here, once rode with the legendary Joaquin Murrieta."

"Well," gushed Pedro immediately, "I think that's just mahvelous. Perhaps he can help me with my part."

"My thought exactly," nodded Roger.

The old man paid little attention to the two men. Instead his eyes branded Mae Lamont. "Excuse my stare, senorita," he explained, "but you remind me of a woman I knew many years ago in this very village. You could be her daughter." His voice was deep and quavered only slightly. The faintest touch of Spanish spiced his pronunciation.

"That's quite all right, big boy," Mae replied with patented boldness, but within her something churned, a kernel of fear or excitement or both. This was not the kind of man she customarily met and her eyes betrayed uncertainty.

"Mr. Tejon owns a ranch near here, and several of the historic buildings in town, all of which he has put at our disposal for a very modest consideration," Roger explained.

Pedro Suarez licked his rouged lips, then sought to interrupt the silent conversation between Mae and the old man. "When exactly did you know the real Joaquin?"

The response was kind but firm: "Your first lesson, my friend, is that here, in this valley, you never ask a man exactly about his past. You allow a man to tell you what he will when he will." Tejon smiled, pausing. "In such a way you survive."

Blinking his eyes, Pedro Suarez seemed hurt by the mild rebuff. "Well!" he huffed. Mae winked at the producer, who grinned.

Returning his attention to Mae Lamont, the old man pointed across the square. "Over there," he said, "is what's left of the fandango hall. The woman I spoke of worked there, it must be fifty years ago now. There is a tunnel running from that hall to a cabin across the street. The lady and I often met there."

"Ya don't say," Mae responded, genuinely interested, though still vaguely troubled by the old man. He had the eyes of a bird of prey. "This musta been a lively burg in its day," she observed.

"It was pleasant to be young here," he smiled. "Let me show you." He extended his arm.

"Yes," gushed Pedro Suarez, apparently healed, "let's do take a look around."

The little pill's on the make, Mae noted. Look at him prance. Well, he's out of his league today. "I think Mr. Tejon was referrin' to me, sweetie."

"Oh," said Pedro, his eyes blinking rapidly.

"Roger," asked Mae, still seated in her folding chair, "is there any chance that we might shoot a scene or two today?"

"Not for a while."

"I figured. Maybe Mr. Tejon and me might take a little stroll and see the sights of Hornitos, if you boys don't mind."

"Of course, my love," agreed the producer, while Pedro Suarez pouted. She stood and grasped the old man's sinewy arm.

A hot breeze gusted east across the valley into the small town, and Mae Lamont, strolling with the old Mexican, thought she heard distant sounds in the moving air: the clatter of hooves, the creak of buckboards, the faint flair of voices. "What's that?"

Tejon listened for a moment, eyes alert, then replied, "There is an old saying, señorita: the wind does not forget."

"Yeah," she said, waiting for him to grin, but he did not. Mumbo jumbo, she thought. "Fascinatin'," she finally murmured, wondering if this character was just another California fake like the Hebrew Spaniards and the Italian Irishmen she always seemed to be cast opposite. No, she could tell he wasn't really like them. This old boy believed himself, she was certain, and that alone lent him credibility.

Outside the crumbling fandango hall Tejon stopped. He pointed toward the second floor window. "That was her room," he explained, "the woman I told you about."

"Ya don't say," said Mae Lamont as she shaded her eyes and glanced up. For a moment she thought she saw something, a shadow, a memory, a windblown curtain, move behind the dusty glass.

"Come in," he urged.

"Whadaya have in mind?" she breathed, humoring the old boy, but he did not laugh, and again his restless eyes locked on her for a moment, and she gulped. Gently, yet firmly, Tejon guided her into the old building, his hand somehow familiar as it directed her movement. "Whadaya have in mind?" she repeated, stammering slightly, but the old man—hardly appearing old at all in the building's dim light—only smiled as his eyes trapped her.

"What happen to you?" gasped Hazel. "You red as a radish! Lord, you got sunstroke?" The dark woman began fanning Mae Lamont with a towel. Looking up from the folding chair into which she'd flopped, her eyes heavy yet luminous, Mae sighed, "Sunstroke? No, I ain't had a sunstroke," she chuckled breathlessly.

"Say what?"

"Never mind. Get me a gin and tonic, willya."

"Lord, lord," crooned the brown woman as she hurried into the trailer.

"And Hazel!" said the red-faced blond.

"Yes, Miss Mae, what now?"

"Tell Mr. Carson I said to let that old reporter from Fresno come back." She paused and the brown woman once more disappeared into the trailer.

"And Hazel!"

Again the brown face thrust from the trailer's door. "Now what?"

"Set out lunch for two," she smiled. "Joaquin will be joinin' me."

"Say what?"

"Mr. Tejon will be joinin' me shortly for lunch."

"Yes, yes." The dark face nodded, then once more disappeared, sighing loudly.

Alone momentarily, Mae Lamont laid back in her chair under the oak and puffed air up over her warm face. She felt languid, she felt good, and she closed her eyes, drifting into easy repose where she heard those hints of sound in the breeze, those memories, as she felt its warm breath press her. Her eyes fluttered open momentarily and through blurring lashes she registered the old post office, the fandango hall, the road up which Joaquin had traveled on horseback only moments before. Her eyes closed and those faint voices, those hidden sounds from a past, returned on the warm wind pressing her gently, gently. From far away the click of a horse's hooves seemed to grow louder as the pressure of the heated wind intensified. She stirred, then without thought opened to it. "Jeez," she sighed.

The Horned Toad

"Expectoran su sangre!" exclaimed Great-grandma when I showed her the small horned toad I had removed from my breast pocket. I turned toward my mother, who translated: "They spit blood."

"De los ojos," Grandma added. "From their eyes," mother explained, herself uncomfortable in the presence of the small beast.

I grinned, "Awwwwww."

But my great-grandmother did not smile. *"Son muy toxicos,"* she nodded with finality. Mother moved back an involuntary step, her hands suddenly busy at her breast. "Put that thing down," she ordered.

"His name's John," I said.

"Put John down and not in your pocket, either," my mother nearly shouted. "Those things are very poisonous. Didn't you understand what Grandma said?"

I shook my head.

"Well . . ." mother looked from one of us to the other—spanning four generations of California, standing three feet apart—and said, "of course you didn't. Please take him back where you got him, and be careful. We'll all feel better when you do." The tone of her voice told me that the discussion had ended, so I released the little reptile where I'd captured him.

During those years in Oildale, the mid-1940s, I needed only to walk across the street to find a patch of virgin desert. Neighborhood kids called it simply "the vacant lot," less than an acre without houses or sidewalks. Not that we were desperate for desert then, since we could walk into its scorched skin a mere half-mile west, north, and east. To the south, incongruously, flowed the icy Kern River, fresh from the Sierras and surrounded by riparian forest.

67

Ours was rich soil formed by that same Kern River as it ground Sierra granite and turned it into coarse sand, then carried it down into the valley and deposited it over millennia along its many changes of channels. The ants that built miniature volcanoes on the vacant lot left piles of tiny stones with telltale markings of black on white. Deeper than ants could dig were pools of petroleum that led to many fortunes and lured men like my father from Texas. The dry hills to the east and north sprouted forests of wooden derricks.

Despite the abundance of open land, plus the constant lure of the river where desolation and verdancy met, most kids relied on the vacant lot as their primary playground. Even with its bullheads and stinging insects, we played everything from football to kick-the-can on it. The lot actually resembled my father's head, bare in the middle but full of growth around the edges: weeds, stickers, cactuses, and a few bushes. We played our games on its sandy center, and conducted such sports as ant fights and lizard hunts on its brushy periphery.

That spring, when I discovered the lone horned toad near the back of the lot, had been rough on my family. Earlier, there had been quiet, unpleasant tension between Mom and Daddy. He was a silent man, little given to emotional displays. It was difficult for him to show affection and I guess the openness of Mom's family made him uneasy. Daddy had no kin in California and rarely mentioned any in Texas. He couldn't understand my mother's large, intimate family, their constant noisy concern for one another, and I think he was a little jealous of the time she gave everyone, maybe even me.

I heard her talking on the phone to my various aunts and uncles, usually in Spanish. Even though I couldn't understand—Daddy had warned her not to teach me that foreign tongue because it would hurt me in school— I could sense the stress. I had been afraid they were going to divorce, since she only used Spanish to hide things from me. I'd confronted her with my suspicion, but she comforted me, saying, no, that was not the problem. They were merely deciding when it would be our turn to care for Grandma. I didn't really understand, although I was relieved.

I later learned that my great-grandmother—whom we simply called "Grandma"—had been moving from house to house within the family, trying to find a place she'd accept. She hated the city, and most of my aunts and uncles lived in Los Angeles. Our house in Oildale was much closer to the open country where she'd dwelled all her life. She had wanted to come to our place right away because she had raised my mother from a baby when my own grandmother died. But the old lady seemed un-impressed with Daddy, whom she called *"ese gringo."*

In truth, we had more room, and my dad made good money in the oil patch. Since my mother was the closest to Grandma, our place was the logical one for her, but Ese Gringo didn't see it that way, I guess, at least not at first. Finally, after much debate, he relented.

In any case, one windy afternoon, my Uncle Manuel and Aunt Toni drove up and deposited four-and-a-half feet of bewigged, bejeweled Span-ish spitfire: a square, pale face topped by a tightly curled black wig that hid a bald head—her hair having been lost to typhoid nearly sixty years before—her small white hands veined with rivers of blue. She walked with a prancing bounce that made her appear half her age, and she barked orders in Spanish from the moment she emerged from Manuel and Toni's car. Later, just before they left, I heard Uncle Manuel tell my father, "Good luck, Charlie. That old lady's dynamite." Daddy only grunted.

She had been with us only two days when I tried to impress her with my horned toad. In fact, nothing I did seemed to impress her, and she referred to me as *el malcriado*, causing my mother to shake her head. Mom explained to me that Grandma was just old and lonely for Grandpa and uncomfortable in town. Mom told me that Grandma had lived over half a century in the country, away from the noise, away from clutter, away from people. She would not accompany my mother on shopping trips, or anywhere else. She even refused to climb into a car, and I wondered how Uncle Manuel had managed to load her up in order to bring her to us.

She disliked sidewalks and roads, dancing across them when she had to, then appearing to wipe her feet on earth or grass. Things too civilized simply did not please her. A brother of hers had been killed in the great San Francisco earthquake and that had been the end of her tolerance of cities. Until my great-grandfather died, they lived on a small rancho near Arroyo Cantua, north of Coalinga. Grandpa, who had come north from Sonora as a youth to work as a *vaquero*, had bred horses and cattle, and cowboyed for other ranchers, scraping together enough of a living to raise eleven children.

He had been, until the time of his death, a dark-skinned man with wide shoulders, a large nose, and a sweeping handlebar moustache that was white when I knew him. His Indian blood darkened all his progeny so that not even I was as fair-skinned as my great-grandmother, Ese Gringo for a father or not.

As it turned out, I didn't really understand very much about Grandma at all. She was old, of course, yet in many ways my parents treated her as though she were younger than me, walking her to the bathroom at night and bringing her presents from the store. In other ways—drinking wine at dinner, for example—she was granted adult privileges. Even Daddy didn't drink wine except on special occasions. After Grandma moved in, though, he began to occasionally join her for a glass, sometimes even sitting with her on the porch for a premeal sip.

She held court on our front porch, often gazing toward the desert hills east of us or across the street at kids playing on the lot. Occasionally, she would rise, cross the yard and sidewalk and street, skip over them, sometimes stumbling on the curb, and wipe her feet on the lot's sandy soil, then she would slowly circle the boundary between the open middle and the brushy sides, searching for something, it appeared. I never figured out what.

One afternoon I returned from school and saw Grandma perched on the porch as usual, so I started to walk around the house to avoid her sharp, mostly incomprehensible, tongue. She had already spotted me. "*Ven aqui!*" she ordered, and I understood.

I approached the porch and noticed that Grandma was vigorously chewing something. She held a small paper bag in one hand. Saying "*Qué deseas tomar?*" she withdrew a large orange gumdrop from the bag and began slowly chewing it in her toothless mouth, smacking loudly as she did so. I stood below her for a moment trying to remember the word for candy. Then it came to me: "*Dulce,*" I said.

Still chewing, Grandma replied, "*Mande?*"

Knowing she wanted a complete sentence, I again struggled, then came up with "*Deseo dulce.*"

She measured me for a moment, before answering in nearly perfect English, "Oh, so you wan' some candy. Go to the store an' buy some."

I don't know if it was the shock of hearing her speak English for the first time, or the way she had denied me a piece of candy, but I suddenly felt tears warm my cheeks and I sprinted into the house and found Mom, who stood at the kitchen sink. "Grandma just talked English," I burst between light sobs.

"What's wrong?" she asked as she reached out to stroke my head.

"Grandma can talk English," I repeated.

"Of course she can," Mom answered. "What's wrong?"

I wasn't sure what was wrong, but after considering, I told Mom that Grandma had teased me. No sooner had I said that than the old woman appeared at the door and hiked her skirt. Attached to one of her petticoats by safety pins were several small tobacco sacks, the white cloth kind that closed with yellow drawstrings. She carefully unhooked one and opened it, withdrawing a dollar, then handed the money to me. "*Para su dulce,*" she said. Then, to my mother, she asked, "Why does he bawl like a motherless calf?"

"It's nothing," Mother replied.

"Do not weep, little one," the old lady comforted me, "Jesus and the Virgin love you." She smiled and patted my head. To my mother she said as though just realizing it, "Your baby?"

Somehow that day changed everything. I wasn't afraid of my great-grandmother any longer and, once I began spending time with her on the porch, I realized that my father had also begun directing increased attention to the old woman. Almost every evening Ese Gringo was sharing wine with Grandma. They talked out there, but I never did hear a real two-way conversation between them. Usually Grandma rattled on and Daddy nodded. She'd chuckle and pat his hand and he might grin, even grunt a word or two, before she'd begin talking again. Once I saw my mother standing by the front window watching them together, a smile playing across her face.

No more did I sneak around the house to avoid Grandma after school. Instead, she waited for me and discussed my efforts in class gravely, telling mother that I was "*muy inteligente,*" and that I should be sent to the nuns who would train me. I would make a fine priest. When Ese Gringo heard that, he smiled and said, "He'd make a fair-to-middlin' Holy Roller preacher, too." Even Mom had to chuckle, and my great-grandmother shook her finger at Ese Gringo. "Oh you debil, Sharlie!" she cackled.

Frequently, I would accompany Grandma to the lot where she would explain that no fodder could grow there. Poor pasture or not, the lot was at least unpaved, and Grandma greeted even the tiniest new cactus or flowering weed with joy. "Look how beautiful," she would croon. "In all this ugliness, it lives." Oildale was my home and it didn't look especially ugly to me, so I could only grin and wonder.

Because she liked the lot and things that grew there, I showed her the horned toad when I captured it a second time. I was determined to keep it, although I did not discuss my plans with anyone. I also wanted to hear more about the bloody eyes, so I thrust the small animal nearly into her face one afternoon. She did not flinch. "*Ola señor sangre de ojos,*" she said with a mischievous grin. "*Qué tal?*" It took me a moment to catch on.

"You were kidding before," I accused.

"Of course," she acknowledged, still grinning.

"But why?"

"Because the little beast belongs with his own kind in his own place, not in your pocket. Give him his freedom, my son."

I had other plans for the horned toad, but I was clever enough not to cross Grandma. "Yes, Ma'am," I replied. That night I placed the reptile in a flower bed cornered by a brick wall Ese Gringo had built the previous summer. It was a spot rich with insects for the toad to eat, and the little wall, only a foot high, must have seemed massive to so squat an animal.

Nonetheless, the next morning when I searched for the horned toad it was gone. I had no time to explore the yard for it, so I trudged off to school, my belly troubled. How could it have escaped? Classes meant little to me that day. I thought only of my lost pet—I had changed his name to Juan, the same as my great-grandfather—and where I might find him.

I shortened my conversation with Grandma that afternoon so I could search for Juan. "What do you seek?" the old woman asked me as I poked through flower beds beneath the porch. "Praying mantises," I improvised, and she merely nodded, surveying me. But I had eyes only for my lost pet, and I continued pushing through branches and brushing aside leaves. No luck.

Finally, I gave in and turned toward the lot. I found my horned toad nearly across the street, crushed. It had been heading for the miniature desert and had almost made it when an automobile's tire had run over it.

One notion immediately swept me: If I had left it on its lot, it would still be alive. I stood rooted there in the street, tears slicking my cheeks, and a car honked its horn as it passed, the driver shouting at me.

Grandma joined me, and stroked my back. "The poor little beast," was all she said, then she bent slowly and scooped up what remained of the horned toad and led me out of the street. "We must return him to his own place," she explained, and we trooped, my eyes still clouded, toward the back of the vacant lot. Carefully, I dug a hole with a piece of wood. Grandma placed Juan in it and covered him. We said an Our Father and a Hail Mary, then Grandma walked me back to the house. "Your little Juan is safe with God, my son," she comforted. We kept the horned toad's death a secret, and we visited his small grave frequently.

Grandma fell just before school ended and summer vacation began. As was her habit, she had walked alone to the vacant lot but this time, on her way back, she tripped over the curb and broke her hip. That following week, when Daddy brought her home from the hospital, she seemed to have shrunken. She sat hunched in a wheelchair on the porch, gazing with faded eyes toward the hills or at the lot, speaking rarely. She still sipped wine every evening with Daddy and even I could tell how concerned he was about her. It got to where he'd look in on her before leaving for work every morning and again at night before turning in. And if Daddy was home, Grandma always wanted him to push her chair when she needed moving, calling, "Sharlie!" until he arrived.

I was tugged from sleep on the night she died by voices drumming through the walls into darkness. I couldn't understand them, but was immediately frightened by the uncommon sounds of words in the night. I struggled from bed and walked into the living room just as Daddy closed the front door and a car pulled away.

Mom was sobbing softly on the couch and Daddy walked to her, stroked her head, then noticed me. "Come here, son," he gently ordered.

I walked to him and, uncharacteristically, he put an arm around me.

"What's wrong?" I asked, near tears myself. Mom looked up, but before she could speak, Daddy said, "Grandma died." Then he sighed heavily and stood there with his arms around his weeping wife and son.

The next day my Uncle Manuel and Uncle Arnulfo, plus Aunt Chinta, arrived and over food they discussed with my mother where Grandma should be interred. They argued that it would be too expensive to transport her body home and, besides, they could more easily visit her grave if she was buried in Bakersfield. "They have such a nice, manicured grounds at Greenlawn," Aunt Chinta pointed out. Just when it seemed they had agreed, I could remain silent no longer: "But Grandma has to go home," I burst. "She has to! It's the only thing she really wanted. We can't leave her in the city."

Uncle Arnulfo, who was on the edge, snapped to Mother that I belonged with the other children, not interrupting adult conversation. Mom quietly agreed, but I refused. My father walked into the room then. "What's wrong?" he asked.

"They're going to bury Grandma in Bakersfield, Daddy. Don't let 'em, please."

"Well, son . . ."

"When my horny toad got killed and she helped me to bury it, she said we had to return him to his place."

"Your horny toad?" Mother asked.

"He got squished and me and Grandma buried him in the lot. She said we had to take him back to his place. Honest she did."

No one spoke for a moment, then my father, Ese Gringo, who stood against the sink, responded: "That's right . . ." he paused, then added, "We'll bury her." I saw a weary smile cross my mother's face. "If she wanted to go back to the ranch then that's where we have to take her," Daddy said.

I hugged him and he, right in front of everyone, hugged back.

No one argued. It seemed, suddenly, as though they had all wanted to do exactly what I had begged for. Grown-ups baffled me. Late that week the entire family, hundreds it seemed, gathered at the little Catholic church in Coalinga for Mass, then drove out to Arroyo Cantua and buried Grandma next to Grandpa. She rests there today.

My mother, father, and I drove back to Oildale that afternoon across the scorching westside desert, through sand and tumbleweeds and heat shivers. Quiet and sad, we knew we had done our best. Mom, who usually sat next to the door in the front seat, snuggled close to Daddy, and I heard her whisper to him, "Thank you, Charlie," as she kissed his cheek.

Daddy squeezed her, hesitated as if to clear his throat, then answered, "When you're family, you take care of your own."

Trophies

"Well sir, they took me outta that wreck for dead," he admitted. "Them ambulance boys just flat give up on me, but this doctor at the hospital he brung me back." Rodney emptied the cup of coffee he had been cradling. "Want another'n?" he asked.

"Sure," I nodded. "Let me get this one."

I walked to the counter and ordered two more, seeing in the mirror not only the large man with whom I had been speaking, but other men, mostly old—retired from the oil fields or broken in them and unable to work—seated in plastic booths with coffee in Styrofoam cups and breakfast on Styrofoam plates. Their faces were creased and sun-darkened, like a collection of well-used baseball gloves, many wearing caps or cowboy hats at jaunty angles. I couldn't help noting how different this clientele was from the one I usually breakfasted with at the hospital in Oakland: no discussion of tax shelters here, not a word about racquetball or recent vintages. These were simpler, tougher men, as my late father had been, quick to laugh, quick to take offense, their passions surging like bunched muscles just beneath their surfaces. In fact, they were what I might have been had education not rescued me: there but for the grace of God . . .

I carried two cups to the booth and said, "Here you go, Rod."

"Thanks, Larry," he grinned and winked, making a clicking sound out one corner of his mouth, a trait I recalled from high school.

High school: if anyone had told me then that I'd one day share a civilized cup of coffee with Rodney Phelps, I'd have considered the speaker crazy. I didn't imagine Rodney would share *anything* in a civilized fashion, or that he could. He had seemed more an irrational, ominous force

75

than a person—a tornado, maybe, or an epidemic—precisely the kind of peril opportunity had allowed me to escape.

In truth, I hadn't thought about him for years—not since I'd gone away to college, I guess—but when I'd spied the large man lurching up Oildale Drive toward the river that first evening home, I'd recognized him even in dusk and had thought immediately of the accident, sensing all the while an ancient discomfort lurching into my belly. I was driving by in heavy traffic, so I couldn't stop—I probably wouldn't have anyway—but from a distance he appeared unchanged by the thirty-plus years; shoulders wide, hair dark, gaze direct and unflinching; he even wore the same costume I'd last seen him in, the one we all wore in 1950: a white T-shirt and Levis, the shirt ghostly. Briefly, I was swept back to my adolescent years and nearly allowed my car to drift into the wrong lane, into an accident of my own.

The very next evening, driving in the same direction on the same street, I once more sighted him, just a bit farther south, but still swaggering and again wearing a bright white T-shirt and Levis. I noticed this time that, below those wide, spectral shoulders, pivoted tragic hips. His walk was less a swagger, I realized, than an elaborate limp—for a moment I wondered if it was a result of the accident. Aware of the degeneration being suffered by my own middle-aged body, I was privately pleased to note that Rodney had not escaped similar disintegration.

I remembered well the times he had bullied me. He had intimidated everyone, of course, and brutalized as many as he could during those days when street fighting was a serious and honored local pursuit. One night at Stan's Drive Inn, Rodney had walked up behind a big, easy-going lunk named Dennis McGee and broken his jaw with an unannounced punch. Another time, he had cold-cocked an East High football player named Bob Meyers while Bob sat on a public toilet; Rodney was much praised for his creativity following that incident. He even won something like a fair fight against a tough little Mexican kid named Trevino who went to the Catholic high school. There were, in fact, numberless stories of his adventures in those years and I was actually present when he duked a shop teacher at Bakersfield High, thus ending his own not-altogether-promising academic career.

Rodney, whose abundant testosterone was not matched by excessive cerebrum, had also claimed to be a great cocksman during those years, and nobody argued. In truth, most of us had toadied up to him, slapping his thick back when he regaled us with the tales of his triumphs at drive-in movies or deserted groves, each wishing he had been the protagonist of Rodney's yarns. It was all so mysterious to us then, so titillating, and he had more than once shown us girls' panties—his trophies, the very sight of which inflamed us—then clicked the side of his mouth.

In any case, Rod's legendary exploits and that terrible automobile accident had returned to me when I'd seen him, because he seemed to be a walking time capsule, bad hips or not. His appearance had even inspired an old, almost primal shadow of fear.

I was back at my late parents' house that week to comfort an aging aunt who now lived there and who was to undergo surgery, so it was not to be my usual one-day-in-one-day-out visit. I was making it a point to contact my few friends who remained in the area, and was even journeying to personal points of interest: the secret spot on the Kern River where I had parked with girlfriends, the church where I had been baptized, the football field where I had warmed the bench. For the first time since leaving town all those years before, I'd succumbed to nostalgia.

As a result, when I'd entered the newly constructed McDonalds on North Chester Avenue that morning, and noticed his broad, white T-shirted back hunkered over a cup of coffee, I'd resisted the antique urge to retreat and had instead approached him. "Rodney," I asked, "remember me? Larry Trumaine."

The heavy face—not nearly as youthful as I'd expected—had swung toward me, and I'd immediately identified ruptured capillaries beneath his tan skin like the red webs of spiders. After a moment, he'd grunted, "Be damned," then grinned and extended a large hand. "Set down, Larry. Set right down."

It turned out that Rod had gone to work roughnecking on a drilling rig after recovering from the injuries he'd suffered in the accident, and had traveled a good deal—Saudi Arabia, Venezuela, Alaska—as a roughneck until, recently, he had badly injured his spine and been forced to retire on disability. Little wonder I had not seen him on any of my many brief earlier trips home. He lived now, he explained, in a trailer court on McCord Street not far from the river. "And you're a doctor?" he observed.

"I wish I'd a knew that whenever I busted up my back. You might coulda helped me."

I only smiled.

His eyes narrowed and his voice lowered. "You recollect ol' David DeJong that was a year ahead of us in school?"

I nodded.

"He's a doctor now, too, a big shot at Kern General. Well he married that Jeanine Garcia that was the good-lookin' song leader. I screwed her." He clicked the side of his mouth and nodded to emphasize the point.

Dave and Jeanine were good friends of mine, so I said nothing, although my belly surged.

Rod seemed disappointed. He added: "And that Miller girl with the big jugs . . ."

"Sherry?"

"Yeah, I screwed her too, and she's on the City Council in Bakersfield. She loved my nuts."

I'd heard enough of his infantile babbling, so I shrugged and looked at my watch. Before I could speak, Rodney continued: "Mary Anne Reynolds that give the graduation speech, I screwed her lots of times. I used to go to her house Thursdays whenever her folks wasn't home and we'd have at it. She'd just beg me for it. I even screwed her that night in her graduation outfit."

I stood, my throat tightening. I *did* vaguely remember him hovering around Mary Anne in the parking lot following graduation. He had lingered there with some other losers while the ceremony went on, probably drinking beer. I started to move toward the door.

One of Rodney's large, knotted hands gripped my forearm. "I'll tell you somethin' else: I even screwed two cousins in one day. Got Marlene Hughes in the parkin' lot at Bakersfield Junior College—remember her? Then I picked up on her cousin, that real purty one from Arvin—ah . . . Terry I believe her name was—and I nailed her that night. Boy, was she somethin': suck your damn sump dry." He again grinned, winked and clicked the side of his mouth.

His face blurred as I moved away from the booth, a force throbbing in my vitals like the surging of an oil pump. I'd seen enough of this pathetic husk of a man, heard enough. I didn't trust myself to speak, certainly not to tell him that I had married Terry. I didn't trust myself to tell him anything.

"You oughta come by the place," he winked, apparently unaware of my anger. "I even got their underpants at my trailer. I always kept underpants off the girls I got. You oughta come see . . ." His voice trailed off and he looked puzzled. "Somethin' wrong?" he asked.

"I've got to go."

"Hey, them gals was big shots and I had 'em."

"How about Leona, do you have her underpants?"

He rose slowly and painfully from his seat—his back clearly arthritic— and I retreated a step at the sight of those huge shoulders hunched toward me. "You sorry fucker," he growled, "don't you never mention Leona's name to me." His eyes narrowed.

The other customers suddenly quieted at the prospect of a little action, but I disappointed them by turning and walking away. I tried to tell myself that, at nearly fifty, I didn't need the hassle that would follow a public fight, but the truth is that I was afraid: I didn't need my ass kicked.

Leona Tedlock had been Rod's steady girl, one of the nice ones who seemed fascinated by him. He had dated her through most of their high school years. A good student, she had been scheduled to go away to college that fall after graduating—Fresno State, I think—but she had been killed in the accident. Rodney had been driving her along the levee, to that spot near the river where we all parked, when he had missed a turn and his car had plunged off the embankment into the stream. Although the water was shallow, it was also cold and swift and its bed was full of quicksand. Leona had been thrown from the vehicle and her body was never recovered. Rodney had been seriously injured.

Whatever he'd said to me that morning, I had no right to mention Leona's name just to hurt him; she had been a good person and she wasn't involved in my anger. It was small of me and I sat in my aunt's parlor that afternoon ashamed and wondering why I had spoken so carelessly. In fact, I was not much concerned by his certainly apocryphal claim concerning Terry, I told myself. Terry had a past—we all do and beautiful women are certainly no exceptions—but not with the likes of Rodney Phelps, of that much I was certain. You have to be mature about such things.

Still, the thought, the possibility however remote that his large hands had slid fine satin underpants from those fine satin hips, that her texture and smell hid within some dark drawer of his trailer, would not leave me. Surges of rage returned throughout the day and, with them, even more disturbing hints of titillation: I could neither avoid nor separate the two.

My behavior that morning also continued to afflict me. I was an educated man, and I had no business behaving so primitively. The more I thought about it, the more I wanted to leave Oildale and its tug toward old, toward raw passions, but I had promised my aunt that I'd remain until she returned home, at least two more days. I suddenly missed not only Terry and the kids, but everything life in the Bay Area represented to me: gentility, rationality, restraint.

Once the sun's heat had begun to dissipate that evening, I climbed into my running gear, needing fresh air and exercise to clear my mind and calm my soul. Out in the somewhat-less-warm evening air, I felt better immediately, breaking into an easy sweat and breathing deeply until I found myself jogging up Oildale Drive toward the river. Far ahead, almost at the levee, I saw in a streetlight's glow the apparition of a white T-shirt lurching in the same direction I was traveling; it had to be Rodney.

Shrugging off an ominous instant of fear, I decided to catch him and apologize for having mentioned Leona but, before I could, he disappeared. I knew he could only be going one place from there—the river's edge was pleasant on summer evenings—so I turned toward North Chester, then ran onto a side street that led to the levee road. In that darkness, I didn't want to run the route he had likely taken because of chuckholes and hidden ditches.

I assumed I'd find Rodney near the cottonwood grove where we all used to park, so I jogged slowly along the narrow track on the levee's top until I reached the curve where so long ago the accident had occurred. Then I noticed something almost luminous on the moonlit water to my left. I stopped and squinted to see clearly what it was.

The river must have been exceptionally shallow that year, because the big man appeared to be walking on top of it about midway out. His arms were extended, I could tell, and he was calling, calling something into the river's hiss. The poor bastard, I thought, all his big talk must have been to cover the guilt he still felt about the accident. I leaned back on a tree's carcass next to the road, fascinated by what I was seeing and troubled that perhaps my thoughtless remark might have triggered this bizarre display.

Beyond the scene on the water, I noted traffic passing on the Chester Avenue bridge—those lights in this darkness little different than they had been thirty years before—and the glow of Bakersfield to the south. Then I scanned back to the white beacon of a T-shirt and realized it had turned and begun moving slowly back toward the near bank.

My heart pounding, I slipped behind the stump as the big man approached the river's edge. Rodney's large body stopped suddenly only a few feet from solid ground and seemed to hover there, arms poised at first, then flailing slowly. I could see him pretty well at that distance, especially his shirt like a soul dancing over the glittering water. I couldn't figure what was going on so, my breath tight, I moved stealthily from behind the stump and down the levee toward the river's edge.

Only when I neared the floundering man did I realize that he was slowly sinking, his arms fighting desperately to reach shore: he was caught in a pocket of quicksand and his movement was a *danse macabre*. Rodney didn't notice me until I stood only a few feet away, then he gasped, "Help me," his voice as thick as the river's hiss. I looked for a branch to extend to him, but even as I did, something ominous as quicksand began pulling at my own hammering core, something as frigid and as old as the river and the sand. I stopped and gazed at him, uncertain what to do. In his desperation, he did not seem to recognize me, and the water was surging over his chest now, gushing around his shoulders. "Please, buddy," he begged, "you gotta help me."

Suddenly, I could think only of Terry, of what Rodney had said about her, and that I could never forget it just as I would never mention it. The wind seemed to cease and I did not move. The night itself waited.

He finally recognized me, I knew—his eyes locking on mine for a moment—but he said no more, and somehow I could say nothing to him as he looked away toward the bank near my feet. He seemed to grit his teeth and I gritted mine. Soon only his eyes were above the gush, then they went under.

In a moment his head submerged completely, the current spilling over it as it would a rock, and I could identify only the phantom white of his

T-shirt through the water above the engulfing sand. Then it too was gone and the water smoothed.

Body shaking, I inhaled deeply, seeking to regain control while I gazed at the surging current a moment longer, at the patterned water below me, then realized fully what had occurred and my absolute absence of remorse. I turned and scrambled into inky darkness up the levee, down the road, then back toward Oildale Drive, running faster and faster and faster.

My Dear Mr. Thorp

⚡ ⚡ ⚡ ⚡ ⚡ ⚡ ⚡ ⚡ ⚡ ⚡ ⚡ ⚡ ⚡

Feb. 3, 1983

My Dear Mr. Thorp:

The world will soon end unless human beings begin to love one another in God's fullness. Thusly, I am submitting to you the enclosed three brief poems celebrating our Oneness with the Eternal. Please note the subtle symbolism and the lyric qualities found in each. As the enclosed resume indicates, I have been widely published in the PIXLEY DAILY RECORD and the TRUE BIBLE CHURCH BULLETIN. It is time, however, for my inspirational poems to reach a national audience and I have chosen your journal, THE ATWOOD REVIEW, to carry the message. If you do a good job with these poems, I have others I might send to you. I hope you enjoy the newspaper articles I enclose, plus the Xeroxed page from WHO'S WHO IN THE TRUE BIBLE CHURCH. *All three of these poems are copyrighted to me.* I also enclose a stamped, self-addressed envelope. I am looking forward to your prompt reply.

Sincerely yours,
J. Elbert Duggan (poet)

Feb. 7, 1983

Dear Mr. Duggan:
Thank you for submitting your work to *The Atwood Review*. While it does not suit our present needs, we do wish you the best of luck placing it elsewhere.

With best wishes,
Roger Thorp, editor
The Atwood Review

83

Feb. 10, 1983

My Dear Mr. Thorp:

Perhaps there has been a mistake. The three poems I sent to you, "Pixley Agonistis," "Heaven Found," and "God's Messenger," have been widely praised as being among my best. Did you confuse them with someone else's? If so, I am still willing to allow you to publish them. They are, by the way, *copyrighted to me,* just in case somebody on your staff has any ideas.

Sincerely yours,

J. Elbert Duggan (poet)

Feb. 21, 1983

My Dear Mr. Thorp:

Since you have not had the courtesy to answer my last letter, I must assume that I have misjudged you. I have today spoken to attorney Randle McQuaid informing him of the possible abuse of my copyrights by members of your staff. We will be watching you closely. Attorney McQuaid is also a member of the True Bible Church.

Sincerely yours,

J. Elbert Duggan (poet)

Dear Editors:

THE BARD HATH LONG SINCE
GRIPPED MY HEART,
SO WITH THESE PRECIOUS LINES
I PART.

ENCLOSED WITH POEMS
YOU WILL FIND
NOT ONLY S.A.S.E.
BUT TIES THAT BIND.

PRAY, DEAR SIR, DO
READ WITH LOVE,
THESE LINES INSPIRED
FROM ABOVE.

Yours for poetry,
Marjorie Marie Rampetti

Feb. 26, 1983

Dear Ms. Rampetti:

Thank you for submitting your work to *The Atwood Review*. While it does not suit our present needs, we do wish you the best of luck placing it elsewhere.

>With best wishes,
>Roger Thorp, editor
>*The Atwood Review*

March 1, 1983

Dear Mr. Thorp:

Please consider the enclosed poem "Wolf's Cry," for publication in *The Atwood Review*. Since you are no doubt familiar with my work, I doubt that you'll require the S.A.S.E. I also enclose.

>Sincerely,
>Morgan Jackson

March 12, 1983

Dear Mr. Jackson:

Thank you for submitting your work to *The Atwood Review*. While it does not suit our present needs, we do wish you the best of luck placing it elsewhere.

>With best wishes,
>Roger Thorp, editor
>*The Atwood Review*

March 16, 1983

Thorp:

You dingleberry! You mote! You feeble excuse for an editor! How dare you refuse to publish a work by "one of the signal poets of our time." Just who do you think you are? No wonder you're stuck in California!

I've half a mind to thrash you. You had best hope that you do not find yourself in my company.

Never again will your journal that publishes only trash be honored by one of my submissions. GO TO HELL!

>Morgan Jackson

March 20, 1983

Dear male:

Here is your chance to undo thousands of years of oppression of Wimin. Are you enlightened enough to allow the truth to be proclaimed? You will note that we have moved beyond the old, male-dominated word "wo" (like halt)-man". We have also moved beyond male imposed sexual roles. Thus the enclosed manifesto: "Personhood!"

For all of history in the supposed "civilized" west the small differences between the sexes have been exaggerated by exploiting males, who created a slave-class of Wimin. Males in sciences such as endocrinology, medicine, and sociobiology have sought to create the illusion that men and Wimin are essentially different. IT'S A LIE!

"Personhood" reveals the whole rotten conspiracy. Here is your chance to participate in the new consciousness that will liberate all people. Are *you* liberated enough to publish it?

> Solidarity Forever!
> Patsy Ross
> Charleston Feminist Collective

March 29, 1983

Dear Ms. Ross:

Thank you for submitting your work to *The Atwood Review*. While it does not suit our present needs, we do wish you the best of luck placing it elsewhere. Please send S.A.S.E. so I can return your manuscript.

> With best wishes,
> Roger Thorp, editor
> *The Atwood Review*

April 5, 1983

Pig Thorp:

You revealed yourself! Your name is on our list! RETURN OUR MANIFESTO, PIG!

> Patsy Ross
> Charleston Feminist Collective

April 20, 1983

PIG THORP:

THIS IS YOUR LAST WARNING! RETURN OUR MANIFESTO!
PATSY ROSS & C.F.C.

April 28, 1983

Dear Sir:

I've never wrote anything before, but here's a poem that makes the boys at the bar where I hang out laugh.

About me—no poet, just a regular guy. Born in Oklahoma in 1937. Fell in the glory hole of an outhouse in 1939. Never been the same. My folks, after some argument, decided to clean me up and keep me. I sold newspapers and once smoked a tampax—like one long filter. I sold crickets to fishermen and ate a couple—crickets, not fishermen—just to see why the fish bit—tasted pretty fair. Also ate a worm and a dragonfly—stick with crickets if you get the chance. Played doctor with the girl across the street in 1948, and 49, and 50, and so on. Better than crickets. Went to high school and even graduated. Tried smoking in 1952—quit in 1953—tasted like shit. Arrested for painting pubic hair on all statues in city park. Went on the road in 55 and worked dipping seed potatoes and waitresses in Utah. Packed grapes and waitresses in California. Army 57–59—prefer crickets or waitresses. Back on the road, drinking a little beer, then a lot. Tried dope, also drugs. Played doctor some more—better all the time. Thinned sugar beets, picked potatoes, tended bar, road rails. Back to crickets. And waitresses. Married a cute one—waitress, not cricket—in 62. Stole a car and didn't get caught. Dipped snuff. Settled down and worked in a feed store. Played doctor with lady that also worked there. Back on the road in 66. (to be continued—life, not letter)

So here's the poem. Hope you like it but, being a realist, I enclose some stamps. Do not smoke them.

Cheers,
Rapid City Robert

May 4, 1983

Dear Robert:

Your poem is lousy. I'd like to publish your letter, however. What do you say?

> With best wishes,
> Roger Thorp, editor
> *The Atwood Review*

p.s. About that girl you played doctor with, was her name Patsy Ross?

May 12, 1983

Dear Sir:

Hell yeah, print what you want. No, it wasn't Patsy, but send me her address and I'll see what I can do. Don't feel bad about the poem. I stole it anyway.

> Cheers,
> Rapid City Robert

May 14, 1983

Roger Thorp, Editor
Atwood Review
Box 102
Atwood, Calif. 94900

Dear Mr. Thorp:

I am sending you three poems in the hope that one may be acceptable for publication in *Atwood Review*. It would be a great honor to be published in your pages since it is a truly great journal and it has always been my very favorite. Please do not think because I am sending you photocopies that I am also sending them to any other journal. It is just that I like to keep the originals in my files.

Well, Mr. Thorp, it is up to you. You can make a poet very happy by honoring him with publication in your great journal. Won't you please?

> Very truly yours,
> Lauren Lafeyette (pen name)
> Bill Schwartz (real name)

May 19, 1983

Roger Thorp, Editor
Atwood Review
Box 102
Atwood, Calif. 94900

Dear Mr. Thorp:

Never mind the poems I sent you. They are being published elsewhere. How long did you think I would wait?

> Very truly yours,
> Lauren Lafeyette (pen name)
> Bill Schwartz (real name)

June 7, 1983

Dear Mr. Thorp:

Well, I'm in love again, as the enclosed poems show. I hope they also show some hint of talent and craft. Being realistic, I enclose S.A.S.E.; being optimistic, I hope you don't use it. Thanks in advance for your time.

> Yours hopefully,
> Rita Lou Bowen

June 14, 1983

Dear Ms. Bowen:

It will be our pleasure to publish your sensitive, original poetry. We all thought the subject had been exhausted, but you have proven us wrong. Thanks.

I will be sending you galley proofs in about three months.

> With best wishes,
> Roger Thorp, editor
> *The Atwood Review*

July 1, 1983

My Dear Mr. Thorp:

Since your thoughtless rejection of my poetry, I have sent it to nine other magazines and all have sent it back. There can only be one reason for this—you contacted other editors and used your influence to convince them not to publish my poems. Well, you have made the wrong enemy. I have discussed this matter with attorney Randle McQuaid and he assures me that your behavior is *actionable*. You have not heard the last of me.

Sincerely yours,

J. Elbert Duggan (poet)

Vengeance

ﻼ ﻼ ﻼ ﻼ ﻼ ﻼ ﻼ ﻼ ﻼ ﻼ ﻼ ﻼ ﻼ

They filled the tiny stucco porch with their bodies and their voices, a thick boy carrying several bicycle tires looped like thick black bracelets over one grimy arm, and a smaller boy shoeless but wearing a tattered shirt. "You better git off my daddy's property, Bertil, or I'm callin' the sher'ff!" shouted the larger of the two. He shook a fleshy fist in the other's face, but the pale, slight boy did not budge.

"Whan I aim a do is git na evinence own nyou, Namar!" the smaller boy yelled back, his narrow arms tight at his sides, his thin fists white. A large hearing aid protruded from one of his ears, and a slim wire extended from it along his neck into the bulging breast pocket of his shirt.

"What the hell's that noise?" roared a voice from within the house.

"It's this dummy, Daddy," called Lamar, then he grinned tightly at the smaller boy: "Now you gonna git it, dummy."

"Whan I aim a do . . . ," the smaller boy was repeating when a vast man lurched through the screen door onto the porch, forcing the debaters onto the small bare space that constituted a yard. Like the heavy boy, the man wore a dirty T-shirt without sleeves; and his thick arms were rippled with fat that stretched his fading tattoos into textured frescoes. Perched jauntily on the side of a head that might have been a pale pumpkin was a greasy baseball cap, and a toothpick extended from the man's mouth like a serpent's single fang. Nearly hidden in the span of one vast hand was a can of beer. "What're you doin' here, boy?" he demanded, his eyes creased with threat.

"Namar snole my nike, Misner Snudly, an I aim a git na evinence own him," the thin boy insisted.

91

"Lamar never stole nothin'," Mr. Studly asserted, wiggling his tooth-pick. "Now git your ass off this property before I let Lamar whup you."

"Whan I aim a do . . ."

"Git!" exploded the man, and Bertil scrambled through stacks of old automobile tires until he stood on the dirt border between yard and street, where he planted himself, shook one small fist, and yelled: "Whan I aim a do is git na evidence own nyou, Namar!" then he turned and walked awkwardly away, arms and legs not quite synchronized.

The man on the porch shook his large head. "Ain't that kid a sorry specimen," he observed, tugging at his jeans so that they hung briefly on the impossible angle of his belly before slipping back to their customary camp below the slope. "What's wrong with him?"

"He's just a dummy is all, in the re-tard class at school, and he's about deaf. He can't even talk right," Lamar explained with a chuckle.

He was still chuckling when his father smacked his face with an open hand. "How's come you to steal that boy's bike?" the man demanded.

The fat boy cringed. "I never," he insisted.

"Don't shit me. I know you never *found* all them bikes I seen you tote through here."

Backing away several steps, the boy asked, "Where'd *you* git all them tires?"

The small, stucco house was an oasis in a black rubber badland, a wilderness of vulcanized pinnacles and peaks, of retreaded dunes and drifts; tentative tracks extended into that rubber wasteland, disappeared into canyons and draws where secret sheds and gleaming piles of hubcaps hid. At the end of one trail, the body of an ancient Chevy lay rusting, its engine suspended from an A-frame like a forgotten sacrifice. The core of the paths was not the house, but a large aluminum building in which Lamar's father mysteriously converted threadbare tires into thickly treaded rein-carnations to be shipped far out-of-state, where their rubber would strip faster than song-leaders at drive-in movies.

Mr. Studly grinned like a clever jack-o-lantern. "Well, I never stole none of 'em *myself*. I cain't say how my suppliers got 'em." The man lifted one thick leg and farted thunderously—"Ooops, stepped on a frog"—he winked at his son and reentered the small house.

As soon as his father disappeared, Lamar shuffled quickly along a path to the small shed in which he secreted his inventory of bikes. Inside, he snapped on the bare bulb, then from under a wooden bench he extracted a warm can of beer stolen from his father's supply in the pantry, and a girlie magazine from his own collection. He took a long pull from the can, and sneezed, warm bubbles having invaded his nose. "Shit!" he said.

At fourteen-and-a-half, Lamar Studly remained in the sixth grade and counted the days until his sixteenth birthday when he could legally quit school. He didn't mind remaining a sixth grader again, because his bulk allowed him to bully his classmates. Among them he was known as a tough customer. Fortunately, most boys his own age or older also treated him deferentially in the hope they might be awarded an occasional tire or hubcap, or perhaps a glimpse at his famous magazine collection, so he moved with blessed impunity through Oildale's streets, little hindered by parental restriction or peer pressure.

Moreover, Lamar had stumbled upon a business when a Mexican man who supplied tires to his father had one day asked the boy if he might be able to provide used bicycles for resale in Los Angeles. Lamar had been doing just that unbeknownst to all Oildale until that fateful day when Bertil had spied him slipping away from the River Theater on the dummy's broken-down Flyer, which had hardly been worth stealing as it turned out. Well, if there was one thing Lamar could handle, it was a dummy. Except this one refused to be handled.

In fact, Bertil had confronted Lamar after school that very next Monday, and right in front of the guys. "I sneen nya Namar! I wont my nike!"

"I ain't got your shitty bike, dummy, now git outta here."

"I sneen nya!"

"You see about as good as you hear," Lamar had said, and the guys all laughed.

"Whan I aim a do is git na evinence own nyou, Namar."

"You better not bother me no more or I'll kick your ass," the large boy had warned, a threat that would have ended matters if a sensible kid had been involved. But Bertil was different.

He lived in a raw wooden hovel near the Kern River, one of nearly a dozen children in a family that seemed desperately poor even in that unprosperous area. Like all his brothers and sisters, his skin appeared perpetually covered by a dirt patina, a mysterious darkness that led some to speculate that they were gypsies, others to suggest that the small house into which the family crowded contained no bath. His hair was permanently burred in a home haircut, and he wore shoes only to school; socks were added for church.

Six mornings a week, shortly after dawn, Bertil's parents, along with several of his older siblings, piled in an ancient truck and drove away, only to return after dark. They were said to be "pickers," a word spoken in hushed, almost frightened tones by townfolks like a dark incantation from their shared past. After school, while other younger children could be seen grazing their lawnless yard—it was considered little short of miraculous in the neighborhood the way those kids stayed home—Bertil delivered *The Bakersfield Californian*.

The boy had for several months covered his newspaper route on foot until he had saved enough money from the small part of his earnings that he kept for himself to purchase an old bicycle at the police auction in Bakersfield. Only a month later, he had spied Lamar Studly pedaling away on it. Although he had told his teacher, and Lamar had been called into the principal's office, nothing had been proven since—as the fat boy knew but did not admit—the wayward bike had already been trucked to Southern California. It had not been a rigorous inquiry in any case, because the claims of students in the Special Class seldom amounted to much; when Lamar's father, a locally respected businessman, had sworn that his son was innocent, the investigation had been terminated. Mr. Studly had dutifully slapped Lamar a couple of times for the real crime of almost allowing himself to be caught, then forgot the matter. Or forgot it until that afternoon when Bertil showed up on their porch.

Sitting in his shed, Lamar sipped warm beer and pondered this new turn of events, the dummy confronting him here, at his own house. Bertil wasn't going to be calling the cops; it was too late for that. Still, some of Lamar's friends were kidding him about bicycles, sometimes in front of other people, and that dumb kid was staring at him all the time at school, and accusing him when he got the chance. A few teachers were now eyeing Lamar closely too. The fat boy considered his options. He could beat the kid up, but some big kid would take up for the dummy sure as anything, and then he would really be in for it. He could lay low for awhile, let his business go, but then he wouldn't have the money he needed to keep his pals happy. Lamar sighed: it wasn't *fair*.

When the fat boy entered the house that evening for dinner, his father grabbed him by the shirt and growled, "I don't want that little turd comin' back here no more, understand?"

"Okay, Daddy."

"And I ain't shittin'."

Mr. Studly's eyes looked like yellow lifesavers and his son suspected that his old man had worked his way through his daily case of beer thinking about that dummy. He also knew that the man was quick to throw punches when drunk, so he decided to say as little as possible. "Okay, Daddy."

"Now go eat," the man grunted, releasing his son. "And go easy. You're gittin' too fat."

"Okay, Daddy."

That next day at school during recess, Lamar and two of his cronies were sneaking cigarettes behind the gym when they noticed Bertil standing across the playfield staring at them. "Looky," observed Talcott, "that dummy's lookin' at ya again."

"Whyn't you just kick his ass?" Buzzard asked.

"Hey, Buzz, I might have to, but I don't wanna hurt the re-tard." Lamar was carefully combing a greasy black curl onto his forehead. He returned his comb to a pocket.

"Here he comes," Talcott said.

Lamar looked up and saw that, sure enough, Bertil was walking straight toward him, and he felt his stomach suddenly churn. Damn him, Lamar thought. Well maybe I *will* just kick his ass. But when the thin boy stood directly in front of him, Lamar felt vaguely sick.

"I aim a git na evinence own nyou, Namar," Bertil said, his beady eyes looking straight into the fat boy's. Belly burning, Lamar said nothing, but he felt as though he was being inflated, pumped full of air so that his skin grew tighter and tighter, while Bertil continued talking.

"I sneen you sneal my nike an' I aim a git na evinence."

For one final instant, Lamar quivered, so full that his skin felt ready to burst, then he snorted—"Nooo!"—and threw a wild, roundhouse punch that smacked the smaller boy to the ground and shattered his large white hearing aid.

"Good punch, Lamar!" exalted Buzzard, jumping in his excitement.

Talcott's voice was less pleasant: "Yeah, but you broke his hearin' aid. I'm gittin' outta here. You're in Dutch now, Lamar."

The fat boy, feeling suddenly free and triumphant, was shuffling a quick circle around Bertil, who held his bleeding ear with both hands and wept quietly, shattered white plastic scattered in front of him like bits of bone. "Come on," taunted Lamar, "you want some more?" His fists were poised.

"What's going on here?" demanded the gym teacher who had just rounded the corner.

Dropping his hands immediately, Lamar gulped, "Uh . . . this kid fell down."

He was expelled from school, and his father had to buy Bertil a new hearing aid as well as pay all medical expenses. On top of that, in order to avoid a lawsuit, Mr. Studly had to settle a sum of money on Bertil's parents. It was the worst time of Lamar's life, and it was all the dummy's fault.

Lamar didn't mind not attending school, but he did mind the daily slaps and punches, the constant nagging, and he resented being restricted to his own yard, a penalty that caused his bicycle business to fall apart. Most of all, he minded Bertil, who each afternoon while wandering his newspaper route, planted himself for several minutes in front of the Studly property and stared. After shouting threats at the boy and making every obscene gesture he knew, Lamar had become frustrated and, in fact, had begun hiding within the house and peeping through drawn curtains at the appointed hour. It was all so crazy: he could kick that kid's ass, yet *he* was hiding.

Nearly a month after the incident at school, the frustrated fat boy determined to escape his confinement in the hubcap hills and whitewall canyons no matter what the consequences. Despite his supply of warm beer and girlie magazines, he felt the need for comradeship. A quick jaunt down to the Tejon Club for a game of eight-ball with his chums was what he needed. Besides, Mr. Studly was gone that afternoon delivering tires, so escape would be no problem.

After traveling sidestreets and alleys, Lamar slipped in the back door of the pool hall; he didn't want any of his father's cronies seeing him. Once inside, though, caution left him, and he called, "Hey Buzz! Hey Talcott!" His pals appeared surprised, then delighted: "Hey Lamar! Hey big guy!" They patted his back and he bought them cokes. While they shot pool, the three boys laughed their way through versions of the fateful fight: "You

really duked that re-tard, Lamar," chuckled Buzzard, who had himself
been briefly suspended from school. "He's lucky that teacher come,"
added Talcott, who had avoided penalty. "That dummy'll never mess with
you no more."

"He *better* not," warned Lamar, feeling easy. Talcott slapped his back.

The Tejon Club's front door opened and a small figure entered wearing
a newspaper bike bag over his shoulders like a serape. He handed the
bartender a copy of *The Californian*, then turned to leave when Buzzard
noticed him. "Hey, it's the dummy. Look, it's the dummy. Let's git him."

"Wait a minute," Lamar said.

"Yeah, come on," urged Talcott.

"No, wait," the fat boy insisted.

Bertil was at the door when he glanced back and saw the trio. He turned
and walked directly to Lamar. "Whan I aim a do, Namar, is git na
evinence own nyou," he said.

"Hit him, Lamar," called Talcott.

"Kick his butt," Buzzard exhorted.

"Git away from me," the fat boy threatened, but Bertil did not move.
"Whan I aim a do . . ."

"Git, damnit!" Lamar shouted and he pushed the smaller boy, who
stumbled to the floor.

The bartender and two customers who had been sipping beer at the
counter hurried to the fallen boy. "What's goin' on here?" demanded the
large man wiping his hands on a bar towel.

"This kid called me a name," said Lamar.

The two customers helped Bertil up, while the bartender growled at the
fat boy: "Maybe you oughta pick on someone your own size."

"That kid better quit callin' me names," Lamar countered.

"He snole my nike," Bertil said.

"I never."

"Oh," said the bartender, his voice even more ominous, "is this the
bully that beat up on you?"

The small boy nodded.

"You three better get outta here," ordered the glowering man, his hands
kneading the bar towel. "I don't want you back ever. Do you understand?"
His eyes were blazing and his voice had become strangely soft. "Ever."

Lamar said nothing. Buzzard and Talcott were already scuttling toward the back door.

"One more thing," the bartender added. "Don't let me hear about you so much as touchin' this boy again or I'll kick your ass so far up your back you'll have to take your hat off to shit, get me?"

"Yeah," Lamar croaked.

"I aim a git na evinence own nyou, Namar," Bertil said as the fat boy turned to leave, and Lamar felt like putting his fingers in his ears.

That night, Mr. Studly raged into his son's room. "Bob down at the Tejon Club called and said you was in there causin' trouble today after I told you not to leave the yard. He said you was pickin' on that deaf kid again. You just cain't leave him alone, can you? Well maybe this'll learn you," he hissed as he began swinging at his son.

Locked in his room the next afternoon, Lamar peered with horrid fascination through drawn curtains at Bertil who was standing and staring at the house from outside the yard, his newspaper bag suspended from his shoulders, his new hearing aid protruding like a wen. He's not just dumb, Lamar concluded, he's nuttier than a fruitcake is what he is. The fat boy felt like crawling under the bed to avoid those hot, beady eyes, but it seemed to him that they would find him no matter where he hid. After Bertil finally departed, Lamar scurried out the window and hustled through foothills of bias plies and belted plies, arroyos of snow treads and tractor treads, to his shed, where he drank a warm beer and tried to distract himself by viewing photographs of naked women in his magazines, but even those rosy nipples reminded him of the dummy's burning eyes. There was only one thing to do, he finally admitted.

While it would be impossible for him to return the bike he had stolen because it was long gone, he could steal another, a better one, and give it to that kid. It would get him off Lamar's back at last, and nobody else had to know. Feeling relieved at having made the decision, the fat boy opened a second beer. There would be nothing to it; the only dangerous part would be sneaking off the yard without his daddy catching him.

The following Saturday, Lamar turned on the radio beside his bed, locked his door from the inside, then crawled out the window and headed for the River Theater where kids would be watching the matinee, and where a selection of unlocked bicycles could always be found. He strolled casually by the bike rack, skillfully assessing the merchandise out the corner of his eye, since he didn't want the lady in the box office to notice him. For several minutes Lamar appeared to be studying the posters of coming attractions when, in fact, he was scrutinizing a luxurious Schwinn. He would present Bertil with a model so good that the dummy would never again bother him.

Finally, after searching up and down the street, he zeroed in on the box office lady, waiting until she was distracted. A few minutes later, the telephone rang and she began talking. Lamar strolled casually to the shining Schwinn, slipped it from the rack, and rode for the nearest corner. There was nothing to it.

Pedaling toward Bertil's ramshackle house, Lamar considered how to present the gift. He couldn't afford to give the impression he was frightened or desperate or anything like that; he was, after all, Lamar Studly, toughest kid in the sixth grade. But if he acted too rough, he might scare the dummy and prolong his own misery. It was a dilemma. He decided finally to be humble and direct but not friendly, to let the runt know this was a favor. He didn't owe the dummy anything, but even the toughest kid in the class could be kind. As satisfying as that resolution was, a nagging doubt remained in Lamar's ample middle: what if the dummy refused to accept the bike? No, he wouldn't do that, he couldn't.

And he didn't. Bertil was sitting on his rickety porch preparing for his paper route, rolling newspapers and placing rubber bands around them, then stuffing them into his canvas bag. Two younger brothers and sisters were browsing over their dirt yard, and another was talking to a lady in the next yard. It was perfect for Lamar, who stopped in the street and climbed off the shining bicycle. Before Bertil could speak, Lamar pushed the Schwinn up to the porch and announced, "You can deliver your papers on this here."

Bertil's little red eyes searched the lovely Schwinn, examined it minutely. Lamar was ready with a lie if the dummy asked where it come from, but he didn't. Instead, he stood up in that odd, crooked way of his, walked to the bicycle and gripped its handlebars. Lamar released the bike and Bertil stood holding his new Schwinn. It was better than Lamar had imagined because the smaller boy appeared to be speechless. Elated by this happy turn, the fat boy said, "Thank you, Lamar," as sarcastically as he could, but Bertil ignored him.

"I don't wanna hear no more about that other bike from you," Lamar advised harshly, "or I'll come back and take thisun away and you won't have nothin'."

Bertil's face was sliced by a mysterious smile, but he remained silent.

The fat boy waited a moment longer for a response, but finally shrugged: what can you expect from a kid in the re-tard class that lives in this dump, he thought. At least I'm shed of him. After pulling out a pocket comb and rearranging his dark, oily hair, the toughest kid in the sixth grade turned and, without saying good-bye, began his trek home at a livelier strut than he'd managed for a long time.

Feverish eyes locked on the stout figure swaggering away, then Bertil whispered, "*Now* I got na evinence," and his visionary smile widened. "I *got* na evinence."

Someone Else's Life

Our fishing trips never really began until we drove past the last houses in the orange grove marking the eastern boundary of town and burst free into treeless, rolling hills, driving east until mountains loomed from smog before us, brown and bleached at their roots, yet ascending into distant blue shafts far above the thick warmth of flatland air—into cool, thin purity. Wade, driving the pickup, visibly relaxed as we passed the grove, rushing away from town; his left arm crooked out the open window; his coarse black hair, straight and heavy as a horse's winter coat, wind blown; his eyes squinting ahead to the point where mountains parted and the narrow road slipped into the sanctuary of canyon and rushing river.

"Light me one a them cigarettes," he ordered.

"Sure." I clamped two of his ready-mades between my lips, puffed them lit, then handed one to him.

"I thought ya rolled yer own," he said, eyes crinkling while his mouth remained grim.

"When I have to."

We were driving over faded sage and tumbleweed country now, passing occasional squares of potatoes or sugar beets or cotton; an irrigator standing near the road stared at the mountains toward which we drove, his cheap straw cowboy hat bright in the sun, his rubber boots drooping near his ankles like elephant's feet.

To our left in the rolling, rising land, a green ribbon of trees, looking like a drunkenly linear forest, hid a river no longer rushing and defiant in its gradual, flattening bed out of the canyon: a river wide and slow and tame like a man grown thick and soft and impotent. We never fished here—"sucker water," Wade called it—but drove instead into the canyon where the current tumbled and threatened and where cool winds blown from alpine crests raced the stream down its jagged course. ("God damn!" Wade used to say as the first high mountain breeze reached us, dragging the smell and taste of the mountains into himself, "God damn it's good to breathe again!")

But now we drew strong, tasteless smoke into us, Wade's lean body calming, his tight shoulders easing back, his jaw muscles showing and softening, his hands beginning to caress rather than squeeze the steering wheel. He was a foreman in my father's packing shed, a tough, stringy man with a face at once emaciated and powerful. He'd drifted into California during the depression, blown off his Missouri farm, and he was the first man hired when Pop started his business. Wade took me fishing for he had no son, and my father had little time or interest. One day, years before, Pop had told Wade what a pest I was about fishing and Wade had volunteered. But several years after Wade and I began fishing together my father angrily told me I was seeing too much of him: "You'll be just like him," Pop shouted, "a lazy Okie working for someone else." Then he explained he'd once given Wade the chance to become a partner, but that Wade had balked at his offer. "He said something about having time to live being more important to him," Pop sputtered. "That's what's wrong with those people!" Anyway, whatever caused Pop's anger quickly blew away for he said no more about it.

Wade taught me far more than how to catch a fish—catching fish often seemed little more than an afterthought on our trips; he had shown me how wildness could strip—as from an ancient, exfoliating stone—layer after layer of civilized complexity from us while we stood, stiff-legged and vulnerable, urinating dark, moving shadow shapes on boulders. And on our trips into it, the canyon itself had taught me timelessness: moments like those I once spent laying rattlesnake bit by the river waiting for, hoping for, Wade to find me, lasted an eternity; the countless hours on the stream pumping my flyrod, daydreaming or watching a water ouzel dip and prance through a shimmering riffle seemed to end before they began yet to require time.

Wade broke through my reverie: "Orta be good today, by God," he breathed with what sounded like a deep sigh.

"Sure do hope so," I replied, relaxing a bit more myself.

"When do ya report?"

"Next Saturday," I answered glumly.

"Well, this'll be our last one for a couple years, then, won't it?"

"Yeah, I guess." I waited for the going-to-the-army cliches everyone else bombarded me with but Wade let it go, knowing I hated leaving my girl and my job, and I knew he hated me leaving too.

We whizzed with bug-splattering speed, snapping through a sudden whirlwind of grasshoppers, jerking our bent elbows in from door-windows to avoid small, stinging collisions. Ahead of us the canyon opened, quite close, still dark with late morning shadows at its narrow mouth; then we were into it, swallowed, blind and cool for a long moment before we could see its sunless walls and its frothing river below. Above and to our left an exposed mountain slope glared in squinting contrast to the shade.

"Damn!" Wade said for us both. "She's always the same." His cigarette smoldered dangerously close to his mouth, held between gently clenched teeth, his lips smile-parted. We traveled unevenly over the road cut into the canyon's wall, speeding straight, level stretches, slowing for curves and steep rises, the rocks on my right out the window blurring, then clearing as our tempo lessened. Quickly we left the flatland an unpleasant memory behind, unable to even see it through the back window after the first few climbing curves of the canyon; away too from the syrupy heat as we drove through coolness morning sun had yet to penetrate.

"Why in hell people live down in that valley I don't know," Wade sighed, "when there's country like this here."

I grinned an answer: "We live down there."

"Because we're stupid or gutless or both," he snapped, then went on more reflectively, "or least I am. I'm a man livin' someone else's life. Yer still a kid. Ya still got a chance."

I didn't reply for I was suddenly in too deep: he was talking about his marriage and the constant tension between him and his wife. During their many years together, Wade had fished alone or with me while Babe, his wife, had quickly tired of drinking alone. In the past couple of years she had drifted away several times, only to return. I knew what my father had told me about Wade and Babe, and that my mother didn't like her; Wade rarely spoke of her. Once, though, when I was still in high school and thought I was in love and wanted to marry, Wade warned me to be sure the girl and I had more than hot pants in common: "I married a good woman," he'd said with husky seriousness, "but we're not good for each other. We're mismated, but knowin' it don't change things. So take 'er slow." That's the only thing I ever remember him saying about his marriage. My father had recently told me that Wade was changing, getting scared he'd kill Babe or one of her men friends. I remained silent for several minutes.

At intervals creeks bubbled under little bridges on their river journey and tiny springs seeped from the canyon's side, slickening road pavement in jeweled dark swaths; our pickup zinged momentarily as we passed over them. Then we were climbing suddenly and steeply so that in a moment we seemed to soar high over the river while far ahead below us we saw an old mining camp next to the stream.

"There it is," I said.

"It won't be long now," Wade replied. "We can hit her upstream from the camp."

Soon we turned from the paved road onto a steeply winding dirt track that switched back, blind turn to blind turn, until we leveled at a wide clearing in a miniature forest that surrounded the river here, and parked the car. We sat for a moment, hearing the sound of rushing water, then crawled from the truck into an unspoiled morning chilled by deep canyon shadow and mountain breeze. Around us dew still glossed green, and I stood, shivering slightly in the shadowed cold, and stretched. Wade handed me a sweatshirt—"Ya look froze," he said—then removed a long aluminum tube containing his spinning rod from the bed of the pickup. "Ya gonna spin-fish too?"

"Naw," I answered, "I think I'll stick with flies." Since Wade had taught me to fly-fish, and had always told me that fly-fishing was *the* way you sought trout, I couldn't resist: "You using worms?" I asked innocently.

He slowly turned his head to face me, still assembling the spinning rod. He was not smiling, yet the cluster of tiny gullies around his eyes had deepened and his lips curved ever-so-slightly upward. "No," he replied with gravity. "I was figurin' on usin' a double bait rig, garter snake low and marshmellow high."

"Sounds good," was my grave response. "Why don't you put a salmon egg in the snake's mouth? That oughta double your chances."

We assembled our rods, adding reels, then rigging line through the rod's guides, Wade finishing long before me, tying a small golden hook onto his gossamer line. I began attaching a long, light leader onto my heavy fly line, fumbling with cold fingers, beginning again, fumbling again, frustration causing me to fumble once more. Wade walked toward the river, calling "I'm goin' fishin'," over his shoulder as he strode away, "be back to untie ya later," then swinging onto the upstream path, his long legs reaching for distance, knees bent in his peculiar Groucho Marx hiking style, hips bouncing low as he moved through trees and out of sight.

It took me a good while to climb into my rubber, chest-high waders and pull on my fishing vest. I sat on a large granite boulder near the truck for several minutes studying my fly box before choosing a tiny deer-hair bug that looked like a blood-engorged tick, then carefully tying it to the fine tip of my leader. One thing I had noticed about Wade during our recent trips: he no longer waited for me before going fishing; when I was small he used to stand patiently, telling me to relax. Other cars often pulled into a clearing next to us, vomiting a clutch of excited fishermen who seemed to sprint in confusion toward the river, their rods half-rigged, their hip boots flopping flatulently. But Wade always waited while my anxious young fingers ruined knots and I had to tie them again and again; he never helped me with a knot after showing me how to tie it, but he waited without impatience and talked to me, telling me to take it easy, the river was older than us and it wasn't going anywhere. Relax. Don't rush pleasure.

So, after attaching my fly, I sat on the warming rock, feeling the cool, blue, high-mountain breeze brush my face, and rolled myself a Bull Durham cigarette and smoked it, drooping from my lips, watching a tiny tan lizard scramble over a nearby rock while it jerkily surveyed its surroundings—its protuberant eyes like tiny polished gemstones—then disappear with an electric swagger into a dark crack. The smoke was harsh and sweet, fading quickly in the wind as I exhaled. Around me the river's roar had long since merged as it always did into smaller sounds, so I could catch birds calling and above on the road, a car passing.

I entered the water where a shallow ripple flowed angrily over small rocks, and I walked into the current and out from the shore, stripping line from my reel for a few moments as I moved, pumping the rod a bit, false casting until I plopped the ivory-colored line and tiny fly well ahead of me upstream. I followed the little deer-hair puff with my eyes as it bounced back toward me over the surface.

Just as the fly passed on my right a small trout rolled up from the stream, as though the formless, pulsing pattern of rocks beneath the clear water had suddenly given birth to a wraith; it tugged savagely at the fly and was gone before I could strike. I retrieved the line and walked forward a couple of straining strides against the pushing current, feeling pebbles sucked from beneath my feet as I settled, then cast the fly in front of me once more.

It was a good day's angling, with many strikes and many trout coming to the net, though they were all small and I kept none. I finally found Wade far upstream at cliff hole, a place where the river had cut a deep, swirling blue-black pool along a mountain's base before straightening into a longer, shallow run and riffle. Standing in that shallow water, I looked ahead into the late afternoon pall where sunlight could no longer penetrate and saw him.

He stood as though rooted, unmoving from the waist down, on a sand-bar that jutted well into the deep water, staring with hunched concentration into the swirl that always seemed especially promising in afternoon shadows below the etched cliff. He didn't see me slosh out of the stream and trudge to within a few feet of him on the sandbar. I hesitated to speak, because Wade appeared intent on some secret communion, bending slightly forward from the waist, holding his rod where it mated with the reel in his right hand while his left hand tested the tense line which ran from the rod's tip into the dark, boiling water. He slowly raised, then lowered the rod's tip, moving his left arm away from his body in a long, careful arc, pulling the line as he did so, releasing it when his arm was straight out from his side like a half-crucified man's; all the while he leaned forward, shoulders hunched, head thrust out on his long, powerful neck.

Suddenly, his shoulders flexing, his neck easing, he straightened and began rapidly reeling his line in, looking not so much tired as spent. I spoke then, shouted really for the river's deep-throated bellow was particularly loud here. Wade turned, still reeling, and grinned loosely, beginning to form a word when, with a terrific lurch, his rod tip dipped nearly into the water and line screamed from his reel; he whirled, lifting the rod high just as the line collapsed and the rod itself lost its tortured bow, quivering as it straightened. Wade froze, couched and alert, facing the pool, then whispered so tensely I heard him through rather than over the river's hissing roar, "Goddamnit!" Retrieving the line once more, he continued walking toward me. "A man can't take nothin' for granted," he said as he passed me. "Let's go home."

We hiked silently back to the pickup, my waders thudding over dirt and sand and rock while Wade devoured the ground before me with his long, hip-bouncing stride. A chilling high-country wind gusted while we walked, making the heat of town seem almost desirable. After removing our fishing gear we rested at the pickup before heading home, me drinking a can of warm beer I'd forgotten to put in the river before starting to fish, while Wade pulled from a carton of half-and-half. "How'd ya do?" he asked.

"Pretty good. But only little ones, so I didn't keep any."

"Did ya fish dry flies?"

I guzzled a mouthful of warm beer before answering: "Yeah. I surface fished." I drank again from the can. "How about you?"

He looked up from his carton, a small white mustache of cream half-circling his upper lip. "I just worked the cliff hole. There's big stuff in that deep if you can just get to the bottom. That's the secret, cuttin' through all the swirl and gettin' to the bottom."

"Uhmmm," I responded, my mouth and nose filled with an eruption of warm beer bubbles. It seemed strange that he'd just fish one hole all day. "What bait were you using?" I asked.

"Eggs. Just plain old salmon eggs." For a moment he seemed to lose interest in our conversation, looking dreamily away toward the river, then his eyes snapped back to mine, "But I didn't get a damn thing, just a few taps and that last real strike."

I bent the beer can in my hands. "You shoulda tried somewhere else," I said. "A spinner would have murdered 'em in the shallows."

"I intended to this mornin'," he said, "but when I seen the river and heard it, I just felt like I had to fish that deep water. Maybe I'm gettin' old or somethin'." He laughed uneasily.

I looked puzzled, I guess, for, as we drove home he read my face, then flipped his cigarette out the truck's open window, the butt spewing sparks like a tiny, errant meteor. "It's like I don't have time no more for fishin' them shallows."

We neared the orange grove as day greyed over the flatland, and before us on the razor-edged horizon lights blinked on uncertainly, since it was neither night nor day: The sky west spread like half a peach skin, pale red and yellow softly flowing up and out from the horizon into a vastness as dark and blue as a crescent inversion of cliff pool.

I sank back into the seat, looking ahead where the town opened brightly to swallow us—lights flashing, streets yawning, cars hurling across our path. Then we were in it. "It's this town," I guessed aloud. "All this part used to be orange groves when we first started, remember? Now look at it."

Wade squinted ahead, jaws pulsing, seeming to look beyond what I saw. "Did ya ever get the feeling," he finally asked, glancing at me, "that somethin' was eatin' ya up?"

"What?"

"I mean did ya ever feel like someone snuck a seed into ya and it's growin' and there's not a damn thing ya can do about it?"

After a long pause—feeling I had to say something—I mumbled: "Don't guess so."

"Naw," he answered his own question, "I guess not. If ya remember what's real—if ya remember that water up there, and them rocks and fish—and don't get caught in all this"—he gestured at the honky tonks and flashing signs by which we now drove—"you'll be O.K. Just always be sure ya remember what's real, and keep a tight hold on it."

He stopped in front of my house and we unloaded my gear. Wade said he wouldn't be able to see me again before I had to leave. I said I'd write and he nodded and said, simply, "It's been good," and we shook hands. Then he drove back up the street toward where honky tonks leered with neon brashness, the shape of his head silhouetted through the pickup's back window.

After basic training, I was sent to Korea where I did little other than drink beer and read a little, waiting for my two years to pass. The letter from my mother came as a surprise. It arrived on a clear winter day and said Wade had "passed away," and not to worry because she was having a Mass said for him. A snake coiled in my stomach, cold and personal, so I did what people do in books: I walked in the woods alone, squinching through thin, icy snow. But it was only a lonely walk in the woods. My father's note came two days later, written with a soft-lead pencil on a tiny page from the vest-pocket tablet he always carried. He wrote: "Thought you would want to know. Wade shot himself with his bird gun. Yr mother and me wish you were home. Yr father."

The Corps of Engineers dammed the canyon the year I returned from the Army. It's a water-skiers' lake now, oily, with supermarkets and trailer parks and honky tonks growing around it, and neon lights to guide lost travelers in from the threatening dark.

The Estero

The road climbs around a hill west of Tomales, passing the old Catholic Cemetery, then bordering a steeply sloping pasture where a dairyman dumps waste from his barn, where grass grows rapidly and dark all year round. During summer when I was a kid I used to walk there and examine the drainage ditch along the road beneath that slanted field; in it muddy offal crusted and split into sharply geometric designs—marvelous to me.

A hundred yards farther southwest, the road crests and veers, and a narrower lane intersects from the right. This one follows the course of a brook and is densely lined by willows as it swoops down the hill's other side, dropping to the eucalyptus border of my uncle's farm where the small creek joins a much larger stream crossed by a wooden bridge. In fact, that one-lane road actually separates our house from our barn and corrals.

The land flattens beyond what we still call Uncle Tony's farm, a wide valley opening into verdant fields dotted with dairy cows and clusters of shaggy sheep. It is in a hidden vale surrounded by rolling hills, one that tourists and even some locals never see. When they *are* here, they usually forget that our place is only four miles from the Pacific and little higher than sea level. The larger stream winding through our property—the Estero—reveals an oceanic link and it too was a source of wonder to my sister Suzie and me when we were small.

It is called the Estero because its estuarial water ebbs and flows with the tides. During wet winters, it can swirl muddy brown, but most of the year it boasts no noticeable flow at all, only a tidal pulsing; it is a sleepy, secret filament of the sea, its channel full of dark water that reveals at unpredictable times the primal surging of its source: vast phantom fish might bulge its surface, gulls might clatter to feast on minnows, an arrant sea lion might appear midstream in our pasture amidst feeding cattle, large brown astonished eyes meeting large brown astonished eyes.

One time when we were kids my sister and I were fishing from the bridge when we noticed something surging up the Estero, a wake without a boat and traveling fast. "Hey, look!" I called, and as it slid directly beneath us, its watery shadow appeared as large as a calf. After it passed, small waves lapped the shore for several seconds. "What was *that?*" she asked.

"I think it was a big giant shark."

Suzie stared at me for a prolonged moment, then began crying.

While I was trying to quiet her, concerned that Uncle Tony might think I'd committed some minor atrocity, old Manuel Gomes, my uncle's only employee, wandered over with his dog from the milking barn to see what was wrong. "Leetle one," he assured my sister, "the beeg feesh no get you. He come up here for bath only." He grinned with his brown teeth and we both smiled. "Yeah, up north pasture een the beeg pool, meester feesh wash hees feens and seeng a feesh song: tra-la-la-la!" He rolled his eyes and his voice grew high and hollow. Then he grinned once more and, while his hard old hand stroked Suzie's dark hair, his dog nuzzled her, wagging its ebony tail. She giggled, shark forgotten.

Manuel was our favorite, mine and Suzie's. He had no family, only Shep—or "Shap" as he called him—not a shepherd at all despite his name, but a one-eyed black labrador who spent as much time in the Espero as he did on land. The man and his pooch lived in a small cabin on the strange stream's bank across the road near the milking barn. He had worked for my uncle since way before I was born, since right after coming over from the Azores, and Manuel had been no kid then, Tony told me. Like his dog, he loved the Estero.

"Een heem I catch salmons and beeg tunas weeth my peech-fork," Manuel once revealed, nodding toward that dark vein of water. Like most local farmers, he harvested the Estero without benefit of rod or reel. He also didn't seem to know one fish from another: his tuna might be a catfish or a carp. "And many leetle feeshes, herreengs and anchov's. And beeg

sturgeons: Ugly! Son a the beetch! I catch heem many times. Juan Bat-
tancourt that works for Dolcini, he say he see beeg whale sweem by the
cows. Son a the beetch! And weeth my own eyes I see the seals many
times. Thees loco dog"—he nodded at Shep—"he theenk he ees one, a
seal." He scratched the ebony head and, I swear, Shep showed his white
teeth in a smile, tail wagging.

One spring day when Suzie was off with our mother, Manuel took me
down the Estero all the way to the sea. He had built an old wooden boat
that looked like a blunt canoe; it was barely large enough for Shep and
the two of us, but we loaded it with lunch and shoved off just below the
cabin and began slowly winding our way westward through lush pastures,
sitting low on the currentless stream, high banks on both sides, our eyes
at grass level. Every few minutes, it seemed, Manuel would say, "Look
at heem!"—and point at a garter snake sliding through the water, at a
long heron spiking minnows, at a turtle plopping into the stream from a
snag—"Son a the beetch!"

Above us and the estuarial pastures through which we traveled shrugged
the hulking shoulders of coastal hills; as it neared the sea, the Estero sliced
through increasingly steep country creating a deeper and narrower canyon.
In places it appeared there could be no outlet, the hills folding so intimately, but an unexpected turn, a secret course, and the channel would
bend on itself, slipping through to another small valley. As we approached
the stream's mouth—not seeing or even hearing the surf, but smelling it
in the strong, salty wind that resisted us—both Manuel and I were forced
to paddle hard in order to make any progress. Shep grinned into that
zephyr, his pink tongue lolling.

Finally the Estero swung wide around a treeless bluff and I began
hearing the dark rumblings of what seemed distant waves. Only a moment
later, to my surprise, we were gazing at the great blue Pacific bursting
against the white sand of a small beach, at a churning expanse as open
as freedom itself. It was low tide and the Estero appeared to be blocked
by a sandbar, so it had formed a small, shallow lagoon on the beach. We
pulled the boat ashore—Shep splashing and romping in that estuarial
pond—then ate our lunch on the steep sand just beyond cresting breakers.
Shep chased shorebirds and the shells Manuel occasionally threw for him.
When we were about to return, lunch consumed, tide rising, a sleek dark

head popped from the frothing water directly in front of us and for a moment, I stared at a sea lion staring at me. Then it was gone. "Did you *see* that?" I asked.

"Son a the beetch! I see heem!" A moment later Shep was exploring the surf where the sea lion had appeared, his own sleek, dark head dipping under water, then popping up. "Looook, another seal!" laughed Manuel.

When the frustrated pooch finally emerged, we all climbed back into Manuel's small boat and paddled home, strong ocean gusts now pushing us, while Shep faced backward, still grinning, tongue still lolling into the wind. "Loook at Shap," said the old man with a wink. "Een hees dreams he ees a seal." Then he reached over and scratched his dog's glistening black head.

Manuel and I always intended to make that trip again, but never did. He grew older and I grew up. Shep-the-seal's snout and paws whitened. The old man and the old dog hobbled around the farm, both troubled by arthritis but both continuing their duties. They even looked alike, those two, Manuel's dark Portuguese complexion seeming to deepen as his hair whitened. Anyway, I finally finished my degree in husbandry at the university and returned to help Tony on the farm; since he had no other family, I was slated to eventually take it over.

Suzie was away at college when the deluge occurred. It wasn't, and isn't for that matter, uncommon for coastal streams engorged with winter's heavy rain to flood these valleys; when storms clear, cattle wander through knee-deep water, feeding alongside egrets and gulls. But that year some of the highest tides on record coincided with profuse rains: a dangerous combination, since tides alone can overflow banks in these low-lying pastures. Combined, they were more than we could imagine.

Uncle Tony, Manuel and I had sandbagged the cabin and the milking barn as a precaution, something we did virtually every winter. Our house sits on a hillock and had never been threatened by rising water. Then we had turned in, Manuel refusing to join us in the house: "Me and Shap no scare a the leetle rain. Son a the beetch!" He and his stoved-up old pooch had hobbled off to their lair and Uncle Tony had laughed, "He's a tough old bastard. Son *a the beetch*," he winked, and we both laughed.

When my uncle awoke the next morning about five, it was still dark and rain was pounding the roof. He usually allowed me to rise on my own, but that day he rousted me immediately. "Come look at this," he insisted.

He'd pulled on his clothes over the long johns he slept in all winter, and I did the same. He walked me to the front porch and in the darkness I saw what looked like a dark, moving mirror. Water was lapping at the porch and our entire valley appeared full: one vast lake. "What the hell!" I grunted.

It was still dark and clouds hung heavily over us, but the rain had lightened to drizzle. "I never seen it like this before," my uncle said.

"Me either."

"We're gonna lose some stock for sure."

That's when I looked at him and said, "Manuel?"

"Oh, Jesus. Let's get the flashlights."

The old man's abode was gone, and by the time we waded to the barn—water chest-deep and cold, footing treacherous—located Tony's bass boat, then got the outboard motor started, darkness had begun lifting, replaced by an eerie luminescence as brown and murky as the water that surged around us. Clouds still rolled above and we didn't know for certain which way to go since water wasn't flowing downstream—it wasn't flowing at all, just curling. We couldn't see the cabin anywhere in our valley, so I said, "Let's head for Dolcini's."

Tony pointed the boat's prow toward the coast and we headed west as rain once more increased. Near the bridge where Highway 1 crossed the Estero, we found the cabin wedged into a grove of eucalyptus, and Manuel was there clinging to the roof. While Tony held the boat steady, I managed to muscle the old man into it. He was stiff, his breath shallow and uneven, but he managed to gasp only, "Shap. Where ees he?"

My eyes caught Tony's, but he shook his head. "We can't look for the dog," he said. "We've gotta get Manuel to the doctor. He's in rough shape."

"Where ees he, Shap?" the old man repeated as we rushed him toward Tomales where a doctor could treat him, then send him to the hospital in Santa Rosa. Tony accompanied Manuel but I returned home and took the bass boat back to Dolcini's just before dark: no luck. That night I telephoned all the nearby places that still had lines up, but we never found any trace of Shep.

The old one-lane bridge at our place was gone—it ended up on our lower pasture—so there was only one route to and from town when the water receded. We brought Manuel home in the pickup a week after the flood and moved him into our house. At first he did not speak no matter what we said to him, but after another day, he dressed and wandered from the house to the remains of the bridge where he stared at the brown water—tides were still running high—and spat into the stream.

He remained there most of that day, and most of the next one. When he limped in for supper, I asked, gently, how things were going. For a minute he gazed at me then away. I didn't really expect a reply, but he fooled me. "I see heem there, Shap, sweemeeng weeth the other seals. He ees hoppy."

I knew he couldn't have seen Shep but it didn't matter. "That's great, Manuel," I said.

He smiled. "Shap."

The following day, we were still busy repairing damage done by the water, so my uncle and I didn't hover around Manuel, although we did try to keep an eye on him. But not close enough, for he somehow put his old canoe into the water and was paddling west when I noticed. Damn! Since I was in the process of pulling a mired cow from a bog with the tractor, I didn't need the added chore of chasing after him, but I had it. Tony was way to hell and gone up in the hills feeding hay to cattle on the upper slopes of our property, so there was no one else to pursue the old man.

By the time I got the bass boat started, Manuel and the canoe had disappeared. I knuckled the outboard down and roared off to catch him, but when I rounded that first bend I couldn't see his head moving over the pasture of the next wide valley as I had anticipated. A moment later, I knew why. I rounded another serpentine curve and there was the canoe with the old man lying in it like some ancient warrior consigned to the sea. His breath rattled and his eyes were open and glazed. I took off my jacket and covered him, then began tethering the two boats but almost immediately the ragged breathing stopped. I checked Manuel for a pulse but there was none, so I reached over and placed his hat on his face, sighed, then finished attaching the towline to the canoe.

That accomplished, I sat for a moment before starting the engine, glancing from the old man's body at the pasture with winter grass flattened by the flood and at the hills ahead. I gazed far to the west where the Estero twisted through secret slopes toward the sea and was startled: I saw the water's surface briefly broken by the sleek black head of a sea lion, or thought I did. It was so far away that I couldn't be certain.

I guess it's not important. It all happened a long time ago when I was a young buck. Now I'm hobbling around this place myself, with grandchildren visiting each summer and with a daughter and son-in-law planning to take over the dairy when I retire, which will be soon. Yeah, a long time ago, but if you climb that road out of Tomales today to the old Catholic Cemetery you can find where Manuel's body rests. I was one of the pallbearers and we placed him there in our family plot next to my dad. Uncle Tony's with him now, and my mother, and my wife. And that's where my bones will rest one day soon.

But Shep isn't there. He's at sea with the other seals, and I'm sure Manuel's spirit is with him. And mine, my spirit is traveling its own Estero, swimming toward Shep and Manuel and the freedom of that secret sea beyond hills or memories or the salty wind of coastal canyons.

The Great Waldorf Astoria Caper

ᴹ ᴹ ᴹ ᴹ ᴹ ᴹ ᴹ ᴹ ᴹ ᴹ ᴹ ᴹ ᴹ ᴹ

Right after Shoat Wilhite made that bundle in the Cuyama oil strike, he wheeled back to Texas in a new Caddy to impress all the home folks. And I guess he done 'er, too, since he come back to Oildale sportin' a wife.

Now you folks might not be surprised to hear that, but you never seen Shoat. If ever a guy was give a true name, it's him. Hell, I seen lotsa hogs better lookin than that sucker. To begin with, he never had no nose, just this little flat nub covered with beer blossoms. He had the teensiest eyes, too, and these pointy ears. His skin was the color of a Poland China's and what little hair he had was cut in a burr, so he even had these bristles a-stickin outta his scalp. Hell of a specimen to look at, I'll tell ya.

Shoat, hisself, he claimed his sister that give him the moniker she meant "Short," but she had too much Lubbock in her twang so it come out "Shoat." He was a squatty little sucker, that's for sure, but one look in the mirror woulda told him to drop the subject.

Anyways, whenever he come back from Texas with that wife, it liked to knocked us boys off our barstools. See, we's settin in the Tejon Club that evenin when him and the new missus blowed in. We never knew he'd got back but we wasn't surprised to see him, cause even if he had hit the big money, he'd never forgot us boys that'd worked with him in the oil field. He never acted like his shit didn't stink.

When me and Earl and Bob Don seen the woman he brung in with him, well, we was semi-stunned. Nedra, ol Shoat's wife, was a looker. Oh, she was all painted up with purple eyelids and lips like slabs a liver, and her hair it was lacquered. She even had false eyelashes about three inches long. But her basic equipment looked damn prime to me. While we's all noddin and shakin hands and sayin how pleased we was to meet her, me I's thinkin baffled'd be a better word.

On top of her looks, she told us she'd graduated the University of Texas, so her and Bob Don that graduated Bakersfield Junior College, they commenced some highfallutin talk while me and Earl gabbed with ol Shoat. Me, I eavesdropped and I heard her talkin French or some such. I couldn't make out exactly what they said, then she give a big giggle and said real loud, "Carpe diem, Mistah Bundy, carpe diem."

I poked Bob Don in the ribs and whispered, "What the hell's that mean?"

He hesitated, then grinned, "Fish of the day," he explained out of the side of his mouth. He's a smart sucker, Bob Don.

Just about then Shoat told us that Nedra'd been third runner-up in the Miss Texas contest a few, quite a few is my guess, years back, and she just kinda give us a Shirley Temple imitation—shakin her curls and puckering them lips—whenever he told us that. She had one hell of a set of knockers, I'll say that much, but she's a little long in the tooth to be actin so damn cute, her drippin them "y'alls" and "sho nuffs" like a jug leakin syrup.

I, at least, was beginnin to get the feelin she was lookin down her nose at us. It was just somethin in how she acted, like she's doin us a favor to even talk to us. Still, we mighta jawed real sociable with the newlyweds all evenin if Big Dunc hadn't showed up. Now him and Shoat had never got along real good. They just sorta tolerated each other because the rest of us was pals. The big guy just nodded and set and ordered him a beer.

Shoat and Nedra was sweet-talkin the hell outta each other, him callin her "Hon" and "Babe," her callin him "Dahlin" and "Sugah Plum." He looked more like a prune than any plum to me, but us boys never said nothin. Ol Shoat he was eatin it up, grinnin like a coyote chewin stink bugs.

Dunc, meanwhile, was sloppin his second beer down. He ordered a refill, then growled, "Ain't you two got no *names?*" Dunc never took no Dale Carnegie course, or if he did he flunked.

Shoat that wasn't afraid a nobody, not even Dunc, he felt obliged to defend the family honor, so he sidearmed a giant dill pickle plucked from the jar on the counter and it smacked the big guy square between the eyes, the juice semi-blindin him. Dunc reared up and took one hell of a poke at Shoat, but he misfired and knocked the third runner-up for Miss Texas damn near outta her girdle, poppin her false eyelashes clean off and lopsidin her boobs.

Me and Bob Don and Earl we jumped between Shoat and Dunc, so the new groom he took to helpin his ol lady out the door, him lookin madder'n a brokelegged centerpede, her lookin like the centerpede itself. I figured Shoat'd be back to settle with Dunc directly, cause ol Shoat'll fight till hell freezes over and a little while on the ice, but his dearly beloved was lookin more like his dearly departed, so he give her all his attention.

A minute or two after he hefted Miss Texas out the door, her head popped back into the club and she screeched at Dunc, "You'll be hearin from mah attorney! Ah'll be seein you in cou't!" Her voice it'd lost all its little girl "y'all" ring.

Then Shoat's gourd thrust through the door and he said, "I'll just plain be seein ya," and all us boys knew he meant it. Dunc never seemed too impressed. The big man was a-wipin his face with a bar towel and he shot right back, "If you're still here whenever I get my eyes clear, you ain't a-gonna see shit!"

Shoat jumped through the door and made for Dunc, but me and Earl and Bob Don got between em again and run Shoat off. As it turned out, it was a good thing we did, cause that ol gal did have her a lawyer, and Dunc never needed no more trouble than he'd already made for hisself.

Next day, this cop showed up at the Tejon Club and he advised Dunc that if he never apologized, he'd go to the slammer sure as hell. Dunc had to do 'er, too. I mean, how can a workin stiff hire hisself a mouthpiece and fight somethin like that. But I'm not sure Dunc got the worst of it when all's said and done.

His wife callin the cops and sickin that shyster onto Dunc really humiliated ol Shoat that was used to settlin matters more directly. He laid low for a long time. When I seen him at Woody's Liquors a week or so later, he told me he couldn't even fight Dunc now that Nedra'd went and got the law involved cause they'd both have to be worried about what his ol lady might pull. He felt like Dunc'd whupped him by default.

Ol Dunc was pissed, too, but more'n that, he's shocked. Damn, he was always beefin guys, and nobody never called no law on him before. It just wasn't fair. It's like somebody went and changed the rules without tellin him. He, naturally, wanted to take it out on Shoat: "I'll stomp that ugly little peckerhead whenever I get ahold to 'im," he snarled.

"Hey," advised Bob Don, "you can't even talk that way anymore."

"Says who?" demanded the big guy.

"The damned judge is who. Don't you remember you're on a restraining order?"

"I always talk thataway," Big Dunc asserted.

"Not now you don't," warned Bob Don that kinda liked to be the expert on stuff, "not if you don't want to vacation at the county road camp."

"Shit!" Dunc spit on the floor. "The damn lawyers and judges and do-gooders have took over! Gimme another beer, Earl." He set there for a minute, then he added: "Can't even kick a man's ass when you want to. Whatever happened to the Bill a Rights?"

Wasn't none of us could answer that.

Right up the street from the Tejon Club, ol Shoat kept this little hole-in-the-wall office. He never had nothin in it but a telephone, a file cabinet, and a bookkeeper. He hung out there most days, and come slippin down to the club ever once and awhile to wet his whistle. All that stopped after he brung her nibs back from Texas.

His wife she hired this queer to come and decorate the office with fancy rugs and curtains and pictures on the wall. She hired a secretary to answer the phone and she leased half-a-dozen more rooms, which that fairy also painted up. On the front window she had wrote in big huge gold letters, WILHITE ENTERPRISES. Right underneath, in letters almost as big, it said: NEDRA MARIE DUBARRY WILHITE & ARDIS DON WILHITE, PROP'TS.

Whenever Bob Don seen her name come first, he just winked. Wylie Hillis, this ol fart that hangs out at the club, he said, "I believe this is one a them deals where a guy's pecker's got him in real trouble." He nodded his head, then added, "The thangs a guy'll do fer nooky."

That ex-beauty queen she sure knew how to spend money if she never knew nothin else. Before long she's drivin to and from the country club in her own Cadillac convertible and she's chummy with all these rich folks. The only Country Club Shoat cared about come in cans. More'n that, she's buildin a damn umpire is what she's buildin. First, she bought that trailer court over by Kern River, then a liquor store by Standard School, and that feedlot out by the Golden Bear Refinery. Directly, she brung in this ol boy from Texas to be her "manager," a young, good-looking kid that wore a suit and I believe was a-gettin in her pants. Shoat never seemed too happy about none a that.

The first time I seen the third runner-up all chummy with her young stud, I wondered if maybe he wasn't her son, then one day I seen em neckin in her Cad where it was parked behind the office. Well, I knew then they wasn't no mother and son. They'd looked semi-hot is how they'd looked. Directly, she went and bought that kid a Caddy of his own. I never said nothin to Shoat about what I seen, but I could tell he's takin the whole business—her phony country club ways, her damn umpire, her fancy man—he's takin it damn hard. He's gettin plenty sore, but I believe ol Wylie'd called it: that gal had Shoat where he lived.

Long about then this article come out in *The Bakersfield Californian* newspaper that said Nedra Marie Dubarry Wilhite was a "daughter of the old Confederacy, a beauty queen in her native Texas, and an honors graduate of the state university." A little farther on it said "this combination of beauty and brains is a dynamic new force in Kern County's business community." It also said she'd been "a well-known chanteuse in her native state at the time she met Ardis Don Wilhite."

I's readin that article aloud to the boys, so I stopped and asked, "What the hell's a 'chanteuse'?"

Big Dunc that was slurpin a beer he grunted, "It means 'whore' in Mexican."

Bob Don he chuckled. "That's a French word for dancer," he explained. Dunc give him a sour look.

The followin Monday a billboard appeared on the big ol vacant lot next to the Tejon Club where us guys parked. "Future Home of the *Oildale Waldorf Astoria*," it said in green letters, then in smaller black print was wrote:

- 100 Rooms
- Gourmet Restaurant
- Olympic Pool

• Two Cocktail Lounges
• Ballroom
• Convention Center

Under that, in red: "the Finest Hotel West of the Mississippi." At the very top of the sign, in bright orange, was the biggest letters of all: "NEDRA MARIE DUBARRY WILHITE presents:".

"Looks like she finally nudged Shoat clear out of the picture," observed Bob Don.

Ol Wylie Hillis he said, "Seems like this is one a them deals where the guy makes the money and the gal makes him."

"Them's some expensive knockers," I added.

A day later No Parking signs showed up on the lot, and directly wooden stakes with colored plastic strips commenced growin there like wildflowers. A couple guys with bulldozers begun scrapin and levelin the lot, and Earl that run the Tejon Club he told us flat out that ol Nedra'd vowed to put him outta business and that her project was already a-hurtin him. Wasn't none of us had seen Shoat for a long time.

It was about then that Bob Don come up with the plan. He busted in the door of the club and he asked—smirkin like a hound chewin bubble gum—"How'd you boys like to help our neighbor Mrs. Wilhite erect her new hotel?"

"Huh?" we all said. We never wanted to help Miz Wilhite do nothin cept go back where she come from.

Still grinnin, Bob Don explained: "You guys remember that sorry old outhouse of Spud Harmon's? It's been years since he got his plumbing, but he's left the old shitter up for black widows to breed in."

"So what?" growled Dunc that couldn't blow his hat off if his brains was nitro.

Me, I caught right on. "We're a-gonna borrow that sucker and haul it onto ol Nedra Marie's lot, right?"

"Right!" snapped Bob Don, "except we've already borrowed it. It's at my place. Let's go paint 'Waldorf Astoria' on it, then sneak it onto the queen's lot."

That's just what we done, cept that I thought up one slight addition: this ol boy named Bo Simmons that used to work in the oil patch he run a taxidermy business outta his garage and somehow he'd picked up this moth-eaten stuffed kangaroo that looked like it come to America to have its acne cured. Well, whenever we swung by Bo's and I told him what we had in mind, he loaned it to us.

After we'd painted "Waldorf Astoria" over the shitter's door and "N. Wilhite, propt" under the half-moon, we snapped this ol brassiere that Earl's top-heavy wife had throwed away onto the kangaroo, then stuffed the cups with newspapers. We set it on the glory hole, the mangy animal lookin semi-dazed, like maybe it'd been waitin to use a outhouse for quite a spell. After inspectin the whole shebang, I painted one more sign and hung it around the critter's neck. It said, "Miss Texas, 3rd."

While the rest of us was working on that decrepit kangaroo—sockin down a few suds to stay loose—Big Dunc that had been actin strange, which wasn't all that strange for him, he snuck off by hisself and made this other little sign he wouldn't show none of us. We's curious, but we got to laughin so hard at the big-boobed kangaroo a-settin there so prim that we flat forgot about him.

Whenever we finally made it to the lot, we unloaded the Waldorf right in front of the sign, then Bob Don and Earl they climbed up and crossed out "Future Home of." "That oughta fix her," grinned Bob Don, and Earl that was still up on the sign he slipped and liked to busted his damn neck. While we's a-puttin him back together, helpin him over to the club for a few medicinal spirits, this other idea it hit me, so I hustled three broke-down ol chairs and a spittoon from the card room, then set em up in front of the shitter along with this other sign I made with a markin pen and a tore-off cigarette carton, "Lobby."

What I never noticed was that Dunc had snuck his own sign onto the outhouse door after I finished fixin up the lobby. Next morning when I drove by, there's already a big crowd and the grown-ups, at least, seemed like they appreciated Dunc's addition, but I never. "Shoats best erecshun" put the blame on the wrong Wilhite, so I jerked the damn sign down.

Didn't none of us but Earl see ol Nedra Marie, us havin to work, but he give us a run down on what happened. Seems that her nibs showed up with her mouthpiece and her manager, and it was none other than the third runner-up that pussyfooted through the lobby and unlatched the shitter's door. Earl said that big-boobed critter—the kangaroo, I mean—

it kinda leaned forward, nodded almost, as if to say, "Howdy, pleased to meet ya. I'm just finished myself. Come right in and use the facility."

Earl claimed that ol Nedra Marie Dubarry Wilhite like to used the facility in her britches she was so scared. She let out a war-whoop and jumped, he claimed, then clutched her blow-dried fancy man that knew just what to do, helpin the poor, faintified thing back to her Caddy. They burned off, the whole bunch of em, and Earl said the kangaroo just kept leaning from the door—one tit in, one tit out—like it's watchin em leave. It done ever'thing but wave so-long, or so Earl claimed. I'd a give a week's wages to've seen it.

As usual, it never took ol Nedra's lawyer no time to get to work. Before lunch that same cop that had dealt with Dunc before, he assembled us guys at the Tejon Club. I think he liked the joke near as much as we did, but he had a job to do. We never blamed him. "Well, boys," he said, "you've really done it this time. You've got the power of Wilhite Enterprises after you."

"Shoat too?" I asked.

"We haven't heard from Mr. Wilhite," he acknowledged, then he went on: "The Chief told me to tell you that if the offensive material isn't removed by 2 p.m., criminal charges will be filed. You also have to apologize and clean up the sign you defaced."

"We never done it," claimed Dunc.

"Shut your face, Duncan," warned the cop. "Well, boys?" he said to us.

"We'll move it," Bob Don replied. "And we'll fix up the sign."

"Good," smiled the cop. "You can make arrangements with Mrs. Wilhite's manager about the apology. She still might sue you for humiliating her, though." He paused then winked. "You boys did a darn good job of that."

"Thanks," Bob Don said.

The cop smiled and nodded. Soon as he took off, I said to Bob Don, "That cop never give us no route to follow, right?"

"Yeah."

"Then let's make a grand tour of Oildale out of it, tour ever' damn street in town on our way out to Spud's." That just what we done, too, with all us boys, cept for Bob Don that's drivin, settin in the bed of the pickup with the shitter and the kangaroo, a-wavin at folks and clenchin our hands over our heads like we just won a championship, folks cheerin and laughin like it's the damn Rose Bowl parade. That kangaroo it looked real proud.

Not two weeks later a story broke in the newspaper that Shoat's bookkeeper had discovered that the ex-third runner-up for Miss Texas and her boyfriend was dippin into the till. Turns out, Shoat'd had his bookkeeper checkin on them two right from the start. There was some complicated stuff in it, but the upshot was that Shoat run em off. One day they's here, the next they's gone, that fast. I heard he told em they could choose Texas or jail. And the third runner-up she had to agree to one a them annulments.

Before another week had passed, that hotel sign was gone; the shyster'd disappeared too; all that gold paint was scraped off Shoat's window, and he'd give them two spare Cad's to the bookkeeper and the secretary. He also give that bookkeeper a raise, or so I heard. Then Shoat come back to the Tejon Club.

"Looky here, it's ol sugar plum," growled Dunc that seen him first. He was semi-drunk.

Shoat ignored him and walked up to the bar. "Boys," he announced, "go back to parkin where you want. The Waldorf is closed."

I slapped him on the back. "Have a beer, Shoat," I said, real happy to see him again.

"Thanks, Gerry Bill," he smiled, "I'll join you for a brew directly. But first I wanta know who put that one sign up on the outhouse."

For a minute nobody said nothin, then Dunc give this evil grin. "Which sign's that?" he asked, winkin at Earl.

Ever'thing went quiet for a minute and Shoat just looked at him, then Big Dunc commenced gigglin, "He-he-he!" He was still giggling whenever that giant dill pickle flew down the bar like a space rocket and—splat!—popped him right on the forehead. He come off his bar stool a-wipin his eyes, but Shoat's on him like a boar on a gopher snake. Dunc never knew what hit him.

Dancing

Dad and I walked into the dinette, where Mom sat drinking tea and smoking a cigarette. "Guess who drove home?" he asked.

She smiled at me. "You got your license."

In spite of my desire to remain cool, I grinned. "Yeah."

"He sure did," my father said with an I-told-you-so nod. He swayed there on his long leg and his short one, the latter embanked by the six-inch wooden sole on his shoe. "He never missed a question on the written test! The guy that give him the driving test said he did real good too. I'm serious as oil, Naomi." He patted my back, an uncharacteristic intimacy. "Serious as oil."

"Thanks, Pop."

"I got these made for you," he said and he handed me my own set of car keys.

"You didn't have to do that," Mom said, her voice suddenly cool. "We already *have* keys."

I ignored her because my father'd had the keys made in advance. He'd *known* I'd pass, and that confidence in me really meant something, since it came from a man who was anything but demonstrative.

"Listen, Naomi," Dad urged, "why'n't we have tacos for dinner. To celebrate, I mean." He winked at me, since he knew it was my favorite meal.

She refused, saying she already had a roast in the oven, but that scene— the three of us together—remains with me. What's more, I still have that first set of keys squirreled away in my desk.

And I retain one other thing: a tint of guilt, for I have since grade school been dragging Pop's deformed leg with me, doing a youthful jitterbug of embarrassment that has mellowed to a secret adult waltz. My awareness of Pop's leg has grown from the time I entered kindergarten and noticed other kids pointing and laughing at his shuffle, and, by junior high school when I heard him called cripple and gimp, I did not defend him but, instead, schemed not to be seen with him.

There was more because, along with that word, "cripple," came fear. As a kid I suspected, even dreamed, that my father was dying. I saw him in a casket like grandpa, but a lopsided one, his face ashy, his white folded hands holding a cross. That image always saddened but also brought relief, then guilt. For a time, even the organ music that was played between matinee movies would bring tears to my eyes. And in those movies cripples died, so it had to be true.

All had returned powerfully when my mother'd called the previous night. Mom had, as was her wont, come directly to the point: "Your father had an accident and he lost the car. He *has* to stop driving."

"He did *what?*" I'd stammered.

"Your father *has* to stop driving!"

"Alright, calm down. Now tell me what happened."

"Your father was driving across town and he hit some fellow's van—it was *awful.*" Her voice was heavy, her tone dramatic. "Then he got confused and had to take a cab home. I'm worried *sick* about him. He couldn't even find the car, so I had to send Michael and his friend to look for it. They said he has to stop driving. So did the insurance gal. *He has to.*"

I'd been thinking the same thing myself, but hated to agree with her, for implicit in her tone was the surging dance their marriage had become since Dad had retired from his service station almost fifteen years before. They never fought, at least not to my awareness, but they did seem to be locked in a deflected intimacy, a step both were trying to lead. Mom seemed excessively concerned about Dad, and I knew it was just that other expressions of her love, and other outlets for her chronic worrying, had dissipated. But there was more: Mom didn't drive, and Pop's ability to climb into a car and leave whenever he wished seemed to burden her more each day. He did that frequently, limping to the Chevy while her words swarmed him, then backing down the driveway and disappearing into the tree-lined streets.

For the past ten years or so, she had been insisting with increasing vehemence that we—which meant I, since I'm an attorney—take the keys away from him. I had explained many times that you don't do such things casually or precipitously, but she continued insisting. It was a subject that she'd bring up when other things bothered her, a festering.

Last year, for instance, one of my sons dyed his hair green and Mom had insisted that we force him to cut it or dye it back to its original color. In response, I pointed out facetiously that his grandmother—her—had blue hair. Mom had sputtered for a moment, then hissed, "And your father's going to *kill* someone if you don't take his keys! I'm worried *sick*."

I drove to Coalinga, my hometown, that next morning and had no sooner entered my parents' house and kissed Mom when she seated me, brought me a cup of coffee, then began whispering—her usual mode of conversation when Dad was the subject. "It was an *awful* accident," she hissed. "The policeman told Michael that your father *has* to stop driving. He could *kill* someone. And that insurance gal said so too."

Well, I shared the fear that he could kill someone. He just wasn't an alert driver anymore. But I know enough about the law to ask some questions. "Did the police officer cite Dad?"

"Cite him?"

"Give him a ticket?"

"Well, no, but he told Michael . . ."

"Michael isn't reliable," I said. He was a forty-year-old boy still living next door with his mother, and much given to neighborhood intrigues. Mom, herself, had frequently complained to me about his prevarications and exaggerations, and in other contexts she didn't trust him.

This time her eyes flared. "*You* may not trust him, but he's wonderful to his mother, and he's been such a help to me since you moved away. Now that you don't live in town, he's one person I can trust to help me."

I had been married twenty-five years and hadn't lived in Coalinga since I left for college nearly thirty years before, but her old resentment quickly returned. No point in getting into that argument again. "What about the insurance?" I asked. I had to get back to my office in San Francisco— nearly four hours away—that afternoon, so I wanted to find out exactly what was happening.

"That gal said they're going to pull his insurance because he *shouldn't* be driving."

"What was her capacity?"

"Her capacity?"

"Her job?"

"She came out to tell us how much it would cost to repair the car."

"I see. And she volunteered her opinion about Dad's competence and driving?"

Mom nodded vehemently. "I told her and she agreed with me. He *can't* be driving."

"Oh," I replied. No point in further upsetting my mother, who was clearly on edge, but the estimator had no authority and probably had done no more than nod her head after listening to Mom. "Do you have any documents on this, anything in writing?" I asked.

"The gal left this deal," she replied and handed me a copy of the estimate of repairs. It came to $470 to mend one fender and a door. "This doesn't say anything about his ability to drive."

For a moment neither of us spoke. The issue hung in the small room like the layers of smoke from her cigarette. Mom's eyes scanned me with what seemed deep disappointment; I had been *her* boy up until that fateful day when my driver's license suddenly veered me into a broader realm, but the special expectations honed between us in my childhood remained. "He *lost* the car," she pointed out as though speaking to a dull-witted kid. "What am I supposed to *do*? You don't seem to understand. I just can't *stand* having him drive anymore." Her voice deepened and her chin began to tremble. "You've *got* to help me."

I knew she was worried for good reason, yet something in me wouldn't allow me to agree, the unspoken implication that I had to be her ally in their soft struggle. She knew how difficult it was to be the wife of an aging man, but she had no notion what it was like to be the son of an aging couple, to be used as a weapon. Again we sat in silence, my coffee cup empty, her tea cold, smoke hovering in the windless room. Finally I said, "Does he still see Doctor McCall?"

"Yes, why?"

I picked up the telephone receiver and dialed the doctor's office. I made an appointment the following week for Dad to have a physical examination, then left a message for the doctor: "Tell him Jim Scannell called, and that I need to know if my father is still competent to drive. This is important. Is there any *physical* reason why he shouldn't drive. If Doc has any questions, please ask him to call me collect at my San Francisco office. He knows the number. Thanks."

I faced my mother then and said, "There. If he shouldn't drive we'll know it and have some documentation. I'll call the state referee about a hearing if Doc has any serious doubts about Dad's ability. Does that satisfy you?"

"I'm hiding his keys," she said.

"You're what?"

"I'm hiding them."

"Don't do that, Mom."

"That policeman told Michael . . ."

"He did or he didn't, but there's a legal way to accomplish it. You seem to want the pleasure of stopping him."

"He has *no* business driving," she snapped as she stood and snuffed out her cigarette. Her face had darkened. "You've *always* taken his side, haven't you?" she demanded, then she huffed from the room.

I didn't see Dad that morning, since he was at an auto-body shop. Just as well in some ways, since he rarely spoke anymore and, even if he did, I didn't want to confront the problem more intimately than I already had. If the issue was merely his driving, it could have been swiftly resolved because I knew that anyone could request an examination of a driver's competency from the Department of Motor Vehicles, and a state referee would conduct a test. But the name of the person making the request would be public knowledge, and I didn't want mine used, since it would humiliate Dad to have me question his competency.

Three days later my mother reached me by phone, her voice thick. "I hope you're satisfied," she said without a greeting. "Your father drove the *wrong* way up a freeway ramp last night. Lucky he didn't *kill* somebody."

"What happened?" I didn't need her editorializing.

"A highway patrolman brought him home and he said your father has *no* business driving. I called and called last night but you didn't answer." We had gone out with friends and returned home late. "Well, I told that policeman my son was a lawyer and that I'd *told* you that your father had no business driving. He said you should've done something. Michael says your father might go to jail." Her voice lurched. "I'm worried sick."

"Take it easy, Mom. He's not going to jail. Where's the car now?"

What I didn't tell her was that this was not a traffic-court offense; Pop would have to face a judge, who would certainly put him on probation for awhile, probably a year, and who would certainly order him to stop driving.

"Michael and his friend are *looking* for it. Your father can't remember where it is."

"Okay. Tell Michael to park it at his place, or anyplace but home. I'll call D.M.V. and make certain a driving competency hearing has been initiated."

"He won't get up," she said.

"He won't what?"

"Your father. He went to bed after that highway patrolman brought him home and he *won't* get up. I told him he has chores to do, but he won't."

"Damn," I hissed.

"*What?*"

"Never mind," I said. "I'll be over later today to talk to him."

"Well, I *hope* so." Her voice edged a sob.

I telephoned the highway patrol office in Coalinga and spoke with an officer who was familiar with the incident. Events were as Mom had reported them: my father had driven out to the interstate east of town and become confused. He'd ended up heading south on a northbound ramp when—thank God—a patrol vehicle happened along and stopped him. The arresting officer had routinely requested a competency-to-drive hearing. That was that. Well, at least I was off the hook, but my hesitation might very well have allowed innocent lives to be lost.

When I arrived at my folks' place later that day, Mom was seated in the dinette talking to someone on the phone, her eyes swollen. "Oh, it's Jimmy," she uttered with relief, "I'll call you back."

I kissed her and said, "Calm down, Mom. Things'll be alright. Is Dad still in bed?" I asked.

"He won't get *up*. I'm worried sick about him."

"Okay, I'll go talk to him."

She lit a cigarette, then said, "I've got the keys, but I think he has a *spare* set. You get them. It's not safe."

"Right." I nodded. Well, there was no delaying, so I walked up the hall to my folks' bedroom.

Dad lay in his twin bed with his back to the door. His eyes were open, but he said nothing when I entered. "Dad?" I said.

He only grunted.

"Are you okay?"

Another weak grunt. His eyes flicked in my direction and his face—without teeth—looked shrunken and empty, as though life was retreating from it, slipping away down his short leg and out.

I placed my hand on his shoulder. "You had a bad day, didn't you, Pop?"

Again his eyes flicked toward me; they were squeezed with pain and a thick tear spilled from each, slowly slicking across his face. "The worst," he mumbled in a voice high and weak.

"Thank God you weren't hurt." I immediately wished I hadn't said it because he *was* damaged. I could see that. "I mean, I'm glad there wasn't an accident."

He did not look at me, but I couldn't help staring at him. He had always been slick, never appearing in public unshaven or without his teeth like some old men—now his face was a ruin.

"You're going to have to stop driving, Dad," I said gently. "It's just getting away from you. If the court doesn't restrict you, the Department of Motor Vehicles will."

He continued gazing away from me, his hollow mouth open slightly: a small, dark hole.

"You know yourself that your reactions aren't what they used to be, don't you?"

The voice was slight, a mere whine, when he said, "Yes."

"You don't want to endanger other people. Why don't you voluntarily forfeit your license, just avoid the hearing altogether." My hand was rubbing his shoulder. "That way it's your decision. No one's telling you what to do."

Breath whistled into his face, but there was no movement. The eyes seemed to recede into their sockets and all was quiet. I could hear no breathing. After a moment, it struck me that maybe he had died there, with my hand on his shoulder. "Dad?" I called.

I heard a sigh and felt his frail shoulders move. "In my shoe," he finally whispered.

"Your shoe?"

"Keys." I could barely hear him.

I reached under the bed and picked up a high-topped black shoe, the heavy one with a built-up sole, but it was empty. I dropped it and picked up the other one. Keys rattled, so I shook them out into my hand, then put them in my pocket. "Thanks, Dad," I said, and again patted his shoulder, but he didn't look at me.

I barely heard him whisper, "Don't give 'em to your mother."

"Don't give them to Mom?"

He nodded.

"I'll keep them, but why?"

His reply was little more than a sigh: "Keep 'er guessin'," he said, then he winked at me.

"I'm proud of you, Pop."

He did not reply, and his eyes closed. I remained above him, touching his shuddering shoulder, my gaze transfixed on that dark hole in his face through which breath softly whistled. When I finally removed my hand and turned to leave, I noticed once more his platform shoe lying where I'd dropped it, empty beside the bed. "Keep 'er guessin'," he'd said: He was still leading their dance and, despite what I saw beneath me, I smiled, knowing that short leg had finally slipped from me as certainly as inno-. cence once had.

An Old Intimacy

Through the kitchen window, I saw Dino swing out of the pickup and stride across the yard toward the house. His brows were knitted, his eyes cast down—which, sadly, I had expected—so I moved to the back porch to greet him. "Hi hon'," he said as he entered.

I put my arms around his neck and kissed his cheek. "Are you alright?" I asked.

"I'm okay."

"What'd the county agent say?"

My husband does not speak easily of serious matters. He poured himself a cup of coffee then sat at the kitchen table, and I waited without probing until he sighed, "Well, it doesn't look good. He's afraid the whole half-section might be poisoned because of that damned dump and that we'll have to pull out all those trees and have someone clean up the soil. Worst of all, he said there's no one to sue. The crop dusters're long gone and the chemical company's gone bankrupt. He's afraid we're stuck, but he referred me to the county attorney and the E.P.A. I don't know . . ."

I didn't know either. This had come up suddenly just when things seemed to be going so well. Dino had noticed that trees on a section next to an old crop duster's landing strip north of our place were sickly. We'd paid a local firm in Chico to come out and test the soil and had heard the worst: it appeared that herbicide and pesticide had been dumped randomly for years at the private airstrip and that our soil—and possibly our groundwater—had been poisoned. Then we'd called in the county agricultural agent, and he'd done more tests: same results. We were drinking bottled water as a precaution.

"And we have to pay for everything?"

"For now, at least," he said with a wry grin. We both knew that we couldn't afford it because we had extended ourselves to plant young trees in the very field now condemned.

"And the E.P.A.?"

"Oh yeah," he smiled but his eyes still looked troubled. "You'll like that. Guess who's coming up from San Francisco to investigate?"

I was too concerned to joke, so I simply responded, "Who?"

"Your old boyfriend, Dale Campbell."

Something immediately softened within me, but I didn't let it show. "Dale," I said, "of all people." We had all been students at the university in Davis when I'd known him, when we both had.

"I guess he finished that doctorate in toxicology like he always said he would. Anyway, he heads that division now. It'll be good to see him."

Good? He and Dino had hardly been friends, and Dino had no idea how close Dale and I had been. He couldn't know. Dale was an episode from my life that I frequently wanted to forget but never could, not completely anyway. "Yes," I said, then, "Oh my gosh, look at the time. I've got to pick up the kids from catechism."

I don't really know how things had started with Dale or, rather, I know but still don't understand. He had been big, blond, and handsome, funny and friendly too, but those things don't explain what happened between us. Maybe nothing does. There had been a mixer dance during rush week when I was fresh from high school, uncertain of myself, and in that romantic atmosphere there had suddenly been his lips on my neck as we swerved slowly over the darkened dance floor, his large hand brushing my breast, there had been the two of us alone in his car later that night. We had swept into two years of . . . well . . . not of dating at all, but of trysts, crazy and secret.

We might meet in the commons and across a table full of laughing friends I'd catch that look, and I'd know, and he'd know I knew, then I'd excuse myself and wander toward the library until he'd follow and catch up. Then we'd go to his car and travel to a lonely road. Or I might encounter him at a club meeting and he'd smile and we'd leave together very casually—"I'll drop you off, Jill"—and go to his place for the night.

And if we didn't date others—each of us had several romances during that period—we might sneak to a drive-in movie together. During the final few months before he and Dino had that terrible fight, I lived in my own apartment and Dale came by every Thursday afternoon when neither of us had classes. I'm sure that no one at school realized what was going on.

When I think about it now, it's all like something I read a long time ago, or an old movie, but it was real. It happened. Except for that afternoon of the fight, I didn't feel guilty, just a little confused. Dale and I never really talked, nothing deep ever developed, yet our . . . what's the word they use now? . . . our *relationship* . . . loomed like a whirlpool between us, huge and engulfing. He had fulfilled some secret need of mine, and not merely a physical one; he offered assurance—I can't call it anything else. In any case, it took falling in love with the man I would marry to finally break the pattern.

I met Dino, who was also on the football team, and began dating him during that very period—near the end of my sophomore year—when I would weekly lie nude all afternoon with Dale, when I would lather his body in the shower, taste his virility. It troubles me now to admit that for awhile I dated Dino following afternoons with Dale, and I would modestly deny the man who was to become my husband more than a caress because I wanted his respect and his love.

When I had them and we had begun going steady, I stopped the relationship with Dale. By then Dino and I had become intimate, so I simply avoided Dale for a long time; I somehow couldn't bring myself to discuss it with him. Then I had encountered him at the student store one afternoon, or he had encountered me and given me that look—he never demanded, never pushed—and, although talking about it made me feel dirty, I told him that everything was over between us. Dale had accepted gracefully.

He'd walked me to class that afternoon and, uncharacteristically, had put his arm around me in public, an innocent good-bye hug. When he did that, Dino had emerged from a doorway and confronted us, almost as though he had been lying in wait. He was smaller than Dale, but not small, and he was intense. He had said simply, "Take your arm off her and put down your books." Dale complied and Dino punched him.

The fight that followed is still a major topic at reunions. The two knocked each other down, beat each other bloody, punched and kicked until fatigue brought on slow motion; still they fought while I stood weeping—realizing for the first time the powerful force I had unleashed—and other students gathered quickly, cheering at first and calling encouragement, but quieting as the fight continued and it became clear that Dale and Dino were injuring one another. Everyone was afraid to interfere, even when I pleaded, "Stop them! Won't somebody please stop them."

Soon all you could hear was the dead smack of flesh on flesh and the explosions of their breath. It went on so long that spectators began flinching, averting their eyes, then bolting from the crowd. When a campus policeman finally arrived, both fighters were on their feet, their faces bloody and swollen with fatigue, their fists bruised, their eyes riveted on one another.

Since they were well-known athletes, the gray-haired officer had addressed them by their first names: "Dale, Dino, cut it out! That's enough!" and he had stepped between them. Each stood with fists poised for a long moment as though waiting for the other to drop his hands, then simultaneously it seemed they lowered them, but had continued glaring at one another.

"Go home and clean up," the officer ordered, "before someone turns you in and you end up suspended." There was in the older man's eyes as he pushed them away from one another something like admiration or even awe. He actually seemed *proud* of them and I wanted at that instant to scream at him: What's wrong with you? Are you *crazy*! Instead, I ran to Dino, put my arms around him, then led him to my nearby apartment so he could clean up.

On the painful walk to my place, I explained to Dino that Dale and I were just friends and that he, not Dale, was my special man, my only one. "He'd better keep his hands off you," was all he had said, his eyes still burning.

Dale had graduated the following June, and I hadn't seen him since the day I watched him receive his degree. Two years later, Dino and I finished school. We were married shortly after commencement and, following our honeymoon, had moved to Chico so he could become a partner at his father's almond ranch, the one we eventually took over and have expanded.

That was twenty years ago, or nearly twenty. That was four children ago, some tears and much laughter ago. Dino and I have built a good marriage; he has remained slim and handsome, and he has become my dearest friend. But Dale was coming here and something in me couldn't be still. Whatever happened, I didn't want to do or say anything that would hurt Dino. And I didn't want Dale to, either.

When the rented car pulled into our place that next afternoon, Dino and I walked into the yard to greet him, me slightly behind. Dale in suit and tie swung from the auto, grinning. A young, red-haired woman, also in a suit, emerged from the small foreign car's other door. While the two men shook hands, I examined Dale—he had aged well: he was heavier, with gray sprinkling his blonde hair, but even his wrinkles seemed to enhance his pleasant good looks. He still smiled easily.

"Chico," he said, "it's great to see you." Back in college Dino had been called that by his teammates.

"And Jill . . . ," he hugged me and kissed my cheek, then stepped back, still holding my hand and placing his other hand on one of Dino's shoulders. "Let me look at you. You two look *great*. You really do. Oh," he grinned, "this is Ginger DiPardo, my assistant." The young woman smiled and shook hands.

We walked into the house and decided that it would be better to take care of business first, then visit, so Dino, Dale, and Ginger hopped into our pickup—it, of course, only seated three—and scooted toward the sick field. I remained home. I had children to keep an eye on, and I wanted to think. I was a little breathless. Dale looked so good and seemed so relaxed and friendly, but I had expected more somehow, a special squeeze of my hand, maybe, or a glimpse of that old look. I don't know what I expected, or wanted. Nothing overt, certainly, since men are so fragile and so burdened by reality: a wife's old loves—even the *possibility* of old loves—damages them, and Dino didn't need anything else upsetting him given our other problems.

We ate that afternoon, Dino pouring homemade wine while I was careful not to drink much because I didn't want to say the wrong thing. Dale had been married, he revealed, and had children of his own who lived with his ex-wife. While he didn't say so, it was also clear that something more than work united Ginger and him, although she was probably fifteen years his junior. As the wine flowed, and talk relaxed, I found myself happy to once more be with Dale but paradoxically tense, afraid he might slip and say the wrong thing. More and more conversation swirled the table, the guys replaying games: "Hey Chico, remember that time at Humboldt when the ball bounced up and hit you in the nuts during warm-ups?"

They both roared and Dale turned toward me, tears of laughter streaming from his eyes: "You're lucky you had any kids, Jill," he choked, and they roared once more. I was more relieved than amused: the conversation was taking Dino's mind off the field that had been burdening him, and it was avoiding the memories hovering just behind my polite smile.

In spite of myself, I kept glancing at Dale seeking vestiges of that other look, the private one we had once shared, wanting and dreading it. It never appeared, so I tried to engage Ginger in conversation—she was bored by the nostalgia—but my English major didn't jibe well with her interests, and my rural life was remote from hers in the city. I did discover that she was a vegetarian after placing a roast on the table, although she was not heavy-handed, and actually referred to herself with a smile as "a reformed hippy." Fortunately, we had an abundant salad and plenty of vegetables.

Dinner was long since finished, conversation slowing, and the large jug of wine was nearly empty, when Dale commented out of the blue, "You know, Ginger, this guy knows me better than anyone in the world. Better than my folks did, better than Marilyn did, better than you do."

It was a tipsy statement but not a drunken one, and it confused me. Dale and Dino had only been teammates, not friends. I said nothing because a tiny kernel of fear settled suddenly into my throat; he was going to talk about me, about us. Suddenly I felt like excusing myself.

"A long time ago, we had a fight where we each gave it all we had, where we fought and fought until there wasn't anything hiding inside us, or in me anyway. All I had was right there. We've never talked about it, Chico, but I gave it everything. I didn't have one thing left."

My husband looked directly at his old rival, and his crooked grin appeared. "I know," he said. "I didn't either. I couldn't've done anything else."

"But we both stood there and didn't quit," Dale said, and I could hear the wine in his voice, but there was something else, something deeper. "We stood there. We didn't quit. Chico, that was the most honest moment of my life."

Dale's large hand reached across the table and grasped Dino's. For a moment they seemed to freeze, their fingers entwined, their eyes locked on one another as they had been so long ago. "Mine too," Dino grunted.

For an instant I felt as troubled as I had when that policeman had so long ago gazed at them with admiration. What was going on? They had almost *killed* one another. My eyes warmed, and Ginger gave me a quizzical glance to let me know that she didn't understand. I only shook my head at her. There was nothing I could say.

Our guests left shortly thereafter, Dale giving me a hug and boozy smack, then hugging Dino too. Ginger exchanged a knowing smile with me as the men did that, then she shook my hand and climbed into the driver's seat and started the car. I stood with my husband in the yard waving in the long summer twilight as their small auto sent a dust plume toward the state road.

"That was good," Dino murmured. "A good visit."

"Yes." I glanced at him and saw that, while he was still grinning, his eyes were clouded. Then I heard him sigh.

"What's wrong, honey?" I asked, squeezing his hand.

"Our field is dying," he said.

The Welder's Cap

That night I was quietly going through my things, trying to decide what to pack and what to throw away, when Brother came home half-drunk and with that tattoo on his arm. Momma's face turned purple when she saw it.

Of course, Brother was contrite, begging her to forgive him, but Momma wouldn't have any of it: "Nosir!" she cried. "Nosir! You're lucky your father ain't alive but only a poor helpless woman that her own chilrin don't love. Wellsir, I'm a-endin' it all. Nobody even loves me!"

Momma thumped into the kitchen crying, "I've had me enough. This is the end! This here is surely the end! Not one soul in the world loves me."

Brother was slinking along behind her, tears starting to trickle down his cheeks and that patch of red-green-blue on one of his forearms spelling "Baboonass."

"Oh Momma," he pleaded, "I'm sorry."

Momma folded her knees and thudded to the floor in front of the stove, then opened the oven door and stuck her head inside—her bottom blocking half the kitchen—and Brother commenced to tugging at her waist: "Don't do it Momma! Pleeease don't do it. I'll git rid of the tattoo, I'll have a guy git rid of it. Pleeease, Momma."

"Turn on the gas, Brother," her voice echoed from the oven. "Just turn it right on and finish the job you done on me."

Well, I stood there and watched those two, more convinced than before that moving away was the right thing to do. I'd seen versions of this act before, like when Brother came home drunk that first time. It was the

141

same. And when he got that hickey on his neck in high school and when he tried to join the Marines Corps when he was fifteen.

"Oh, Momma, I'll cut this arm right off. Swear to God I will. Sister, gimme that butcher knife," he called to me. "Gimme it!" He was still tugging at Momma with one arm, waving the other at me, his face like a wet tomato.

"Turn on that gas!"

Brother looked at me. "Sister, aren't you gonna do nothin'? Aren't you gonna help me save our own momma?"

From inside the oven Momma echoed, "No she ain't. I'm a-endin' it because there ain't one soul in this world that respec's me. Turn on that gas, Brother."

"Help me, Sister! Sister!"

No wonder I couldn't seem to tell Momma that I'd accepted a promotion at work requiring me to move to Fresno—I never knew how she'd act. And Brother too, for that matter. I looked at those two posed there, then reached over and turned on the gas.

Momma jerked out of the oven so fast that she sent Brother sprawling. "Oh, thank God!" he cried and commenced blubbering for real.

Momma glared at me. "Listen here, Missy," she huffed, struggling to her feet, "you wanta blow this house up and it the only thang I own in this whole world. What's the matter with you, anyways? Is that what they taught you in that *school*?"

I turned off the gas and walked into the other room without answering.

She lumbered after me. "Now you looky here, Missy!"

"*You* look, Momma," I turned around and snapped, "it wasn't me made a fool of myself squatting down on the floor and sticking my head in the oven! Now leave me alone! I've got things on my mind."

I'm not one to snap at other people, but enough's enough. My response shocked her. She stammered, "Well . . . well you just mind your own beeswax when I'm a-talkin' to my boy," then she huffed off to the porch where she might find a neighbor lady to sympathize with her.

Me, I cooled off then found Brother out in the yard working on an old Chevy—he always had one car or another torn up in our yard. He acted just like nothing had happened, except that he'd put on a long-sleeved shirt. "Whatever possessed you to get that stupid tattoo?" I demanded.

The old car's hood was open like a giant mouth and he was half-swallowed by it. "Sister," he confessed, from inside the Chevrolet's jaws, "it was the beer done it. Me and Fat Larry and Manuel, we was just drinkin' beer and throwing horseshoes at the park yesterday and this Mexican that Manuel knows he come by and said he'd give us tattoos half-price. He had his tattoo deal with him. Anyways, we never had no money, but we give him some beer and pretty soon he just give 'em to us, tattoos, on credit and half-price."

"I didn't know you even wanted one."

"Well, I never, but they was *half-price* and *on credit.*"

He's a caution. "What if *poison* was half-price and on credit? Would you buy some?"

He blinked for a minute then said, "Nope," his eyes hidden in the shadow from the car's hood. "Anyways, it was one a them beer deals."

"And why in the world did you have *that* put on your arm?" I reached over and jerked his sleeve up to reveal the colored scabs that said "Baboonass" and what looked like a curved American flag above it. "I swear, Momma should put *you* in the oven."

"Don't be hateful, Sister."

"Why 'Baboonass'?" I insisted.

"Well, I told that Mexican I wanted 'Coonass' in honor of our own Daddy that he was from Louisiana"—he gave me a reproachful look—"but the Mexican he's drunk too and I just never noticed what he was doin'. Whenever he got done, it seemed real funny." He ventured a tentative chuckle.

"And that flag? What's it about."

"Manuel he said that deal's the baboon's ass."

"A grown man with a monkey's rear tattooed to his arm." I swear, I can't figure Brother out. He's three years older than me, but still treading high-school water. "It's just what you get," I finally spat, more frustrated than angry because he doesn't ever foresee consequences of anything, "no job, hanging around the park with those . . . those *losers.*"

He pulled his sleeve down and came completely out of the car's maw like Jonah escaping from the whale. "Sister, me and the guys we look for work, but we can't find us nothin' but nigger work—packin' sheds, mowin' lawns, them deals. We hold ourselves to be white men."

He puffed up a little as he said that last thing, but I deflated him in a hurry. "You and the other *white men* maybe deal a little dope or something to find beer money, though, don't you?"

That stunned him. "You got no call to say that. You got no call." His eyes were suddenly wide and ragged because he knew I did indeed have call.

I'd heard that Brother and his buddies were small-time dealers. I wasn't going to say any more, but I wanted him to know that I knew. I wanted him to think about that. "And you were too smart to finish high school, weren't you?" I added. I'd been trying to talk him into going to adult school to finish an equivalency program.

"We're not into that dope deal, me and the guys."

"Right," I said, "and Manuel didn't serve time for peddling either, did he?"

His brows thickened. "Well, don't be throwing that school deal into my face again. I coulda done good if I wanted to. Besides it was just a buncha kiss-assed fairies that did, and the teachers they was dumb."

"And you and your smart buddies, you're throwing horseshoes at the park, picking up money some way, and getting stupid tattoos."

"If I could get me a *good* job . . ."

"I know, like doctoring or lawyering," I said, "or maybe some company needs a president." Then I returned to the house. Talking to him's like spitting into wind.

I'd been taking junior-college courses ever since I finished high school, and I had to get to a night class, but Momma stopped me. "That boy's gotta get that awful *thang* off'n his arm."

"That *boy's* nearly twenty-five, Momma. What he needs is to grow up, go back to school and finish, then find a steady job."

"Your father worked steady."

And drank steady, I thought but did not say. "My father's dead. Now I'm the only one that's got a job."

Her eyes clouded and she gasped, "Why're you so hateful, and your brother's as good as he can be to me."

"Ohhhh!" I just wanted to shake her teeth loose. A half-hour before she'd been ready to strangle him. It seemed like she was always playing one of us against the other.

"He never says nothin' hateful to his own mother that carried him in her *womb.*" She pronounced the "b," so the word always sounded like she dropped it, "wuuum-bah." I didn't pay her any mind. Lord knows I'd heard all this before. Then she extended her hand and said, "Looky what I found in the garbage."

It was a small black welder's cap I had secretly thrown away the day before.

"This ain't what your own Daddy that he was a welder give you, is it? And you wore it ever'wheres when you was little, so cute?"

"Yes. It doesn't fit anymore, Momma."

"Your own Daddy that he was so proud of you and now you're a-throwin' it away?"

"I've gotta go or I'm gonna be late for class, Momma." I turned for the door.

"*Class!*" she spat.

The next morning, as usual, she was pouting. I just went about my business, putting on my make-up and drinking my coffee. She entered the kitchen still carrying that little black cap and said, sounding real hurt, "When I was your age, I was married and had me two younguns. I wasn't a-paintin' my eyelids to make *men* look at me. I wasn't goin' to no *classes* at night. No ma'am. There's a whole lot *school* don't teach you. I don't know why you can't settle down and get married and give me some gran-chilrin."

I put my coffee down and stared at her. How many times do I have to hear this? I intended to tell her that I had to move, but instead I said, "Well, I can quit at the bank and go to the park, drink beer with Brother and his buddies. I'm sure one a them'll be *happy* to give me babies . . . and probably VD. Maybe *all* of 'em will. I can even get a tattoo just like the rest of 'em."

"What a way for a girl to talk! Listen, Missy, you don't have to be so uppidy! I worked myownself! I waited tables for a spell when you was little. I know all about *work*—men a-pinchin' you and all. Hah!"

I just shook my head. "And how about Mr. Baboonass that's still in bed, probably with a hangover—when's *he* gonna settle down?"

"The poor boy's just a-findin' hisself."

"Tell him to look in the park," I snapped, and turned to leave.

"Boys they don't grow up as quick as girls," I heard her say as I walked out.

That afternoon I came home from work determined to tell Momma the good news about my promotion, and what did I find in the kitchen but one of those pit bull dogs, short and ugly with a big, thick head, and a little stub tail. It didn't look real friendly. "What's this?"

"That's Buster. I got him from Manuel at the park," grinned Brother.

"Who's gonna feed him?"

"He don't eat much."

I shook my head. "Well he won't eat much around here because I'm not gonna pay for dog food. You'll have to take it out of *your* . . . ah . . . income," I added, and he winced.

That's when Momma lurched through the door and said, "You will so. That there's the dog my boy brung his momma to protec' me when I'm left here all alone while you're off a-workin' or a-takin' them *classes*." She smiled at Mr. Baboonass.

"Brother can stay home and protect you, or maybe he has to protect Fat Larry and Manuel at the park."

Momma stopped and put her hands on her hips. "Why're you so hateful to this poor boy? I believe you're jealous because me and him're so close."

I looked at Brother and Buster, both of them tilting their heads and staring at me. "Yeah," I said as sarcastically as I could, "that must be it."

I went into the kitchen, put water on to boil for coffee, then made myself a sandwich. I had another class that night.

Momma and Buster joined me. She still carried that small black welding cap. "You was cute as a bug's ear whenever you wore this, 'member?" she asked.

"I remember." I looked up. "I got a promotion at work, Momma. I won't be a teller anymore. They're gonna train me to be a loan officer, but I have to move to Fresno."

"You *what*?"

"I'm transferring to the Fresno branch."

"You'll do no such a thang!"

"Wait a minute, Momma," I said, putting down my sandwich. "I'm twenty-two years old and I've got a career started. Nobody helped me but *me*. I'm only going a couple hours up the road, so I won't be far. We've got this place paid off and you've got your check from the widow's welfare fund, so you'll get along. And I'll send you some money. Brother can find a job, so he won't starve. But I'm *not* gonna throw away this chance."

She plopped onto a chair and shook her head like she was lost. "It's young girls nowadays wanta act just like *menfolk*. They don't stay home with chilrin. They don't cook no more. They don't sew. They don't even get jobs. Nosir, they get *careers*. Always takin' *classes*." She looked at me then and pleaded, "Why can't you just *settle down*?" Then she glanced away, her hands kneading that little cap, and her eyes began blinking.

Momma hadn't attended much school back in Arkansas before she'd met Poppa while she was visiting a cousin in Baton Rouge. The way she tells it, there wasn't much school to attend. Anyway, they got married then moved here to California to make their fortune. She'd managed to live right in Oildale in this neighborhood of other one-time migrants, rural folks like herself from that part of the country, while Poppa'd worked as a welder in the oil fields. He drank at a honky tonk just up the street and listened to Hank and E. T. and Lefty on the juke box, and Momma'd gone to a Pentcostal church a block from this house where she heard the same comforting sermons she had in Pine Bluff. As far as I know, all their close friends lived right here.

Brother and I'd grown up here too, but after grade school we'd gone into town to Bakersfield High where there were different kinds of folks and the beginnings of different dreams. It had offered us another world and I, for one, intended to pursue it. Poor Momma didn't understand and Brother, I suspect, didn't care one way or another.

"I'm not *leaving* you Momma," I said. "I wouldn't do that. But I am going away for this promotion. I can go to school at Fresno State while I'm up there, maybe finish my degree, but I'll be home too. I'm not running away. If I'd wanted to do that, I'd've done it a long time ago."

Momma watered up. She just sat there, her big shoulders shaking. "I don't know why thangs always have to *change*," she moaned. At least she didn't stick her head in the oven.

"I don't either, Momma." I reached over and rubbed her back. The world was moving too fast for her.

"And you even threw away your own daddy's cap."

I sighed. What could I say? "That was just an accident, Momma. Let me have it back, please." She handed it to me, soggy from her tears.

Just then Brother busted in the door wearing a sleeveless Harley-

Davidson T-shirt so his baboonass tattoo was on display. He grinned, as charming as could be, and said, "Say, Sister, could you let me have five bucks till tomorrow? Me and Fat Larry got these dates."

That perked Momma up. "Oh," she smiled, wiping her puffy eyes, "ain't that nice. Who're you boys a-goin' out with?"

"Don't ask," I advised.

"Oh just some ol' gals we picked up at the skatin' rink. I don't 'member their names, but Fat Larry's she's got this big horse deal tattooed on her chest." He grinned.

"You see, Momma," I said, "*everything* doesn't have to change." At the same time I was thinking as I gazed at her, you'll get your grandchildren Momma, even if Brother won't know the mother's name. I put that little cap on my head, took five dollars out of my wallet, and handed them to my brother.

"Thanks," he grinned as he swung out the door to join Fat Larry and the maidens.

Momma beamed at him, hesitated, then said to me, "What horse deal?"

Missing in Action

"Not long after they come back, Mirahashi he got himself worked over pretty good by Bo and Babe Purvis. You remember 'em, don't you? They was guys I worked with and their brother, Johnny Lee, he got killed on Okinawa. Anyways," Pop continued, "when the Japs come back, them boys they was laying for the old man and they sure got him, sent him to the hospital."

"I didn't know."

"No, I guess not. You was just a little shaver," Pop said. "Funny thing is that Mirahashi he never pressed charges. Said he understood how the Purvises felt because he'd lost a boy himself. After that, nobody bothered him."

"Huhm," I nodded.

"Him and his wife was the only Japs in town."

We were sitting on my porch drinking beer that warm afternoon, Pop having just arrived for a visit. The drive had tired him, and the brew seemed to be hitting my father more than me. I'd read an item in the local newspaper about Congress voting on reparations for Japanese-Americans incarcerated during World War II, and had mentioned it to him. He'd snorted more vehemently than I'd expected that liberals were selling out the working man, grumbled about the sad state of the modern world in general, and then begun telling me about the lone family in my home-town that had been taken away.

"Yeah, they run a little truck farm just outside the city limits. I guess they made a good living. They sure as hell grew good vegetables, the Japs. They're good at that."

"I really don't remember them."

"You don't remember that old lady that always pulled a kid's wagon loaded with junk?"

"Oh," I said. I did remember her. As a school kid I had often seen the old woman, shuffling through alleys mostly, picking up stale produce from grocery store garbage cans. She'd always worn men's argyle socks, house slippers, and a stocking cap. Sometimes my friends and I would follow her chanting "Ching Chong Chinaman." We were real cards. Later, when I was in college, memories of that little stunt had caused me to gnash my teeth. "*That* was Mrs. Mirahashi?"

"You bet."

"But I thought you said they owned a truck farm. What was she doing taking wilted lettuce out of garbage cans?"

"Oh yeah, they had nice little place. Everybody bought from them. Your mother and me used to drive out nearly every Saturday to buy vegetables. A real nice little place, neat and clean. Fact is, we thought they was nice folks. They used to always play with you when you was a baby and we brung you out. Their own kid was real polite. He worked on the farm after school. He could really run too, their kid. I seen him in some track meets for the high school."

I was intrigued by this addition, so I asked, "And their boy was killed in the war?"

"Not killed, I don't think. Missing in action, that's what I heard, in Italy. He never turned up. His name's on the war memorial, you know."

"And he was an athlete?"

"You bet. He run in the state meet the year before they got took away. Fast as greased lightning. He was one fast Jap. He even beat all the colored boys."

That remark made me laugh—maybe it was the beer—and Pop laughed with me, his voice a little louder than usual, his grin a little loose. "Fast as greased lightning," he repeated.

For a moment neither of us spoke, then I said, "Old Hokie Hall could really run, too. Remember him?"

"That kid in your class with the bugeyes?"

"That's him."

"Sure do. He was a pistol himself, that kid," Pop agreed.

"He ran 9.7 for the hundred."

"Is that right? He run 9.7?"

I grinned. "It used to look like a bunch of black kids chasing a white boy down the street every time he raced."

Pop got a kick out of that. "You bet," he chuckled.

I asked Pop if he wanted another brew, and he continued smiling as he said, "Naw, I've drunk about enough." I could see that he had, and my own numb cheeks told me that I had too, so I didn't bother walking into the kitchen.

Again a boozily comfortable silence settled over us, each secure in the presence of the other. My father pulled a plug of tobacco from the breast pocket of his shirt and offered me a chaw.

"No thanks," I said.

He again grinned. "I forgot you learned better in that college."

"I even wear shoes on weekdays now," I replied.

Pop bit a quid from the plug, then hesitated and asked, "Lorie don't mind if I spit on the flower bed, does she?"

I thought he was kidding, but I could see he wasn't, so I suppressed a cute response and said only, "No." After another moment of silence, that question reoccurred to me. "If they owned a farm, why was that old woman digging in garbage cans?"

"Huh?" His mind had obviously been on something else, and he appeared confused.

"The Mirahashis, if they owned a farm, why was that old woman digging in garbage cans?"

Pop looked grave. "Well," he explained, "they lost their place, and when they come back they lived in a little trailer house over by the river. I don't know if the old man ever went out again after that beating. If he did, I never seen him. He died years ago. So did the old lady, not long after you graduated from college."

"Huhm."

"It was funny, though," Pop went on, "because they was like different people, the Japs, when they come back. Or maybe they was just being their true selves, I mean with the war lost and all, they never had to fake anymore. They could act like, well, real Japs."

"How did they lose their place?"

My father sighed, and shifted his weight. "I guess they never kept up the payments on it, so the bank got it. Some rich guy that owns big acreage out there he bought it up, or that's what I heard."

"How could they?"

"Eh?"

"How could they make payments if they were away in one of those camps?" I asked, curious about the logistics involved in the relocation. My father's response surprised me.

"The Japs bombed Pearl Harbor!" he snorted, his voice suddenly thick.

Even though I knew better than to kid him when he was drinking, I couldn't resist saying "They did?" with mock wonder, then smiling.

"It's not funny!" He seemed angry in that explosive way I remembered from my childhood. "There was thousands of our boys killed."

"I wasn't smiling at that Pop," I explained. "It was just that you changed the subject so quickly."

His brows knit and he looked away. "They never coulda done that to our boys without help from Japs right here in our own country."

"Maybe not, but . . ."

"No maybe to it! It's a true fact. I was there. You was just a baby."

He still sounded hot, so I decided to let it slide. Beer did that to him sometimes, and I hadn't meant to stir him up. "Well," I said, "that's all ancient history now. There're Japanese-Americans in Congress, and the chief of surgery at Memorial is a Japanese-American, and even Tommy's soccer coach is Japanese-American, so . . ." I shrugged and smiled.

"It wasn't my idea to burn their place, though," Pop said, looking away from me. He spit a brown stream into the flower bed.

"Burn their place?"

"Their house, the Japs'," he said, his eyes still wandering.

"Somebody burned their house?" Why had he even mentioned it, out of the blue like that?

He turned to face me then and I could see how the beer had affected him, his face seeming to slide down and to the left, his eyes red. "You bet," he finally replied. "See, the Japs they had this antenna up on their windmill that they used to send messages to Japan, so a bunch of us went out there the night after they got took away and we searched the place to find, you know, their secret code and Jap flags and all that."

"A bunch of *us?*" What he had said was sinking in.

"Sure, real Americans." That indignant tone crept back into his voice.

"And did you find what you expected?"

"Well, no, we never." His voice had eased again. "The Japs they was too smart for that, but we found something worse—we thought it was worse. Mirahashi he'd burned this American army uniform in the fireplace, but we found parts of it. We was drinking pretty good, and we got sore. I don't know exactly who done it—I never—but pretty soon the Japs' place was on fire."

"What did you do?"

"Nothing." He seemed to avert his eyes for a moment. "We just let her burn. We never wanted the Japs in the first place, and damn sure never wanted them coming back."

"So they couldn't have returned to their house if they'd wanted to?" I couldn't soften my own tone as I asked the question, and Pop's face hardened.

"Don't you remember the Corregidor Death March that the Japs done?"

"Not really," I responded, troubled by what I had heard. My father had never broken the law. He was a hard-working, conservative man, an elder in the church. He'd worked an extra job to help me through college. During World War II, he'd been deferred because of his job in the oil fields, but he had volunteered for every task open to a civilian. Now he was telling me that he'd virtually helped torch a neighbor's house. "Jesus, Pop, how could you just let someone's house burn?"

His reply was sharp. "Don't take the Lord's name in vain!"

"Okay, I'm sorry, but how could you just watch?"

"The Japs they was doing terrible things to our boys, and there was that uniform, an *American* uniform . . ." His voice seemed to linger on the final word.

"But you said we bought produce from the Mirahashis, that you knew them. You sounded like you even liked them."

"They're tricky, the Japs. They had me fooled. Your mother too." His voice had changed. It was still a little beery, but there was a deeper note in it, an uncertainty that I didn't remember having heard before.

His lingering on the word a moment before, caused me to ask, "What about that uniform?"

"Uniform?"

I wasn't certain he really hadn't understood me although his voice did retain that uncertain note. "The one you found at the Mirahashi place," I prompted.

"Oh, that." He seemed to be staring at something in the sky above the house across the street. "Did you know the Japs they threw babies up in the air and caught 'em on bayonets? It's a true fact. And they stuck bayonets in pregnant women. They was uncivilized. They bombed women and children. They never fought like white men."

"Yes," I replied, "but what was that uniform all about?"

He sighed, then said, "We took it to Nate Peters, the sheriff, and he said it wasn't important."

"But what was it doing there at all? It sounds incriminating."

Pop cleared his throat, then spit. "Incriminating? I don't know. Anyways, it turned out to be his."

"His?"

"Mirahashi's."

"What was he doing with an American uniform?" I asked.

"He was a veteran. I guess he served in the Great War. But *not* overseas," Pop quickly added. "Anyways, what kind of man would burn his own country's uniform? Answer me that."

"His *own* country? But you said he was Japanese."

There was no uncertainty in my father's reply, only an emotional surge that led him to grasp one of my arms. "They're *different*. They're not like us. We never wanted them coming back but they did, and they stayed even after the old man got beat up, and that old woman always around like a ghost to remind us. They don't *feel* like normal people do, the Japs. They don't." His eyes were welling and his mouth appeared ragged.

I should have shut up, but instead I let slip out, "Pop, the Mirahashis were Americans, you said so yourself, and they lost their boy in the war fighting for us."

His hand seemed to fall from my arm and he once more looked away at that spot across the street. "That's easy to say today. So easy. Thousands of our boys tortured in them prison camps. . . ." His head was slowly shaking and his eyes were damp.

"I'm sorry, Pop," I said, touching his back. "I didn't mean to upset you."

He stood, half-turned away from me and his shoulders began to shudder, and his voice sounded like a cry: "Everybody took *their* side after they come back. Just because that boy of theirs won some big medal and got missing in action, just because me and Bo and Babe . . ." His voice dissolved into muffled choking.

"Pop," I called, "it's okay. Never mind." I didn't want to hear any more, and I didn't want him crying. I'd never seen him do that before.

He turned his crumpling face toward me and moaned, "It's so easy nowadays, but you wasn't there. They done *awful* things to nuns."

Lives Touching

"You know a Darleta Sims?" that stranger asked.

Of course everyone in McFarland knew Darleta. She was real strong in the Prophet of Light Church and she worked over at Morine's Beauty Salon. Before I could answer, though, the stranger went on. "Me and Darleta usta be sweet on each other. I haven't seen her since I come back from Korea in '54."

I glanced out the window and seen the Oregon plates on the new Continental the man had parked in front of my diner. "You from around here?" I asked.

"Born and raised," he grinned, his front teeth bracketed with gold like porcelain pastures. "Course I live up in Portland now. I come home for the reunion tonight."

"That's nice," I said. "Yeah, I know Darleta. She comes in here for a snack ever' afternoon."

"Is that a fact? Tell me, is she still no bigger'n a minute? Usta weigh about 90 pounds soakin' wet, and with the teensiest feet."

Darleta Sims dressed out at a good 200, wet or dry, and she wasn't much over five foot tall. Her neck was rolled by years of bacon gravy, the gravy knotted and bleached under her collar. "Her feet're still small," I replied, not wanting to say too much.

"Listen, my name's Huel Lester," the stranger announced, thrusting a large paw toward me like he's fixing to snap my bow tie.

"Jim Fitts," I said while we pumped hands.

"Jim," Huel said, "I'd surely like to see that ol' sweetie. You reckon she's goin' tonight?" He had relaxed as soon as we'd shaken, no longer standing stiff across from me, but slipping onto a stool and resting his elbows on the counter, cupping his coffee in both hands like he was home. His tone sounded dang near like *I'd* been his high-school honey, not Darleta. "Yessir, Jim, I'd surely love to see her."

"She'll be by," I acknowledged, then added: "I heard her talking about the reunion, so she'll be there too."

Up the counter, Mutt Walsh, my only other customer during that slack, post-breakfast hour, tapped his cup noisily with a spoon, signaling for a refill. He was nearly deaf, Mutt, so he always made a loud racket. He also always managed three refills—with lots of sugar and cream—for his two-bit cup. While I poured him fresh coffee, he whispered in what me and you would call a low holler, "Who's that ol' boy?"

Mutt's voice was raw. He was one of them fellers that always seemed to have his back hair up, always claiming he was gonna whip this guy or tell that one off. He kept a pit bull at home he claimed could kill any dog in town.

"Friend of Darleta's," I answered, winking at the stranger. "Name's Lester."

"Ya don't say," replied Mutt, pouring my expensive sugar into his cup. "Usta be a family of Lesters lived here. Come from Arkansas. I worked at Guimara's with the ol' man. Is that feller's name Hugh?"

"Huel," I said.

"Ya don't say. Why I knowed his daddy." Mutt turned his attention to Lester. "I b'lieve I knowed your daddy, ol' Ned Lester. You'll have to speak up. I'm a tad deef," he added.

"Is that a fact? I'm surely ol' Ned's boy." Huel picked up his coffee and moved next to Mutt. Them two warmed stools and yacked until the merchant's lunch crowd begun drifting in, Mutt holding me up for one more refill while Huel took two. There went my profit.

Mid-afternoon, like always, Darleta waddled through the doorway. I only had a couple of regulars in drinking coffee when she called, "Hello ever'body!" and we greeted her. She waved a plump, pink hand that looked like it'd been boiled till it swelled, then she made her way to a stool and plopped, her hindquarters obliterating the seat.

"I'll have some a that *scrumptious* banana cream pie," she announced, "with a nice scoop a vanilla, and a glass a lo-fat milk."

"I'm out of lo-fat," I told her. "Charlie's late with the deliver."

"No lo-fat?" Her face crumpled till it looked about like one of them mask-of-tragedy deals they used to show us in high school. "Oh *darn!*" I thought she might cry. "Well, gimme a Coke," she sighed. "Make that a cherry Coke."

After she got started on the pie, I asked: "You all set for the big shindig tonight?"

She glanced up at me, and her face looked like I'd just told her I didn't have no whip cream. "I ain't goin'," she mushed, her mouth full.

"You're not! That's all you been talking about for a solid month."

She pulled on that cherry Coke, then explained: "Well, me and Momma was consultin' our Ouija board last night and it spelled D-A-N-G-E-R-U-S just bigger'n you please."

"Is that right?" I said. Darleta's ol' momma that lived with her was touched, no doubt about it. She'd never been out of the house for a good five years, maybe more.

"And that ain't all," she continued, raising her penciled eyebrows. "Guess what the next word was."

I never had no idea.

"R-E-U-N-Y-U-N is what! Momma's not lettin' me go against Ouija."

"Is that right?"

I told Mutt the story whenever he come back in. "Ouija!" he snorted— pronouncing it "wee-gee"—sounding right away pissed. "Why one time this ol' boy had me ask a question on his and I felt that pointer a-movin' so I give it a little tug and you know what that sumbitch done? He said *I's* movin' it. I said, 'How the hell could you *know* that if *you* wasn't movin' it first!' I kicked his ass right on the spot!"

Mutt never weighed but a hundred pounds. His arms was damn near big as toothpicks. I said, "Oh."

After he'd slurped down a cup of my coffee, Mutt groused on. "Just as well Darleta ain't a-goin'. I b'lieve ol' Huel'd be disappointed whenever he seen her."

"Maybe so," I granted, "but she looks real nice, what with her hair beehived and all."

"Hah!" snorted Mutt. "That's about like fixin' up the fuzz on a bad peach. It don't make the peach no better. She ain't too good a ad for that beauty saloon."

"Darleta's not a bad peach."

"You know what I mean," he scowled.

Darleta come in a second time that day just after work. She looked low and ordered a cup of coffee and a donut for a pick-me-up. I was bustling around trying to keep my early supper crowd happy, balancing chicken-fried steaks and lima-bean specials, but I took a second to talk to her. "You look beat Darleta," I said.

"I shore am. I'm wore to a nub."

"Maybe that coffee'll pep you up."

"Maybe so," she said, and her little eyes that usually sparkled just set there like tacks in a board.

The next time I passed, I said, "Friend of yours was in this morning. I forgot to tell you before. Name's Huel Lester. Said he really wants to see you at the reunion."

Them tacks livened up and blinked at me. "Huel?" she said. "Huel's here?"

"He sure is, and you're all he talked about."

"Huel Lester talked about me?"

"Not a thing in this world else. He's really lookin' forward to seein' you."

A small smile creased her face. "Who'd a thunk it?" she mused, then she slipped heavily from the stool. "And he's goin' to the reunion?"

"To see you," I said.

That crease turned into a grin. "I gotta get goin', Jim," she said as she turned and passed through the door, her hips brushing both jambs. On the counter sat almost half a doughnut, the only time I ever seen her leave a crumb. I considered having it bronzed.

Mutt sidled in a few minutes later for the special—he always ordered the cheapest thing—and hollered up the counter at me: "I seen ol' Darleta damn near runnin' up the street. She got aints in her paints?"

"Not as I know of."

"Eh?" he cupped one hand around an ear, deaf as a turd.

"Not as I know of!"

"Gimme some a them lima beans," he shouted.

"Soup or salad?"

"I don't eat no rabbit food," roared Mutt, then he give a horse laugh. He slurped up the lima beans and pork neck, talking all the time about how lucky it was for both of them that Huel wouldn't see Darleta at the reunion. "That's one time ol' Wee-gee done its work. I ever tell ya about the time I kicked that ol' boy's ass that tried to trick me with one of them deals? Wellsir . . ."

Five o'clock comes early in the morning, but I open the diner then so the farmers and short-haul truckers can have their coffee and eggs. I don't see many neckties and corsages at that hour, in fact, I'd hate to be paid by how many neckties and corsages I ever seen in my place.

I seen some that morning, though. No sooner'n I'd got the coffee started than up drove that big old Continental, then Huel Lester jumped out and scurried around the car and opened the passenger's door. Out popped Darleta, dressed to the teeth. Well, they come in and grabbed the corner booth, giggling like teenagers.

Huel waved and called, "Mornin' Jim!"

"Mornin' Huel, Darleta," I said.

"Mornin' boys," Huel waved to the other customers at the counter.

I carried two glasses a water to their booth. Huel had a menu in his hands. "You shoulda went to that reunion, Jim. Did we have fun!"

Darleta giggled, "Oh *Huel*."

"What a time!"

"Oh *Huel*!"

I smiled.

"Give us your best, Jim," Huel ordered, "your very best. Eggs, bacon, pancakes on the side. The whole works."

"With lotsa that scrumptious blueberry syrup," added Darleta.

"Yessir," said Huel, "lotsa that. And coffee for me."

"I'll have lo-fat," Darleta smiled demurely.

Well I give them breakfast and they ate, carrying on, giggling with one another, then whispering, then giggling again—and them grownups too! It was plain silly, if you ask me. But I never complained when Huel stripped bills off his roll to pay, then told me to keep the change. Tips in my place're about as common as lipstick at the Assembly of God.

Out them two went, Darleta waving like she'd just won Miss Kern County, Huel opening the door for her, then jogging around his big car and jumping in. That Lincoln swooped onto the road then headed north toward Delano. I never seen no more of them that day.

Mutt was setting there downing my coffee at a terrible rate whenever

Huel come in the next morning. He looked low. "Howdy Jim, Mutt," he nodded, then sidled into a stool. "Coffee," he said.

Mutt winked at me. He'd been aching to find out what'd happened when Huel seen Darleta—"I'll bet that ol' boy'll never recognize her"— so he couldn't wait to give him the third degree.

"How'd you and ol' Darleta get along?" Mutt asked in a pleasant shout.

"Oh, fine," replied Huel, staring into his cup.

"You don't look too fine."

"I got things on my mind."

Mutt wasn't letting go. "How'd she look to ya?" he hollered, winking at me.

Huel Lester looked up and a tiny smile curled the corners of his mouth. "Well, at first I never recognized her. She'd surely put on a little weight and aged some"—Mutt winked again—"but soon as we started talkin', I could tell she was the same ol' Darleta, sweet as a yam. Lemme tell you boys, all I could think was thank Heaven, there's more a Darleta to love! That's a fact."

Mutt blinked. "You *did?*"

"Why so sad then, Huel?" I asked.

"Well, I ast that little darlin' to marry me last night—I'm a widower myself—and she said she'd have to talk it over with her momma that never liked me. The old lady remembers me from when I was a kid and a little wild. Anyways, this mornin' Darleta tells me—and she's real broke up, cryin' and carryin' on—that her momma won't leave McFarland and move to Portland with us, and that she cain't leave her momma that's old and sick. So there it is. My business is up there."

Wasn't much I could say. It seemed like to me that Huel and Darleta was stuck.

"And Darleta's momma claims she shoulda not went to the reunion at all," added Huel. "The ol' lady she claims that the Ouija board warned her that trouble was comin'."

"Trouble for who?" I asked. "Sounds like to me Miz Sims is lookin' out for herownself, not Darleta."

"That ol' armadiller!" bellowed Mutt. "You can bet she'll get her way. She used that board trick on ol' Melvin, her husband that was so henpecked. I worked with him way back when. Hell, I'd a kicked her ass!"

"Did you talk to her, the old lady I mean?" I asked.

"No, Jim, I never," he answered. "Darleta said she didn't wanta talk to me."

"Why hell's bells," hollered Mutt, "if it'uz me, I'd go nose-to-nose with the ol' armadiller. She needs to git told is what she needs. Her and her damn Wee-gee board! Did I ever tell ya 'bout the time I kicked that ol' boy's ass over a Wee-gee board?"

Huel ignored him.

"What I think," I volunteered, "is that ol' Miz Sims needs to let Darleta live her own life. The old lady's been off for a long time, and poor Darleta's been the victim, nobody else."

"Darleta wouldn't hear of it," Huel said, "Besides, I wouldn't wanta cause trouble. I surely never meant to do that, but it looks like I have. Life gits complicated, don't it?" he smiled sadly.

"You reckon Darleta'd listen if a Wee-gee board was to tell'er to go with ya, Huel?"

We both looked at Mutt. Huel finally said, "If it's somethin' crooked about it, I cain't do it."

"You don't have to do nothin'," Mutt told him. "Hell, me and Jim here can handle things, cain't we? Gimme some more coffee."

I poured his fourth cup. "I guess."

"Well, I still got the board leftover from whenever I kicked that ol' boy's ass. I'm a-bringin' it in."

Darleta and Huel had 'em a date for lunch that day, so I let Mutt tote his Ouija board in and set it up in the corner booth. He was hovering there like a Jehovah's Witness with a handful of *Watchtowers* whenever Darleta arrived.

She slunk in, looking mighty low, and before she could order a Coke Huel had steered her into that booth. Things was slow that day, so I slipped over myself to watch. Soon as I got there, Huel said, "Sit down, Jim."

"I got work to do," I protested.

"But you *said* you'd handle things."

Well, I had. Or at least I'd let Mutt say that for me. *I swear.* Sometimes I wished I never knew some folks. I looked around then give my apron to Huel. "Keep an eye on things, willya?"

"Sure 'nough."

Mutt he was just aching to get started. "Looky here, Darleta," he shouted. "You need to git a readin' from this here board so's you and Huel there can decide what to do."

"Me and Momma already done a readin' and decided," she told us, her face sagged with pain.

"No sir!" busted Mutt. "Cain't do 'er thataway. Ol' Wee-gee ain't reliable if the folks involved is in on it. What ya need is guys like me and Jim that ain't got no special inter'st."

While Mutt talked, I's thinking that this could get real uncomfortable, since he can't even spell M-U-T-T. I was sure hoping Darleta wouldn't notice. I never had much time to consider it, because a second later we had our hands touching that pointer and it's sailing over the board, picking out letters like a kid plucking black jelly beans. "Where should Darleta go?" Mutt'd asked, and Ouija spelled out "P-O-R-T-L-A-N-D." I give Mutt a hard look, because that pointer liked to flew over the board. He needed to ease up some so's not to give the plan away.

After the question "What about Darleta's momma?" the pointer liked to jerked me out a the booth when it hit for the letters. I give Mutt another glance and he's looking real strange right back at me. "I-N-C-O-M-P-E-T-E-N-T," the pointer spelled, and I *really* give Mutt a stare then. He must've looked that big devil up in a dictionary. I was beginning to think I'd underestimated him.

"What's that spell?" Darleta asked.

"Incompetent," I answered.

"Ohhh," she said real thoughtful. "What's it mean?"

"It means she can't take care of herself."

"What oughta Darleta do about it?" asked Mutt, and that pointer gave me another jerk. N-U-R-S-I-N-G H-O-M-E," the pointer spelled. "E-X-C-E-L-L-E-N-T C-A-R-E. I-N P-O-R-T-L-A-N-D."

None of us said nothing. Me, I was stunned. Mutt sure had did his homework. Darleta just set there. Mutt, himself, he shook his head. Finally, Darleta called Huel: "Sugar, we gotta have a talk. In private."

Soon as Darleta and Huel'd went outside, I hissed at Mutt, "You spelled real good, but you damn near broke my arm jerking that pointer so hard."

"*Me!*" hollered Mutt. "Hell, you'uz a-doin' it. I'us about to git sore. How's come you to jerk it thataway? And where'd you git them damn big words? Hell, Darleta's probably out there right now askin' ol' Huel what they mean."

"*My* words?" I looked out the front window of the cafe and seen 'em in the front seat a Huel's Lincoln, so close that they looked like a two-headed guy kissing himself. Mutt still seemed genuinely baffled. Finally, I just shook my head. I turned back toward him. "She got the message," I said. I glanced down at the old Ouija board with the pointer resting on it, wood on unmoving wood, then shook my head.

Another California

Wellsir, the way I heard it, Vanderhofen he walked directly into that . . . that *torrent*, and he never give a try to swimming. The deputy sheriff he'd just told him about the two girls, about not finding their bodies I mean, and Vanderhofen he'd stood there for a minute, then wandered real slow toward Coyote's Cataract right below his cabin like he was looking for his poor lost kids, then he was in the current before anyone realized what he was doing. It was like the river just swallowed him, that deputy told me. They never did find the body. They never found none of 'em. The Kern River there, that danged cascade, it just chews folks up, batters 'em to pieces. A terrible thing.

So now he's dead, and that big project of his is too. His cabin's still there across the river above what us locals like to call Nee-Chee-Say-Too, that's Indian for Coyote's Cataract. The cable's rusting and the suspension car is locked on this side. No one but me's used it since his relatives come and cleaned out his and the kids' personal effects. He never had a wife that I saw or heard about. All that's left of his work is what's in these papers of his, and they sure don't amount to much.

"When the world was dry and all the things was so dry and thirsty, Coyote begun fasting and dancing and singing until finally Earth Father come to him and asked what he wanted. Coyote said, 'The people are dying of thirst, the plants are dying of thirst, the animals are dying of thirst, the rocks are dying of thirst, we are all dying of thirst.' And Earth Father took pity and tore open the great mountains and they bled the purest, coolest water to save the world. That is how Mother River was born and that is why Coyote loves her."

> Sally Joe, informant
> (recorded by R.L.V., 3/18/22)

I still recollect that first time Vanderhofen ever come by here. He was with a group from the Kern County Museum that stopped at my place for coffee on their way on up the canyon. They was looking for Indian stuff—you know, mortars, rock drawings, old campsites—so I give 'em a few tips, exchanged a few snappy sayings with this one cute little number. The rest, they looked like if you put 'em on the street the cops might mark their legs with yellow chalk.

I come here from Kansas City over three years ago, running this juice joint, and doing real good too I might add. If you can't make money in California, you can't make money is what I always say. But, anyways, those flatlanders that come up here, well, they're all something, and that bunch wasn't no exception: a bunch of squirrels.

This one guy, though, tall and big-shouldered, with puttees and wearing a tie tucked into his flannel shirt, he never smiled, never joked, but he did give me the eye when I was sweet talking that looker. The guy he was real grim and impatient, all the time tapping his foot until the rest of 'em finished their coffee, then he growled something and they all took right off.

Wellsir, two, maybe three weeks later, he was back. He didn't even order coffee like most would, but just asked, "Can you tell me where a woman named Sally Joe lives?"

"That old Indian?"

"She's a Tubatulabal."

"A what? Old Sal's a Indian."

"A Tubatulabal."

"We just call her Indian Sal up this way," I pointed out. I didn't cotton to flatlanders coming up into the canyon and trying to tell me stuff. If he'd been a little smaller I sure would've told him off, you can bet on it.

"Where does she live?" he asked tonelessly, those big shoulders at my eye level, that tie tucked into his flannel shirt.

"About a mile up the canyon, you'll see a dirt road from the right where a little arroyo empties. Her cabin's a half mile farther on up that road."

"Thank you," he replied without smiling, then he was gone.

"He's a strange one," I told Smitty, the guy that pumps gas for me.

"And a big one," he added.

May 7, 1922: I have determined that the woman known as Sally Joe (79 yrs) and the man known as Pasatiempo (84 yrs) are the last living speakers of Tubatulabal—a Shoshonean language that was restricted to Kern Canyon—Kroeber says it never had more than a thousand speakers—They are in poor health—The other informants (Roscoe Redbird 49 yrs, Robert Redbird 41 yrs, Julian Lopez 62 yrs) are no more than quarter-bloods and although they recall some traditional stories, their recollection of the language is slight and incomplete— To date I believe I have been able to identify most Tubatulabal phonemes and many morphemes as well—It is clearly a polysynthetic language—It will never be heard again on this Earth after these two informants die—I must work fast.

> R. L. Vanderhofen, Ph.D.
> (diary entry)

Not more'n a week later, he come back and he had Indian Sal, another old-timer called Pasatiempo, and those two little girls that looked a lot like him in tow. One was, I'd say, maybe four years old, and the other was about a year, year-and-a-half, younger—cute little muffins. Like I said, I never seen a wife with him and he wasn't the kind of guy you questioned too close. Anyways, he walked right into my cafe with those Indians and kids, sat in one of the booths, and bought 'em lunch—I'd never had Indians inside before, never even thought about it, and they probably never had either, I'll bet. They never had any money ever.

You know, there's those bleeding hearts that cry about the poor Indians this and the poor Indians that, but until *we* got here, nobody wasn't making any money up this canyon at all. Those darn Indians was up here for years before Americans come and never made a penny, just ate trout and pine nuts is what I'm told. Why, in only three years I turned this place into a gold mine.

Well, anyways, there was a lot of talking all through lunch, and I kept noticing Vanderhofen—he might even've been one of those bleeding hearts himself—taking notes in this book he carried and saying things to the kids. It was real strange, *he* was. Robert Lafayette Vanderhofen was the big man's full name, *Doctor* Robert Lafayette Vanderhofen, but he wasn't any real doctor, the kind that can give medicine.

Wellsir, he pretty soon was up here all the time, bringing those two old Indians into my place three or four times a week, always with those little girls, too, and sometimes he'd have other Indians in tow—Robert Redbird, Roscoe Redbird, and old Julian. I couldn't for the life of me figure what was going on, but he paid hard cash.

Then Vanderhofen he bought the Starrett cabin across the river close to my cafe just above Coyote's Cataract. It was a nice little place, the cabin, on an old mining claim. To cross the river there you had to ride that suspension car that Starrett he'd installed back when he thought he was going to be in the chips: a real heavy cable anchored in rocks on both sides with a little car dangling from it that you operated with a pulley. Since it's next to impossible to cross the river anywhere up here in Kern Canyon except in real dry years, there wasn't nobody going to bother him when he was on the other side of it with his cable car pulled over there. To me, it always seemed like a real lonely place.

> "One time Coyote wanted Mother River to love him and he visited her all the time and talked to her and begged her, but she was true to Earth Father. So Coyote—he was white then like the moon—he determined to trick her into loving him so he rolled himself in mud and dirt until only his d—— belly was white, and he came to her and said he was Earth Father, but when she let him touch her, some of the mud and dirt washed off and she was very angry and almost drowned him before he escaped. After he ran away he realized he could not wash the mud stains from his back and his head, and that is why he is still stained brown."
>
> (Pasatiempo, informant
> (recorded by R.L.V., 4/21/22)

Wellsir, one day I run into Vanderhofen in the grocery store up at Kernville and, seeing as we was neighbors, I just asked real casual why he'd chose such a out-of-the-way location, there above Nee-Chee-Say-Too. He measured me for a minute and I wished I hadn't said nothing, then he almost whispered, "My work requires privacy." That was all. He had those two little girls with him and they both give me the sweetest little hellos, but a second later while I tried to make pleasant conversation with their father, I heard or half-heard, really, them talking to each other in some sort of strange mixture of lingos, English but all messed up by something else. I couldn't savvy 'em.

Their father *the doctor*, he never did say *what* he was working on and, looking at those big shoulders and that grim face, I decided not to push the issue, but I was curious because I'd every once in awhile see him toting Sally Joe or Pasatiempo across the river in that cable car, them looking real scared at Coyote's Cataract that had all the Indians spooked, or he'd bring them into my place of business, along with his two girls. In fact, it seemed like those two Indians was always with the little girls. I'd've been careful if it was me, I'll tell you.

More and more when they'd come in, they was jabbering, even old stone-face Vanderhofen some of the time, but mostly it was those two little kids and the old Indians, Sal and Pasatiempo, chuckling and carrying on like they was with their own grandchildren. They'd go on and on and I never really caught what they said—I was afraid to get too close because I didn't want that Vanderhofen to think I was eavesdropping—but they seemed like they was having a big time. And that Vanderhofen he was scribbling notes, always scribbling notes.

Feb. 27, 1923: Sally Joe died suddenly but my plan has worked beyond my wildest dreams—Both Betsy and Martha are now fluent in Tubatulabal—We have saved a language as old as time—It happened far more quickly than I had imagined possible—My own efforts to learn the language are slow and halting—It is a singularly difficult tongue to master but somehow the children grasp it easily— Thanks to my girls, we have defied history!

R. L. Vanderhofen, Ph.D.

(diary entry)

Anyways, not long after old Indian Sal passed away, this young guy that worked for the Kern County Museum he come up from Bakersfield to visit *the doctor*, and he stopped at my place to ask for directions, so I give him a cup of coffee on the house and quizzed him a little, and danged if he didn't come right out and tell me what was up. It seems that Vanderhofen he was making a *book* of that Indian talk, such as it was.

Wellsir, I'd heard Indian Sal and old Pasatiempo once or twice over the years myself when they was around my place and let me tell you they never had no *real* language at all, just a lot of grunts. And *that* was Vanderhofen's big work. Me, I'd had him pegged for some kind of mad scientist, making a bomb or something important, not just writing down how a couple broke-down old Indians talked. A waste of danged time if you was to ask me. It sure as hell takes all kinds . . .

"One time Coyote he couldn't find no woman to, you know, stick his p—— in, so he snuck up to Mother River where she was all soft and slow and real pretty and he unrolled his big long p—— and, you know, stuck it into her. Just when he got to pumping, the river she clamped down and he couldn't pull out and his p—— it started jumping like a trapped snake and Coyote he was roaring and scratching and the river there she churned all up and churned all up until finally, you know, she snapped his p—— off and that's why he's got just a little red nub now, all sore. And the place where he did that to her it's that big cataract, you know, Ni'chisa'tu—that means p—— of Coyote—still churning and you can still hear Coyote roaring if you go there. And sometimes Indians would go there to fish and not come back and nobody could ever find them. That's because Coyote's p——, you know, it lured them and got them. And that is where all the Indians have gone. Coyote's p—— is angry because Mother River loves them, and it, you know, likes to trick those Indians and take them."

Roscoe Redbird, informant
(recorded by R.L.V., 3/1/23)

Wellsir, old Pasatiempo he had a stroke and when they found him at his place they rushed him down to the county hospital in Bakersfield. I heard that he was paralyzed and couldn't talk no more at all. I don't know for sure because he never come back. Robert Redbird he told me that Vanderhofen visited the old man down there real often. I wouldn't know that either because by then *the doctor* he'd stopped coming into my place much, except once in a great while he'd bring those girls by for a Coke. Mostly, though, they kept to themselves over there across the river just above Nee-Chee-Say-Too with their cable car pulled to their own side.

Once when I was out fishing I saw him sitting near the cabin on a log with those cute little muffins and it looked like he was reading something, and so was they, as little as they was. He looked different that time, not so stern, and the girls they was laughing. I waved and those two cuties waved back. Vanderhofen nodded. It sure did seem like a lonely life to me.

May 6, 1923: Not only have Betsy and Martha learned the language, they have now committed to memory the tales I recorded from Sally Joe, Pasatiempo, Roscoe, Robert, and Julian—They are my loves and my life—Why has no one else, not even Kroeber, thought to record these God-given languages as I have—Children must be taught a language by native speakers so that it will truly live and be perpetuated; it is the only answer—With children the cultures can be saved before they are entirely lost—Whole ways of seeing and being may be saved—Another, nearly forgotten, California may be preserved.

R. L. Vanderhofen, Ph.D.
(diary entry)

I don't know what possessed those two little girls to try to ride the cable car across the river on their own or how they got up strength enough to pull themselves out as far as they did. It just don't make sense and it's so danged sad. Anyways, this truck driver he happened to be going by uphill on the road and he seen them fall into the river, almost like they was jumping in he said, so he pulled into my place and I right away called the sheriff, then me and Smitty and the driver we rushed over to the river, but there really wasn't nothing we could do, I knew, except hope to find the bodies. Folks they fall in or try to swim here every year and if you don't get to 'em right now, they're gone. Poor little muffins.

Where the hell was Vanderhofen, that's what we all wanted to know. He never left those kids alone. Never ever. We finally managed to get over to the cabin to look for him—me and Smitty had to snag that suspension car and pull it over then ride it back over to the other side of the river while the sheriff's boys tried to find the bodies. Wellsir, we discovered Julian Lopez asleep—you know how old guys nod off. I guess he was the baby-sitter, but it didn't matter no more, did it?

When I told what'd happened, old Julian he just collapsed. I figured him for dead, but he wasn't, so me and Smitty, we got him to that suspension car and across the river so the ambulance boys that was there could look at him. And the truth is, he's never been the same since that day. It's like he died too. Anyways, that's when Vanderhofen drove up. He'd been down to Bakersfield visiting Pasatiempo at the county hospital. I was already back at my place then so I never seen what happened next, him walking into that cataract I mean, but they never found his body, we never, because us locals kept looking for a good week. The river got 'em.

Wellsir, since there wasn't no local relatives, I made a offer through a lawyer on the old Starrett place and it was accepted. It was a real good buy if I do say so myself, and I'm not noted for making bad ones. Vanderhofen's kin from back east they'd pretty much cleaned out all his valuables, but I found this one box full of junk. There was a diary full of crazy notes and all these papers, some with a kind of code on them, squiggles and dashes and funny letters, plus a bunch of silly stories, just kids' stuff like this one:

> "Here is what my grandmother told me: Many years ago there was no world only empty sound and Mother River was sad. 'I need children and a world for them,' she said, and she called to Earth Father but he couldn't understand her words because they were only empty sound. So she prayed and prayed until she kept getting smaller and tighter and her sound kept getting tighter and smaller until it was a terrible hiss that shook the heavens and opened the earth, and finally Earth Father understood and he said, 'You will be my wife and we will make a world and we will make our children.' That is how she made our language and how our language made our world."
>
> Julian Lopez, informant
> (recorded by R.L.V., 6/9/23)

You see what I mean? Can you imagine a grown man, a so-called *doctor*, spending all his time writing down that kind of stuff and not taking good care of his kids, letting them fall into Nee-Chee-Say-Too? Not me, I can tell you that much. Where I come from his kind wouldn't be tolerated.

And his work, his *great* work—hah! All that paper'll do is start a fire for me. It's not worth a dime.

The Hearse Across the Street

𝄞 𝄞 𝄞 𝄞 𝄞 𝄞 𝄞 𝄞 𝄞 𝄞 𝄞 𝄞 𝄞 𝄞 𝄞

He heard the metallic grappling of key in lock—his daughter had never learned to open the door without a struggle—and knew it was Laura. He wished she'd knock first, but no: because she had been raised in this house, she thought there was no need for that common courtesy. What if he was naked? What if he was naked with a woman? Wouldn't that shock her!

"Dad?" she called.

"I'm in the kitchen."

"Good. I can use a cup of coffee."

She stopped in the doorway. "Dad," she gasped, "*look* at you," clucking and shaking her head.

He wore carpet slippers, boxer shorts, and an undershirt. "What?" he replied, surprised.

"Go put some trousers on. After *all*."

Ignoring her, he sat at the small kitchen table, and sipped from his freshly poured coffee. "This is my kitchen and I just got up. Besides, I've got more clothes on than you wear in the summer."

"What if I'd brought the girls? Think how *they'd* feel."

Think of how I feel when you walk in on me like this, he thought but did not say. At least she came to visit, unlike some people's kids, and he didn't want to lose that. He also didn't want to seem eccentric, since he knew that his son-in-law coveted this house and would happily consign him to a nursing home. "Just a minute," the old man finally said, slipping into the bedroom to pull on a pair of slacks, then returning to the kitchen. He hesitated in the doorway, sighting the middle-aged woman sitting in the same chair where her mother had sat, as shapeless as her mother had been, but not the same, not his best friend, just a friend.

"What's that hearse about?" asked Laura.

"Hearse?"

"There was one pulling away from little Mrs. Crumpacker's place across the street when I drove up, one of those fancy maroon ones that O'Meara's has now."

Another hearse. Those damned things seemed to be stalking him and everyone he knew, coming closer, closer. "Jan Crumpacker? Are you sure?"

"Right across the street at little Mrs. Crumpacker's."

"She's not *little*," he snapped. "She's as tall as you."

"Well," Laura's voice betrayed shock at his response, "I only meant . . ."

The old man did not wait for her reply—she referred to everyone his age as "little"—but walked instead into the living room and raised a shade, then gazed across the street at the small house. The hearse was gone, but two neighbor women in robes stood in the driveway talking. Jan Crumpacker dead, it didn't seem possible. She'd been fine yesterday. But it was possible, he knew, anything was.

"You don't have to snap my head off!" Laura, recovered and indignant, called from the kitchen. Her mother's daughter, he thought, but did not say.

Instead, he scanned the small, neat house across the street, its row of rose bushes along one side, its wysteria in front of the porch. He could almost smell the sweet blossoms as he had that warm summer evening— how long ago?—when, shirtless as usual, he'd been watering the lawn and he'd waved at Jan, who was weeding her flower bed in front of her house.

She had been wearing shorts and a halter top, her long legs were still youthfully lean, unlike his own wife's veined stumps, and he had, as he often did, gazed at her for a long moment before she'd noticed him and smiled. Then he'd waved, on the edge of embarrassment. He and Jan weren't kids. Laura was already in high school then, dating and certain she had discovered great and personal secrets in the new uses she was learning for her own body.

His daughter had been out that night, as was her mother, so he'd strolled across the pavement and joined Mrs. Crumpacker in her front yard. "Hot enough for you?" he'd asked.

Jan had whistled through her teeth, "You bet." She had reached up and awkwardly touched the bright bandanna that hid most of her auburn hair.

It was common for neighbors to talk like this on long evenings when everyone was home from work and watering their lawns. That evening, for some reason, no one joined them, so they discussed their yards and gardens. "Where's Clyde?" he'd asked.

"Working nights this week."

"Too bad, but at least it's not so hot."

"Oh," she'd said, as though surprised, "he wanted me to ask if we can borrow your pipe wrench. We've got a leaky sink."

"Sure thing. I'll go get it."

On his way back across the street, he heard Mrs. Newhouse, Jan's next-door neighbor, call from her porch, "Trouble?"

"Leaky sink," Jan had called back.

"Well, you've got the block handyman to fix it up," laughed Mrs. Newhouse, and he had turned to wave at her.

"I'll take a look at it," he volunteered.

"If you don't mind."

He trailed Jan into the house, eyeing the long legs and slim hips, the strands of auburn hair fringing pale skin at the back of her neck. In the kitchen he had knelt, examining pipes under the sink, then tightened a coupling. She had been standing next to him, her legs beside his tan shoulder while he worked, and twice their flesh had touched. Each time he had felt a jolt within himself, the magical sensation of skin kissing.

Just as he finished, her leg again touched his arm and shoulder, and he heard a tiny sigh. This time her leg did not move, and he had gazed up into her eyes just as her warm hand touched his neck.

It had been dark when he emerged from Crumpackers' door, and no neighbors had noticed him. He'd returned home and consumed a beer, then gone to bed. Although he and Jan had remained friends, perhaps more than friends, he never again entered her house. There *was* something special in their relationship: the way their eyes would meet, their laughter coincide, and it had thereafter been enough.

That next evening, while he was watering, Mrs. Newhouse had called to him: "That was *some* job last night. It took long enough."

"It sure did," he'd responded pleasantly, "but we got that sink fixed."

"Well," Mrs. Newhouse had said, "my shower's on the blink. Maybe you could look at it."

"Sure thing." Across the street he had seen Jan Crumpacker standing in her shorts in front of the wysteria smiling at him, and he'd waved.

His daughter's voice jolted him: "You know, that little fellow who lives down from us, he passed away."

The gray man said nothing.

"Dad? Are you alright?"

"I'm okay," he answered.

When he did not pursue the conversation, his daughter stood and walked into the living room. "Dad?" she called, her voice hesitant. "Bob and I've been thinking. You're so lonely here. Wouldn't you feel better around other people, people your own age?"

He did not turn, but continued gazing out the front window. He could see Jan Crumpacker over there working in her garden, her long legs folded beneath her, that bright bandanna curled around her auburn hair, a few wispy strands against the fair flesh of her neck.

"Dad?"

"I'm fine," he responded without looking at her.

Across the street, Jan looked up, seemed to notice him, and smiled. He began to wave, then restrained himself. She was still smiling as he pulled down the shade like a guillotine slicing time.

Tower Power

Love Sister Sunshine sat unmoving, eyes closed. A thick man stood behind her, hand extended palms up on each side of her head, large ring bright on one pinky. Suddenly Sunshine's lips curled and she crooned: "I be Naomi. Oh, I be so happy . . . so happy to be back. It's been so long . . . so long. . . ." Her reedy body swayed and tears began flowing from her eyes.

"All thought survives. All vibes survive. All energy survives. We survive from incarnation to incarnation." Love Sister began shaking and the crowd gasped as she called, "Still yourself for the inner voice."

"Who be thou?" asked the man standing behind her—Archbishop Roland Bundy from the Berkeley University of the Psychic—and she replied in an off-key, chanting tone, "Naomi. I be Naomi."

The pinky-ringed man waited until spectators quieted, then explained, "This is a *real* powerful visiting entity that hasn't had a body for a *real* long time, so this could get *real* rough." He clenched his fists beside the quivering woman's head and rolled his eyes toward the ceiling as though straining to control some invisible force. Again the crowd gasped.

"Why have you chose this channel?" asked the man.

"I knew her in past lives," sang the voice of Love Sister Sunshine, and the crowd once more stirred.

Sitting on one side of the stage with other New Age practitioners, teeth gleaming, the Divine Len Schwartz dared not reveal his agitation. Not only had he been billed no higher at this Psychic Faire than the charlatans with whom he shared the platform, but now he had been trumped by his arch rival. His bad back began tightening.

177

As the audience responded breathlessly to Sunshine's latest scam, the Divine Len could only smile—that dazzling, phony grin—as his innards swirled. This was too much, too damned much. He had been carefully planning to introduce this latest scheme locally himself, reading all he could about it, consulting friends in the Bay Area where it had been perfected, and now it was all wasted because this ex-palm reader had jumped right in and grabbed the market. If he announced he was a channeler now, he would seem to be following her, *imitating* her, and he had far too much pride for that. "The Divine Len Schwartz doesn't imitate anyone," he assured himself.

His arm was tapped lightly and Reverend Dale Daley, who sat beside him, whispered into his ear, "Isn't it *wonderful*. As a *clairvoyant*," she added, "I can like *feel* the power of the deal she's, you know, channeling."

The Divine Len only grunted and nodded. Daley, her face painted like porcelain mask, her hair dyed and lacquered, was an aging hippie who was cashing in—an ex-reflexologist. No class, no pride. You can bet *she'll* be a channeler soon too. Hell, he groused, she'd examine toad bowels if people took it seriously, or took *her* seriously.

This whole damned scene was humiliating. "The Divine Len Schwartz, sharing the stage with every Johnny- or Jill-come-lately," he groused to himself, then looked around at the others: the Right Reverend Cindy (the guru of crystals was an ex-hooker), the Very Right Reverend Arnold Gonzalez (a youthful healer whose motto was "Enlightenment starts with a clean colon!"), Bishop Bev Howard (past lives, I Ching, and nutrition—meaning she also peddled vitamins to the gullible), and, worst of all, the Reverend Doctor (that title!) Paul Madruga (who claimed, among other things, to be a mediator between whales and people).

Even the can-you-top-this war of titles demeaned New Age commerce: Archbishop this, Reverend that, Doctor whoever—all self-proclaimed. At least the Divine Len has trumped them all there. When, as a college drop-out, he had entered the consciousness-raising business, he had called himself "Eaglehawk." Later, in response to a changing market, his "Krishna" period had ensued. Just three years ago, when he'd realized that Yuppies yearned for souls as perfect as their teeth and were willing to pay handsomely, he'd decided to use his real name, but with one significant addition. No others dared designate themselves "The Divine," and they'd better not if they didn't want to see him in court.

After all he, the Divine Len Schwartz, had introduced New Age Consciousness to this market, reading auras and interpreting smudges on snapshots as spirits. And he had done very well indeed until Love Sister Sunshine, who'd barely been scraping by, had also recognized the commercial potential of the churchless-but-yearning commuters who had moved into the area.

With no originality, she had claimed to read auras and interpret snapshots, but had added iridology and high colonics. To his astonishment, the woman had immediately attracted gullible clients with her florid, theatrical style, forcing the Divine Len to think up his very profitable "Totem Pole Seminar." But that hadn't fazed Sunshine: she had begun her "Faerie Seminar" and stolen many of his customers. Matters had been escalating ever since. Schwartz crossed his legs and sighed, still smiling, and watched with a certain desperation the show on the stage. "The Divine Len Schwartz doesn't give up," he said, grinding his teeth. "You've got trouble, lady." His back was aching.

In front of him, his enemy was intoning: "Get real tight with your intimates—pets, fish, flowers, mothers—*real* tight, like *karmic* bonding. You've gotta keep a tight hold on your chakra and activate your kundalini. And beware of corporate mergers this month. There's some evil wind, evil wind, out there. . . ." Her voice trailed, she swayed, and the crowd once more gasped. No question, she had them.

"The Divine Len Schwartz hates these damn theatrics," he told himself. "*Hates* them. And *not* because he's jealous, either," he assured himself. "No, because they detracted from true New Age awareness like his." He nodded, comforted by his own revelation.

He surveyed the members of the audience, well-dressed and prosperous—at a hundred bucks a pop to attend this soiree, they had to be. Their blue-collar equivalents were probably at a tent meeting somewhere listening to a Pentecostal preacher talk tongues. That he could once more be losing this upscale market to a woman who was herself no better than a tent preacher particularly galled him. It hadn't seemed possible when only six months before he had introduced fire walking and, he thought, blown her away.

He had, as usual, taken time to research the subject, actually attending three fire-walking sessions in Los Angeles. "Overcome your limitations by eliminating fear," the brochure on fire walking had read, and he had indeed been terrified until Reverend Dougal Divine, who ran the seminar, had explained why he wouldn't be burned if he just walked firmly and quickly across the coals.

And Dougal, an old friend, had been correct, so when the Divine Len brought his own "Empowerment Through Fire" seminars to the valley, they had been an instant hit. Local papers had at first pooh-poohed them, but eventually letters to the editor demonstrated how thoroughly successful this latest technique was. In one sweep he had regained symbolic leadership . . . until this damned woman had beaten him to channeling, anyway.

Within days after she had revealed she was a channel, Love Sister's ads began appearing not only in local New Age publications, but also in mainstream media. And they were tacky: A full-page, much-retouched photograph of her with the boldface message, "Transform your Corporate Life! Embellish your Business! Listen to Your Past!" Below that she had included what appeared to be a personal resume, that read:

SUNSHINE, LOVE SISTER

Profession: Psychic, Counselor ("Hah!" Len had scrawled in bold green ink on his copy.)

Background: Naomi Montez, Spain, 1647–1692 ("Oh, bullshit!")

Jane Wenden, England, 1705–1789 ("More bull!")

Oliver Trumaine, New York, 1799–1844 ("Bull!")

Wendy O'Mara, Ireland, 1851–1937 ("Moo!")

Present Reincarnation: Love Sister Sunshine, 1959–date ("She cut fifteen years.")

Education: Th.D., Berkeley University of the Psychic, 1980 ("She diddled Bundy and he gave her one of his unaccredited degrees.")

Goals: Unlimited ("Prison for fraud.")

A few days after the ads appeared, the Divine Len confronted the "Psychic, Counselor" at the opening of the Right Reverend Cindy's "Essence Channel—Woman Magick—Massage Institute," which was her same old dive, redecorated and without hot tubs and glory holes because, Len suspected, of the AIDS scare. Anyway, he finally cornered Love Sister near the salmon loaf and she had been as vague as usual, her I-am-a-spirit bit, so he hit her with his question: "Look, you say everybody's got a spirit that's been in lots of earlier bodies, right?"

"That is correct," she sighed in the measured English she had lately affected.

His voice lowered to a hoarse whisper. "There's five damned *billion* people on earth right now, more than all who ever lived before this century *combined*. Where'd all those extra spirits come from?"

"Huh?" For a moment, the begowned woman seemed not to understand, and her green eyelids fluttered. She touched the large crystal that hung at her throat.

"*Five billion,*" he hissed. "Where'd they come from?"

She drank rapidly several times from her cup of punch, then seemed to regain composure as she replied, "Other worlds, other spheres of existence . . . ," her voice grew stronger as she spoke, "from which they emerge through a crystal portal to act as spirit guides to help integrate consciousness . . ."

"Bullshit," he hissed. "It doesn't work, Sunshine . . . or should I call you *Señorita Montez?*" he sneered. "The Divine Len Schwartz says there's no way five billion spirits could have had multiple lives on Earth—or even have existed. No way! Figure it out. Just *count* 'em."

She spilled her punch then and, as she frantically wiped her diaphanous gown with a napkin, snapped at him, "You're so fuckin' left-brained, Len," then she spun away.

He loved it because he had wounded her. But she soon fought back. The Reverend Dale Daley phoned Len to tell him that the very next night at Love Sister's weekly channeling session, his rival—in the guise of "the Naomi entity," of course—had explained that all spirits were really multiple and that they just divided like amoebas in order to accommodate all the new bodies in the world, so everyone would always host an entity that had experienced many lives. No doubt about it, she was clever.

For several days following that revelation, the Divine Len searched New Age publications for some edge, some activity that might once more thrust him ahead of the despised Sunshine. He had long been planning to add the word "Men's" to all his seminars, since the addition of "Women's" to Dale Daley's had increased her gross considerably. He was certain that "Men's" would soon be hot because he had tried it once successfully— his "A Man's Journey" weekend—but even that would not leapfrog him beyond the despicable Love Sister. It wasn't money he wanted—he had plenty of that, more than he had ever imagined this market could pro- duce—but what he wanted, needed really, was ascendancy, and he was determined to have it. "The Divine Len Schwartz will *win*," he said, gazing into the mirror where the face of a winner dazzled him.

Before long, Daley, Cindy, and Madruga did the expected and revealed that they, too, were channels, which he knew would somewhat dilute Love Sister's impact. "The Divine Len Schwartz will *not* jump on that bandwagon," he said to himself with considerable satisfaction. No, there had to be something else he could do . . . rebirthing? no, old business . . . pelvic chakric centering? no, he'd leave that to Cindy . . . past-life regressions? maybe, but really too much like channeling. There *had* to be something no one else had thought of. There *had* to be.

Len sat in Mister Kit's Hair Salon two weeks after the Psychic Faire, still glum, still searching, while Mister Kit himself snipped at the divine locks, shards of which fell onto the pages of a *National Geographic* open in the divine lap. He had picked up the magazine out of habit but was not reading it.

"Boy," he heard Mr. Kit croon in that nasal tone of his, "I'd hate to do *tha-at*." The hairdresser dragged two syllables into the word. "That'd be a lot harder than walking on those coals." He had been empowered at one of the Divine Len's sessions, so he knew whereof he spoke.

"Huh?" The psychic had not been listening.

"Those colored fellows in that picture, jumping from that tower, I'd hate to do *tha-at*," Mister Kit explained.

Leonard Schwartz, the Divine, looked at the magazine in his lap and saw a photograph of New Guinean natives leaping head-first from a high tower. Their ankles were tethered with long vines to prevent them from striking the ground. Then he smiled. "The Divine Len has just had a flash," he announced.

"Really?" sang Mister Kit.

A flash indeed. A whole new level of prestige, of prominence, even of monetary reward. It would be a thousand-dollar-a-session experience, at least a thousand. "This is the Divine Len Schwartz's greatest scheme, maybe *anybody's* greatest." It all came together magically as he sat there having his hair trimmed—some greater force directing him: destiny.

First, the test: he telephoned a friend who coached gymnastics at the local junior college, and was given advice on the kind of rope to use and how to secure it to his ankles. "It's for my back," he had explained, not revealing that he was really honing a new method of empowerment. "Listen, Lenny, you gotta have play in that safety line or you'll only make one jump—*Boing!*—and you'll have a skeleton hanging there with a puddle of guts underneath." The Divine Len hadn't laughed and he had purchased exactly what the coach recommended.

The second step was critical. With a diving instructor from the swim club helping him, he climbed the platform at the indoor swimming pool and, ankles firmly tethered, stood fifteen feet above the water. They had calculated that the actual line should be seven-and-a-half feet long. "The Divine Len Schwartz is *not* afraid," but he was and, as he hesitated above the pool, he thought of being hanged, then gulped and leaped.

For a breathless second he saw the water surging toward him, then a sharp jolt momentarily disoriented him. "Allll Right!" he heard the diving coach call as the divine form swung slowly just above the water—and it was indeed all right. Hanging upside down, he began laughing to himself: "The Divine Len Schwartz is *empowered!*" he called. In fact, he had not only empowered himself with that leap, he knew, but had likely become considerably more wealthy.

Only when the coach pulled him to poolside and released him, did he also realize that his bad back no longer hurt. He leaped twice more that afternoon, and his tutor dove once, successfully each time. "That really *does* help your back doesn't it," the coach'd remarked, and Len had smiled and nodded, his plan working to perfection.

Driving home, he purposely passed Love Sister Sunshine's small compound—it was crowded with expensive, late-model cars, and the fancy neon sign in front flashed simply, "Love Sister Sunshine—Psychic," but underneath on the stucco you could still see where "Tarot, Reflexology, Auras and Cranials" had been painted over if you looked closely. "The

Divine Len Schwartz will send you back to 'cranials' and 'anials' after he blows you away with Tower Power," he chuckled. The divine one couldn't remember ever having felt better.

He slept fitfully but not unhappily that night, mind churning over how to best market this new knowledge. There had to be more than mere seminars in something as spectacular as this. Of course, he could even sell towers to those who graduated from his seminars, call them self-empowerment tools. But they'd have to be classy towers, expensive, hand-made—BMWs of empowerment. He had no desire to appeal to the tent-meeting types. This was to be strictly a class operation for the upscaled who were, for the time being at least, *into* New Age awareness: chrome towers that could enhance anyone's yard and maybe double as objects d'art. No, not merely chrome, muted gun-metal gray too, give folks a choice. His initials—D.L.S.—could be tastefully if prominently etched on the major support bar. He arose happy and relaxed, his back feeling fine.

That next morning, he placed ads in all the local papers, plus *The New Age Voice*, announcing his new empowerment seminar but not offering any details—he would not reveal this inspired scheme to anyone. "The Divine Len Schwartz is nobody's fool," he conceded. A telephone call to an engineer chum began the process of building towers, and he ordered more rope from the supplier recommended by the gymnastics coach. He was gambling considerable capital in this venture, but it was really no gamble. This was a winner if ever there was one and it was entirely secret because he had not divulged all his plans to anyone, just a little here, a little there. His prototype tower was being clandestinely assembled out-of-town.

As the date for the first seminar approached, the Divine Len was un-troubled even by the relatively slim enrollment his vague ads prompted. After the premiere, he would no longer need to advertise—customers would line up to become empowered. And he would surprise them. He had learned one thing from the hated Love Sister: make an impression. He was having a bright tux with crimson cape designed to wear the first time he climbed the tower in public, the first time he freed others from fear and empowered them, and collected a fat fee from each.

Then, driving by Love Sister's compound just a day before his secret empowerment session was scheduled, the Divine Len noticed something that chilled his blood and almost caused him to nose his Mercedes into a ditch: a tower was being erected there, higher and more ornate than his own. Once he controlled his auto and stopped it, he gazed with unbelieving eyes. A tower! A damned tower! How could she have known? "Someone is spying on the Divine Len Schwartz," he choked. Feeling as though his throat was swallowing itself, he pounded the expensive steering wheel, then spun gravel as he sped home.

He telephoned the Reverend Dale Daley and bluntly asked what Sunshine was up to. "Well, it's supposed to be like this *big* secret, but I have it on reliable authority," the Reverend Dale gleefully announced, "that she's discovered that the earth is a mega-crystal, so she's like having a seven towers built. She's gonna put like *six* in the shape of a hexagon with a big crystal at the top of each one, and number seven—her own personal tower—is gonna be like an *apex* with this *amethyst* on it. It's gonna be this *beacon* and it'll be so far-out because it'll like send *karmic* messages to the beings that, you know, run the universe." After a pause, she added, "And it'll like *collect* all this cosmic harmonic *energy* just like Stonehenge does."

"No shit," said the Divine Len Schwartz sarcastically, but the Reverend Dale Daley seemed to miss it.

"Isn't it *great*?" she gushed.

He hung up, but was seething. That woman was copying him and he was going to have it out with her. He dialed her number and a man's voice answered. "What be thy name?"

"I be Naomi," spit the Divine Len. If they wanted to play games, the Divine Len would outplay them.

"Okay, Buster, who is this?" demanded the voice that suddenly sounded like the Archbishop Roland Bundy's.

"This is the Divine Len Schwartz. I want to talk to Sunshine *now*."

The voice on the other end hesitated, "She's not available."

"Bullshit! I just drove by and saw her car."

"She's not . . . well." Bundy's voice faltered.

"She sure as hell isn't, and she's going to be worse if she doesn't talk to me."

"Okay, Schwartz, but just for a minute, and take it easy on her. She's *real* . . . ah, delicate . . . right now."

Bundy was trying to tell him something, but didn't seem to know how. Well, the Divine Len wasn't backing off. "Yeah, she's a tender flower," he snorted. While he waited for Sunshine, he speculated about Bundy's tentative language. It was strange.

"Yes?" she finally said.

He did not mince words. "I want to know what's going on, Sunshine— how've you been getting information about my plans. What're you up to?"

"What entity be this?" she replied, her voice ethereal.

"What *entity* be this? You know damn well who this is. What entity be *that?*

"I be Naomi."

"You be nuttier than a damned fruitcake, Sunshine."

There was no answer, but the Divine Len heard a scuffling sound from the other end of the line. A moment later, the Reverend Roland Bundy's voice said, almost sobbed, "I *told* you to take it easy on her. Sunshine's stuck. I think she gave Naomi seniority and now Naomi is creating her own karma in Sunshine's body. We can't get her back."

"You mean she's finally fallen off the edge," the Divine Len asserted, unable to hide the triumph in his voice. "She's hallucinating."

"No, it's just that Naomi's karma is real heavy . . ."

"She's psychotic, Bundy, looney tunes, and you'd better take the Divine Len Schwartz's advice and get her some medical help."

"No, no doctors!" Bundy's voice was firm on that subject. "No unen- lightened AMA butchers that don't . . ."

"She's off the damned edge. Hah!" Schwartz hung up the divine phone. Stuck my ass, he thought, she's just caught in her own scam. She always had seemed a little spacey, and now the Divine Len's suspicion had been confirmed. It was terrific.

That next evening he dressed, not nervously, but with anticipation. From an anteroom, he watched the crowd trickle in, regulars most of them, rich or becoming rich, young or desperate to be young, overedu- cated, undersatisfied, with Mastercard or Visa bills higher than the na- tional debt. BMWs and MBs and Jags gleamed in the parking lot. A few special customers were escorted to him, women mostly, smartly dressed, with crystals exposed and vocabularies at the ready, anxious to "share," to "relate," and to invite him to their expensive, unpaid-for homes. This was a distracting but necessary ritual, as necessary to his business as cures were to a faith healer's.

The session finally opened as Len had planned. He sat alone bathed in blue light on stage as the curtain was lifted. A single flute played, then was joined by a harp—music properly spiritual. He remained motionless until sufficient murmuring from the crowd told him he had thoroughly milked it, then he slowly rose, raised his arms so that his crimson cape extended like wings, then he intoned, "We are responsible for ourselves. We are responsible for our lives. We must take control of our lives. We must assume control of our lives, and the power for them because we *are* power." As he had expected, a warm murmuring and scattered applause followed his final word. He knew the empowerment crowd and how to please it.

Again he waited, then intoned, "Fear is our enemy. Fear is what holds us back. We must believe in ourselves and conquer all those forces, that old psychological and spiritual baggage that burdens us. *We must take care of ourselves.* You must take care of yourself and not feel any guilt for doing it because when *taking care of yourself you will find your quiet center, your chakra, your karma, your mantra, your dogma!*" The applause was deafening. *This* was why the Divine Len Schwartz was and would always be Number One, he assured himself. He could feel the intensity as he sensed warm vibrations from the audience engulf him. He was growing, growing.

"We must push *back* the boundaries of fear, push *back* the boundaries of the possible. And when you conquer one fear, you threaten all fears. And when you conquer fear, you *enhance*, you *expand*, you *increase* all your possibilities."

He basked again in their applause and their warm, venerating vibes. With a grand sweep of his right arm he pulled the cord that revealed his gleaming chrome tower and posed silently while the crowd first gasped, then chattered, then applauded.

At last the crowd quieted and the Divine Len Schwartz intoned: "Who will *climb up* this great tower with me?" Shouts from the audience told him that many would.

"Who will *stand upon* this great tower with me?" More shouts, most of the audience this time.

He waited until there was absolute silence, then called, "Who will *leap from* this great tower with me?"

Dead silence. He cautioned the crowd, "Do not allow fear to determine your actions," then swirled his cape as he turned toward the gleaming ladder.

As music from the flute and harp wafted from the stage's elaborate stereo system, he began the long climb, whipping his cape with each thrust of his arm, hearing with satisfaction the crowd's growing murmurs while he ascended. Each upward swirl of his crimson wrap generated a louder gasp from the throng.

Three-quarters of the way up, feeling weightless in their adoration, the Divine Len Schwartz heard an even louder gasp followed by applause and shouts of encouragement. Glancing back, he saw the wispy form of Love Sister Sunshine sliding across stage toward the tower. Frantically, he waved at his stage crew to restrain her, but they only waved back.

He hurried to the tower's top, then struggled into the ankle braces of his jump cords—looking down in the dark, it all seemed so much higher than before so he wanted those safety cords attached right away. Moreover, he saw the small woman slowly making her way up the ladder, her gossamer white dress billowing in gentle wind. Far below on the stage, Archbishop Roland Bundy suddenly materialized, speaking frantically to the stage crew, then he too began mounting the chrome spire. "Oh, *great*," groaned the Divine Len. The crowd was coming apart, losing concentration, and he even heard sprinkles of laughter from it.

Gathering himself—but unable to resist glances at the slowly approaching forms of Sunshine and Bundy, the Divine Len Schwartz waved his cape-clad arms to regain the crowd's attention, and called: "Who will *stand* upon the great tower?" His back had begun to tighten.

No reply for a moment, then he heard from the crowd a man's voice respond: "Damn near everybody," followed by laughter.

The Divine head felt like it was swelling—this was all going wrong. After a deep breath to regain control, he called once more: "Who will accept the challenge of the great *tower?*"

At that very moment, Archbishop Roland Bundy slipped from the ladder, barely caught himself, and the crowd sucked its collective breath, then applauded as the chubby archbishop wrapped both arms around the ladder and ceased climbing at all.

Fine! Now no one is even watching me, the Divine realized. They're watching that fat clown with the pinky ring. I'm losing them, he told himself, so he quickly played his trump card: "Who will *leap* from the great tower?" he shouted, but just as he did, Sunshine's dyed hair, then her entire head, appeared at the platform's edge, and the Divine One heard voices from the now-milling crowd—"All right, Sunshine!"

Quivering, temples pounding, back aching, the Divine Len kicked at the crazy woman who was pulling her body onto the deck next him, but his anger ruined his aim and he missed, and his crimson arms suddenly flailed for balance while he teetered, teetered—the assemblage gasping then chuckling—until he plunged out and away, arms extended like a flightless bird, screaming "Oh Shiiiiii . . . ooof!" With a numbing jolt, the cords arrested his fall.

The New Age leader hung senselessly upside down, red cape dangling over his head like a harlot's skirt. After several moments swaying at the end of the tether, he began to register chuckles and cheers and even catcalls from the crowd. Desperate to salvage some shred of dignity from the fall, the hallowed one wrestled that ridiculous cape, struggled to grasp the tower so he could right himself, the crowd laughing louder as he punched and tugged at the bright red cloth. Finally, he managed to wrestle himself free from the crimson prison and his hands at last grasped the tower's cold metal.

Then he heard above him the chanting voice of Love Sister Sunshine: "I be Naomi . . . ," followed by warm applause from the throng below.

Len Schwartz ceased struggling. At least his back didn't hurt.

Tarzan's House

Maybe it wasn't a real desert, the kind with sand dunes and Arabs and camels, but it was brown and dry, almost toasted, and there weren't any trees at all except in people's yards, that's why even the idea of a jungle around here seemed so . . . so *strange*. But Gary, my older brother, he told me about this place called Tarzan's House. He said it was one, a real jungle, all green and tangled and that he went there sometimes with other big kids. I thought he was teasing me.

That day, though, Gary loaded me onto his bicycle's handlebar and peddled out Chester Avenue past Standard School to Decatur Street, then over the canal bridge and onto a dirt track that skirted an oil refinery. We pedaled past horse pastures and finally some scrawny trees where a few cattle tried to find shade. There were lots of ground squirrels there, too, scrambling in every direction ahead of us like little beige darts. It seemed like a long, long way, bouncing on that hard handlebar.

But Gary still didn't stop. He kept pedaling us away from the last corrals toward where the dark line of the Kern River swung underneath big, scorched bluffs. They looked scary and my brother told me there were caves up those waterless slopes where robbers and bats lived.

Once, a long time ago when my Daddy was still living with us, he drove me up there and I walked with him through dry tumbleweeds and short, crisp weeds that looked like a burr haircut. I saw where the river wound around below like a giant snake and I remember that when we were up there he asked me that funny question, "Listen, Marlise, does a man come visit mommy when I'm at work?"

"A man?"

"When I'm at work."

"No, Daddy."

"Okay."

There was a big green strip of trees all along the river underneath us but, beyond it, the round hills where my Daddy worked didn't have any green at all, just lots of oil derricks sticking up and a few shiny tanks. The day was real hot and everything over there seemed like it was swerving, like water was running in front of them. "Why're those hills all wet?" I asked.

"Heat waves," my Daddy grunted.

"Heat *waves*? At *me*?"

"It don't wave at *you*, honey. It don't wave at no one. It just . . . well *waves* is all."

"Oh."

Off to one side a heavy cloud of black smoke was swirling up real slow like octopus ink I saw one time in a movie. "What's that, Daddy?" I asked.

"What's what? Oh, they're burnin' a oil sump, honey," my Daddy explained. "You *sure* no man comes to visit her?"

"Yes," I said, uncertain what an oil sump was. Not too far from where that smoke was rising I saw the red brick buildings of Standard School. "That's where I go," I told him.

"Good," he replied. "You study hard." Then we drove home.

Before that year we'd lived in a trailer house and moved all the time so my Daddy could find work, but by then we'd been in Oildale longest of all, and not in a trailer anymore. I had a real house, just like other kids did and my own school where I knew other kids' names and they knew mine. But I didn't have my Daddy anymore. He and the trailer were gone.

Anyway, those big brown bluffs loomed ahead of us as Gary pedaled over a dusty trail, and close in front I could see bushes, then trees, real big ones, tall and green, not like the little stubby sticks in town. The closer we got, the darker that forest looked, until we slipped into it and the temperature dove.

"Gary, it's really real," I gasped.

"Just wait," was all he said.

He kept pumping and the bike bounced farther into the woods, cooler, denser, like green walls on both sides of us, with vines dangling from the tall towers, with birds flitting all around, and little side paths that looked like tunnels in the bushes. Finally, we reached this big clearing where the sun lit everything up, grass and wildflowers and even a sheet of flat water that barely moved. It was a little side channel of the river, Gary said. There were big giant trees all around with long green vines hanging down. I couldn't even see the main river at all.

"This is Tarzan's house," my brother said, and I really could imagine a crocodile sliding into that water.

"It's neato," I told him. Just then leaves rattled behind us and I jumped. Turning, I saw a large brown man lunge out of the woods, then another one followed him. They looked like the dark people in Tarzan movies. My eyes fled to Gary's.

"Hi," called my brother, and both men smiled. Each carried a stool, a bag, and a long bamboo pole.

"How you chil'rens today?" said one that had white hair.

The men put down their stools and bags, then stood for a moment holding their long, skinny poles. I stared at them because I'd never seen people like them before, not in real life anyway. "You be careful, sugah," the white-haired man said to me. "That watah dang'ous. Don' you be fallin' in it."

"I'll watch her," Gary said. "I'm gonna leave my bike and show my little sister some secret trails."

"You chil'rens go 'head," the other man smiled. "We watch yo bike."

As soon as he led me into a leafy tunnel, I asked my brother, "Why're those men so brown? Are they *natives?*"

Gary hesitated, then said, "I don't know." He shook his head. "Anyway," he added, "they come here to fish. I seen 'em before."

"Like natives?"

"Yeah, just like 'em," he grinned. "You ask some dumb stuff."

"Are they nice?"

He stopped. "Sure, everything's nice at Tarzan's House. Come on."

My brother led me through green passage after green passage. At one place we stepped onto a soft bank and the Kern River's main channel hissed past. I was scared and grabbed his hand because Momma had told me about all the children who'd drowned in it. "That brown man says there's real quicksand in there but it's okay," Gary said, "I won't let you fall in." Then he led me back into the safety of the jungle.

When we said good-bye to the fishermen and left the cover of those trees on our way home, everything seemed hotter than I could ever remember, and those swerving hills with their oil derricks looked like the worst desert in the whole world. We left the last bushes and pretty soon scrambling ground squirrels gave way to lizards. The only trees left were snags where cows clustered. Jolting home, I still wondered if what we'd seen had been real at all.

Just as we rode up to the house that day, Mr. Carlton, the man who'd begun to call on Momma, he was driving away, and she stood there waving at him in her blue and white waitress dress looking real pretty. I was so proud of her in that uniform and wanted one for myself when I grew up.

"Hi Momma!" I called.

"Where've you two been?"

"Gary took me to Tarzan's House."

"He took you *where?*"

"I just showed her the woods, Momma."

"Not to the river, I hope."

"I just showed her the woods."

That next day my Daddy visited. He drove up in the old car we'd always had, but when he got out he had on a brand new Hawaiian shirt and a pair of those neato sunglasses like pilots wear, with clean jeans and brand new boots. He looked like a movie star. Momma waited on the porch with Gary and me in front of her, and Daddy kind of leaned on the car for a minute like he was posing, a cigarette hanging from his mouth. Then he said, "Hello, Marie."

"Hello, Frank."

"Hello kids. No kiss for your old Dad?"

"Give your father a kiss," urged Momma, so I walked to the car and gave him one. He smelled like the aftershave my brother'd given him for Christmas. Gary, who was 12, waited until I was finished, then he thrust his hand forward.

"Well, aren't you the little man now," my Daddy grinned, and he shook Gary's hand.

Then my father turned to Momma and he stopped smiling. "I'd like to talk to you, Marie, ah . . . privately . . . before I take the kids for a ride. Can I come in?"

"We can talk on the porch. Gary, you take Marlise to play around back, please."

My brother escorted me to the clothesline behind the house, found an old tennis ball and began underhanding it to me. It was fun, especially when it bounced off a rock and I got to chase it. Then we began to hear their voices, Momma's and my Daddy's, louder and louder, just like we had before my Daddy'd moved away.

"I won't have that Carlton guy . . . !"

"None of your business . . . !"

"I pay for it, another guy gets it . . . !"

"Foul-mouthed . . . !"

"No *respectable* parent . . . !"

"No *decent* husband . . . !"

"My lawyer'll get . . . !"

"No judge'll grant . . . !"

"You always were a . . . !"

Then my Daddy, his face purple, was around the house grabbing my arm and Gary's, pulling us toward the car. Momma was behind him, warning, "You get them home on time today, Frank, or I'm going to report you!"

"Come on!" he jerked us toward the car, then stopped before he opened the door. "Where're my glasses?" he demanded. He let us go and searched the porch, then returned. "Did one of you pick up my glasses?"

"No sir," Gary replied.

I shook my head.

"You sure? I just had 'em. What're you grinnin' about?" he asked Gary.

"I'm not."

"Yes you are. I can see your stupid face and you're grinnin'. You hooked 'em, didn't ya?" He stood directly in front of my brother.

"No." Gary backed up a step.

"Yes you did. What're you gonna do, give 'em to Momma's boyfriend? Do *you* like him better too?"

"No I . . . ," my brother couldn't finish because my Daddy smacked him hard on the face and knocked him into the dirt. I got scared and ran toward Momma, turning once and seeing my Daddy pick Gary up then hit him again, bloody his mouth. "Bawl you little son-of-a-bitch!" my Daddy was demanding. "You're not the man of this house yet. Bawl, damnit! Bawl!" Then he hit him again, but Gary wouldn't cry.

"I called the sheriff, Frank," Momma shouted as she rushed out of the house, scooped me up, and hurried toward her son.

My Daddy stared for a second, looked at his own hands, then climbed into the car and roared away. Gary sat bloody but dry-eyed on the ground that was our small yard. Neighbors were already gathering: "The poor boy. What happened . . . ?"

When the doctor finished, and the deputy sheriffs were through talking to him, Gary was put to bed and Momma stayed home from work. I heard her on the phone talking to Grandma, so I went to our room and found Gary dressing. "What're you doin'?" I asked.

He talked funny, like he had cotton in his mouth, when he said, "I'm gonna go to Tarzan's House."

"What for?"

"I'm gonna stay there and live from now on."

"But why?" I felt my face warm suddenly. I didn't want my brother to go away.

He just shook his head.

"Can I come with you?"

"No one can."

I couldn't keep from crying. "But whyyyyyy?" I sobbed.

"Marlise, I just . . . ," he looked at me through his swollen eyes, then gave in. "Okay. You can come, but hurry, before Momma's off the phone."

We slipped out the back, climbed on my brother's bicycle, and retraced the route we'd taken the day before. When we reached the place where cattle lounged under those bare snags, Gary stopped looking back, but he kept pumping hard toward the jungle. The track curved into the bushes and squirrels flashed away in front of us. All but one. Ahead, we both noticed a small squirrel, unmoving as we approached.

When we were right next to it, the little head turned and it made a scared sound—"Cheepcheepcheep!"—but only its front stirred. The rear legs were spread flat in opposite directions and motionless.

Gary stopped the bike and jumped off. The squirrel cried again and pulled frantically with its front legs, dragging its hind end in a circle. "It's just a baby," I said.

"Yeah." Gary's voice sounded real sad.

"What's wrong with it?"

"I don't know, but it's hurt."

I tried to reach down and pet it, but it cried and again struggled to escape, then stopped and suddenly its eyes half-closed and it seemed to just lie there panting.

"It's hurt real bad, I think," my brother said. Then he didn't say anything for a long time. He just stood there looking at it.

"Can't we help it?" I asked. "Can't we take it to the doctor?"

My brother didn't reply. He just kept watching that little squirrel panting with its eyes almost closed.

"Gary?"

"It's gonna die, Marlise."

"No. No it's not," I countered. "No it's not!" I didn't want it to.

"It's gonna die and its hurtin' real bad right now," he said.

"No, Gary," I pleaded.

"We've gotta help it." His eyes had not left the little animal.

"We could go home and get it some medicine," I urged. "Momma's got some."

"Look over there." He pointed toward a steam plume rising from the Golden Bear Oil refinery, and when my eyes followed the line of his finger, he moved his leg fast and I heard a light thump.

The little squirrel was spinning down the trail when I looked back. It stopped upside down and its legs were jerking, jerking. My brother ran up to it and kicked its head again, sending it bouncing into the bushes.

"Gary, no!" I cried. "Gary, don't! You'll hurt it! No! No!"

He was ahead of me running to where the squirrel landed. He stopped there but did not kick again. When I arrived, the little animal was not moving and its head was bloody and mis-shaped. I began to weep and turned toward my brother and tried to hit him, to hurt him, to punish him. "No Gary!" I gasped. "No Gary! Gary!"

But he did not seem to hear me. Instead he stood above the dead squirrel and his shoulders began to surge, his face suddenly slicked with tears, and his head fell to his chest as though it had lost connection with his body. He started sobbing and that really scared me, so I touched his arm. "Gary?"

After awhile, he looked up, his face all red and wet, and he gazed for a minute ahead toward Tarzan's House, then he turned from it and walked back to his bike. "Let's go home," he said.

Library of Congress Cataloging-in-Publication
Data

Haslam, Gerald W.
   That constant coyote : California stories /
Gerald Haslam ; foreword by Ann Ronald.
      p.   cm.
   ISBN 0-87417-160-1 (alk. paper) —ISBN
0-87417-161-x (pbk.: alk. paper)
   1. California—Fiction.   I. Title.
PS3558.A724T4   1990
813'.54—dc20   89-70764
                                    CIP